Sometimes love and luck collide . . .

When sultry British Baroness Piper Darrow falls on desperate times, she needs a diversion—and cash. As a talented photographer, she jumps at the chance to travel to the U.S. for a Manhattan Marauders football event. But she gets more than she bargained for when buff quarterback Wyatt Hunter's errant pass lands...in her face. And when it results in Wyatt's comeback of a lifetime, the superstitious athlete is convinced Piper is his good luck charm . . .

With his sights on the Super Bowl, Wyatt will do anything necessary to keep Piper close. The fact that she's a feast for the eyes is a bonus. And as they get closer, he discovers that beneath her proper English surface is a sweet, sexy seductress. Soon the notorious playboy finds himself genuinely smitten, and surprisingly open to love—until his powerful family uncovers something about Piper that threatens to shatter his trust. Now he'll have to decide whether to team up with his fears, or his heart.

Visit us at www.kensingtonbooks.com

I0677390

Books by Mackenzie Crowne

The Players Series
To Win Her Love
To Win Her Trust
To Win Her Heart
To Win Her Back
To Win Her Smile

Published by Kensington Publishing Corporation

To Win Her Smile

A Players Series Novel

Mackenzie Crowne

LYRICAL PRESS
Kensington Publishing Corp.
www.kensingtonbooks.com

First Electronic Edition: July 2017
eISBN-13: 1978-1-60183-997-8
eISBN-10: -60183-997-9

First Print Edition: July 2017
ISBN-13: 978-1-60183-999-2
ISBN-10: 11-60183-999-5

Printed in the United States of America

For Crowne's Crew, my awesome street team, who understand, encourage, and support, and never question my sanity as I entertain the voices in my head.

Acknowledgements

I've been blessed with the most amazing editor. Thank you, Jennifer, for your calm voice of reason and unwavering support.

A special thanks to my critique partners, AJ, V, and Kelly, for their patience, wisdom, talent and humor. They are a bright beacon of sanity in the midst of madness.

Chapter 1

Wyatt Hunter hated to lose.

He glared at the game clock. Eighteen seconds. Time for two plays. Three, if he was damn lucky. Three plays to move the ball from midfield to the end zone. If he failed, he'd spend the next hour bombarded by reporters demanding to know how the reigning champions had lost to a team not expected to make the playoffs, and the next *week* reading about how he'd let the franchise down.

He needed a fucking miracle.

Dipping his knees behind the Manhattan Marauders' veteran center, he swiveled his head back and forth. "Thirty-six blue. Downtown. Hut."

Gabe Tillman snapped the ball into Wyatt's hands. He backpedaled several yards as the opposing lines crashed together. Determined grunts and the crack of pads competed with the thunderous cheers of the home team crowd. Settled deep in the pocket, Wyatt searched the pass patterns.

The right side of the field was covered. No hope there. Twenty yards downfield, Kevin "Tuck" Tucker stutter-stepped, then cut sharply toward the Marauders' bench in a square out route.

Wyatt sidestepped one of three blitzing linebackers. Another second ticked off the clock as he scrambled right, avoiding a second rushing wall of muscle. Racing toward the sideline, Tuck had temporarily broken free of the man-to-man coverage, but Albuquerque's left safety was closing in fast.

Wyatt cursed under his breath. No time to waste. Still in motion, he twisted his upper body and bulleted the pass. Like Superman in a helmet and pads, Tuck leapt into the air, hands outstretched toward the ball speeding his way.

Hit on his blindside, the air whooshed from Wyatt's lungs. His world tipped on its axis as two-hundred-eighty-seven pounds of all-pro linebacker rode him to the ground. A collective groan pulsed through the stadium. On his back beneath Dwayne Williams, Albuquerque's defensive captain, Wyatt desperately craned his neck to follow the play.

At least three yellow flags littered the turf and the Marauders' bench was going ballistic. Tempers flared and two separate shoving matches broke out between members of the opposing lines. Several players flanked Sam Fitzpatrick, holding the offensive coordinator back from lunging after Dante Grovers, the Rattlers' cornerback. Wyatt couldn't see Tuck, but a medical crew raced toward where he should have been.

"Son of a bitch." Wyatt shoved at Dwayne.

"I guess that shoulder injury story wasn't bullshit after all." Dwayne rolled free and rose. "You can't hit the side of a barn today, Hunter." With a taunting sneer, he spun away.

"Asshole." Gabe glared after Dwayne and offered Wyatt a hand, then tugged him to his feet.

"What happened?"

An earsplitting cheer erupted as the head linesman announced defensive pass interference against the Rattlers. Gabe pitched his voice to be heard over the roar. "Your throw was dead-on. Tuck would have had it if Grovers hadn't clipped him."

"Shit." Wyatt's gaze whipped back to the bench. "Is he hurt?"

"Grovers spun him like a top, but he's on his feet."

As the offensive line gathered around him, Wyatt scoured the sideline. He spotted Tuck near the end of the bench where the medics huddled around someone lying on the ground. Wyatt's tensed shoulders loosened as relief edged out over concern. An injury to anyone on the roster was a problem, but losing their number one wide receiver in the opening game of the season would be disastrous.

They'd dodged a bullet, but weren't out of the woods yet.

He cast a quick glance at the game clock as Tuck returned to the field in a loping gait. Ten seconds left. Thanks to the Albuquerque penalty, the Marauders were facing a first down inside Rattler territory. They'd been handed an opportunity they couldn't afford to squander but, down by four, a field goal wouldn't do. It was end zone or nothing if they were going to pull off a win.

He clenched his teeth. Considering the clusterfuck the afternoon had been so far, that was a big *if*.

"Who's hurt?" he demanded of Tuck as he joined the loose huddle.

"A lady photographer. The ball tipped off my fingers and drilled her in the face."

A chorus of grunts sounded from the men.

"She okay?"

Tuck nodded. "I didn't actually see her, but I heard one of the medics telling her she'll probably have one hell of a shiner."

Wyatt winced and shot a quick glance toward the medics.

Mario Davis, the team's bulky left tackle, sucked air through his teeth. "I'll bet. That pass was a damn cruise missile."

Gabe nodded in sober agreement. Tuck's lips twitched as if he were fighting a smile.

Wyatt frowned. "Why is that funny?"

"It's not, but the lady was. I'm not sure, because none of the words were actually profane, but I think she was cussing a blue streak."

On the other side of the circle, Jamal Knight didn't bother hiding his humor. The seven-year running back flashed his teeth in a grin. "Damn, Wyatt. You're on a roll. Looks like you've got *another* babe pissed at you."

"Yeah, man." Gabe leered and waggled his brows. "What happened to that legendary charm you *used* to have with the ladies?"

Wyatt grunted at the reminder of the fallout from his off-season injury. Caroline Wainwright, the team's owner, had docked him one hundred grand for skirting too close to the dangerous activities restriction in his contract, and V, his friend and the team's redheaded PR babe, was still giving him the stink-eye every time he visited the front office. He shoved his residual frustration over the situation aside to focus on the moment at hand.

In truth, his teammate's taunting snickers were a welcome change from the sober silence he'd faced throughout the afternoon. Gabe, Jamal, Mario, and Tuck were the best of the best. The starting line. All four had played at Wyatt's side since the Marauders had signed him as their starting QB. Over the course of seven seasons, they'd developed a solid comradery based on mutual respect, determination, and friendship. Mockery and laughter were a big part of the easy cadence that normally allowed them to work like a well-oiled machine.

So far today, that cadence had been off, but hell, it wasn't every day a team started the season with the possibility of making history by becoming the first team to win three consecutive Super Bowls. As their quarterback, it was Wyatt's job to set the pace, but nothing he'd tried had worked to overrule the men's understandable nerves.

Until now.

He flicked a pained grimace toward the group of medics working over the lady press photographer. While he hated knowing his tipped pass had hurt the woman, it looked as if she might have delivered that miracle he'd been hoping for. He'd have to find a way to make it up to her. Later.

"Yeah, yeah." He eyed the play clock that had begun to tick off once again. "In case any of you forgot, we still have a game to win."

Sam's voice came through the speaker in his helmet, delivering what would most likely be the last play of the game. Not surprised by the ballsy call, Wyatt's grin was sharp. Nervous jitters hadn't been their only problem today. Albuquerque's defense had so far held the Marauders to fifty-eight yards in the air. With time running short, the Rattlers would be looking for the long pass, and *that* was just the advantage the Marauders would need to pull off their scam.

"All right, gentlemen, what do you say we dazzle these assholes with a little bait and switch?"

Tuck dipped his chin. "What's the call?"

"Eighty-two post left."

Wyatt was met with anticipatory grins all around. He reminded each player of their responsibilities, then broke the huddle. The men spread out on the line of scrimmage. Wyatt used the time on the play clock, uttering bullshit audibles designed to settle the defense deeper into their stances, then scrambled back into the shotgun formation, barely avoiding a delay of game penalty.

With his defensive line out of position for the developing play, Dwayne frantically shouted instructions for the shift. Wyatt didn't give them the time. He called the snap.

Jamal cut from the right, tucking his arms and bursting toward the left side of the field as if he'd accepted the handoff. The move drew several members of the defense with him and opened a hole in the line much smaller than Wyatt would have preferred.

No time for hesitation. He sprinted through the crack, continuing straight down center field, and hoped like hell he could stay free long enough to clear the route for one of his receivers. If he couldn't, time would run out, the Marauders would lose, and there was an excellent chance he'd end up in traction.

A wall of determined muscle pivoted toward him. His path to the end zone was blocked, but he kicked on the afterburners, drawing the defenders and eating up a few additional yards. The clock showed three seconds and he'd neared the line of scrimmage before Albuquerque realized what was happening. By then it was too late. Distracted by Wyatt's run, the Rattlers' right safety had fallen behind Tuck. For the league's quickest wide receiver, a step and a half was more than enough.

With two seconds left in the game, Wyatt launched off his right foot and let the ball sail. It flew past the confused defense to drop into Tuck's hands. The stadium exploded in frenzied celebration as he strolled into the end zone unopposed for the win.

* * * *

Piper Darrow jumped as the curtained divider jerked open.

Eyes wide and full of concern, CC Tucker rushed to the side of the emergency room bed. "Getting out of the stadium was a nightmare. I followed as quickly as I could." The petite blonde cringed at the wad of gauze protruding from Piper's left nostril. "Oh, God. Is it broken?"

Touching a gentle fingertip to the bridge of her nose, Piper bit back a wince. "Slightly."

"Slightly?" CC dropped her gaze to Piper's blood covered sweater, then back. "That's an awful lot of blood for *slightly*." She crossed her arms. "Are you going all stoic English gentry on me?"

At her childhood friend's narrow-eyed complaint, humor overrode the dull throb of pain pulsing in Piper's nose and cheekbones. "I can't help myself. I *am* English gentry. We're reserved by birth and my stoic gene is dominant."

CC smirked. "I remember, *Baroness Delaney*. I also recall you participating in several very unreserved pranks during our summers in Italy. Especially one in particular that involved Signora Altobello's garden gnomes."

Piper laughed at the memory. "I was twelve and hadn't yet accepted the responsibility of my title." She pinned CC with an accusing grin. "And I wasn't alone in that mischief."

CC's eyes glittered with silent laughter. "Don't blame me. The gnome thing was Kris's idea."

"If memory serves, your cousin was the mastermind behind most of our pranks."

"Yeah." CC sighed happily. "We did have some fun, didn't we?"

"Great fun."

They shared a grin, then CC sobered. "So, what's the verdict? Will you require surgery?"

Piper shook her head. A mistake. The headache brewing at the back of her eyes intensified. She dragged in a cleansing breath. "No. Thank God. Actually, I was pretty lucky. The doctor said it's a mild break and expects the bruising will be minimal. He prescribed rest, ice for any swelling, and an over-the-counter pain reliever."

CC's cheeks puffed on a windy sigh. "Oh, Piper. I'm so relieved."

"You and me both. I'll be released as soon as my paperwork is in order." Piper smoothed the sheet over her legs. "Apparently, American emergency rooms are the same as in the UK. They're a tangle of red tape."

"Give me a few minutes." CC adjusted the strap of her purse over her shoulder. "I'll take care of it for you."

"It's being handled. Caroline Wainwright's personal assistant is down the hall dealing with the hospital administration." Piper glanced at the door and frowned. "I have to say, I don't feel right about the Marauders paying my medical bills, especially since none of this is the team's fault."

"Of course, they're paying. As a contributing artist for the team's biggest fundraiser of the year, you were on the sideline as Caroline's personal guest." CC cocked her head and squinted. "Please tell me you aren't blaming yourself. This was an accident. You were simply in the wrong place at the wrong time."

"I realize that but, you have to admit, it's obvious I have a major case of bad mojo when it comes to professional athletes."

"Mojo?" CC laughed.

Piper grinned and shrugged one shoulder. "You know what I mean."

"Don't even go there, girlfriend." CC's lips pulled tight in an affronted line. "It's not your fault Cody Beckett is a class A prick."

"There is no arguing that." Piper sighed. "But heavens. I haven't had a single incident with the normal men who visit Delaney Manor on a weekly basis, yet ten minutes surrounded by a field full of your American footballers and I'm a bloody mess." She touched a fingertip to the slight swelling between her eyes. "For my own safety, I believe I should limit my exposure to jocks while I'm here."

CC snickered and shook her head. "You can try." She propped a hip on the edge of the bed. "But it won't be easy. Especially with the Marauders players required to attend tomorrow night's fundraiser."

Piper chewed her bottom lip and winced. "There is nothing I can do about that, but I hardly think I'll have to watch out for flying footballs. With millions of dollars of art on display, I doubt the owners of the gallery will tolerate that type of tomfoolery."

CC grinned but her humor quickly died. She took hold of Piper's hand. "God, Piper. That ball had to be traveling at close to sixty when it hit you. When I saw you go down, I was scared to death."

"I admit, when I opened my eyes and found a crowd of uniformed behemoths standing over me, so was I, but I'm fine." She squeezed CC's fingers. "I promise."

"Okay." CC's chest expanded on a shaky sigh. "What can I do?"

Piper glanced down at the streaks of blood staining her sweater. "Have you a fresh jumper handy? I look like an extra from a horror film and don't want to frighten the hotel staff."

The concern in CC's eyes eased further with her laugh. "You don't have to worry about the hotel staff. I'm taking you home with me."

"That's not necessary."

"Yes, it is. You are *not* spending the night alone in a hotel room."

"Don't be silly." Piper tugged her fingers free. "I'm perfectly capable of caring for myself. Besides, I don't want to impose."

"Please. It's no imposition. The house has six bedrooms. We're only using two." Piper opened her mouth to make a further argument, but CC cut her off. "I should have insisted you stay with us from the beginning."

"Dearest, you know I appreciated the offer to be your guest then, as I do now." She softened her refusal with a smile. "But really, you have enough on your hands with a new baby, not to mention your handsome groom."

CC dismissed Piper's argument with the flick of her hand. "Tuck and I are hardly newlyweds and Huey is almost a year old. Anyway, bringing you home with me was Tuck's idea. If you want to refuse, you'll have to take it up with him."

Piper frowned. Having missed her friend's wedding because of scheduling difficulties at the manor, not to mention a decided lack of funds, she'd yet to meet CC's husband in person. "Why ever would he suggest such a thing? He's never even met me."

"Because you're my friend." A muffled jingle sounded from CC's purse. She bent over the bag and dug in search of her cell phone. "He didn't realize *you* were the lady photographer who'd been hurt. When he heard your name after the game, he called me from the locker room and insisted I convince you to come stay with us." She retrieved her phone and straightened, meeting Piper's gaze. "He feels guilty for not catching the ball."

"That's ridiculous."

"That's Tuck." CC shrugged and checked the phone's screen. Concern wrinkled her forehead as she answered the call. "Wyatt? What's going on?" She listened for a moment, then held a fingertip over the cell's mic to whisper, "It's Wyatt Hunter."

The name meant nothing to Piper, and she arched a questioning brow.

"The Marauders' quarterback," CC added, then spoke into the phone. "Besides a broken nose, she assures me she's fine." The deep rumble of Wyatt Hunter's voice reached Piper's ears. Whatever he was saying made CC laugh. "You can tell her yourself. She's sitting right here."

The headache in Piper's temples pulsed with renewed vigor. She waggled her hands in an *I'm not here* motion.

"He just wants to apologize." CC held out the phone.

Mackenzie Crowne

Piper bit her bottom lip. Well, bother. So much for limiting her exposure to the Marauders players. Still, refusing to speak to the man would be rude and God forbid the Baroness of Delaney ever be discourteous. Swallowing the familiar frustration that came with the need to always do the socially correct thing, she accepted the phone and held it to her ear. "It's so kind of you to call, Mr. Hunter, but an apology isn't necessary."

"I disagree, Miss…Darrow, is it? After all, I did break your nose."

She blinked. "I beg your pardon?"

A moment's hesitation, then, "CC said your nose was broken."

Piper met CC's questioning stare. "Technically, yes, but the ball simply grazed me instead of hitting me straight on. The break, as well as the resulting damage, are minor."

"Well, there you go. I broke your nose."

She mentally shook her head at the satisfaction in his tone as if he were actually pleased to have his culpability confirmed. "Seriously, it's nothing to be concerned about, and accidents happen. Please, don't blame yourself."

"Why wouldn't I? I threw the ball."

Oh, for heaven's sake. Why was he arguing when she was clearly attempting to excuse him of any fault? "Are you saying you were *trying* to hit me?"

CC slipped her fingers over her mouth, but her eyes twinkled with silent laughter.

The Marauders' quarterback was silent for a moment. When he finally spoke, his voice held a hint of humor. "Make no mistake. If I had *meant* to hit you, I would have. There would have been no grazing involved and the damage wouldn't be minor."

CC dropped her hand to her chest to whisper, "What's he saying?"

Piper cupped her fingers over the phone's mic the way CC had and whispered back. "If I'm not mistaken, he's bragging about his accuracy and prowess." A bark of male laughter came through the earpiece and Piper finished on a squeak, "in his sport."

"Nice clarification, sweetheart, but it ain't bragging when it's the truth."

Piper's mouth dropped open and she barely suppressed a distressed whimper.

CC's wince slid into a helpless grin. "He heard you, didn't he?"

Wyatt Hunter's deep voice came through loud and clear. "Every word."

Piper groaned and nodded, but CC waved her off. "Don't stress it, Piper. Professionally, Wyatt has reason to brag, but he's never been thin skinned, especially when the jab comes from a woman."

His easy laughter vibrated in Piper's ear. "CC's right. When it comes to jabbing women, particularly those who do so with sexy British accents, I'm a total pussycat."

Oh, dear Lord. Piper opened her mouth, but if there was an appropriate reply to his taunting gibe wrapped in a semi-flirtatious compliment, she couldn't think of it.

"You still there, sweetheart?"

Beyond embarrassed, Piper nonetheless chafed at the teasing laughter in his question as well as the endearment. "Yes, of course." Years of practice kept her voice even, controlled. "However, I'm afraid I must be going. It was lovely of you to ring me up, even it if was unnecessary. Good day."

"Wait, I actually called to..."

Thumbing the screen, she cut off the call and handed the phone to her wide-eyed friend. "And *that* man is at the top of my list of jocks to avoid."

Chapter 2

"I'm a *huge* fan, Mr. Hunter."

Wyatt paused in his search of the packed art gallery and turned his head. At six foot three, he towered over the petite blonde waitress with the smoky feminine purr. Arching a brow, he offered her his patented grin.

"That makes my day, sweetheart. It's always a pleasure to meet a fan."

She batted the thick fringe of her false eyelashes. "Can I get you anything?"

He bumped his chin toward the tray of crystal flutes she carried. "Why don't we start with one of those?"

She fingered the lapel at her bust line, drawing his attention to the mouthwatering view framed by the deep plunge of her white cotton blouse. Dipping two fingertips into her impressive cleavage, she retrieved a card.

"I work for the company that serves the private skyboxes at the Marauders' complex, and I never miss your games." She plucked a glass of sparkling champagne from the tray and handed him her card along with his drink. "Maybe we'll run into each other sometime."

His grin broadened. Though his taste in women tended toward curvy redheads, variety was the spice of life. That, and he'd never been a man to ignore a pretty woman with an invitation in her eyes. "That's a definite possibility," flipping the card over, he read her name, "Bethany."

The pink tip of her tongue appeared, briefly licking the dip in her full upper lip. Anticipation gleamed in her brilliant blue eyes and she matched his grin. "If there is *anything* else you need, anything at all, you just let me know." After a moment's hesitation, she turned and walked away.

As yet unnoticed by the milling crowd, Wyatt brought the rim of the glass to his lips and followed the deliberate swing of her hips. Her slim, black skirt molded sweetly proportioned curves. He hummed in appreciation. Bethany might be a tiny thing but, damn. She had a great ass.

For a moment, he considered taking her up on her blatant offer and to hell with the consequences. Shit, considering his playboy reputation, no one would be surprised if he tossed the pretty waitress over his shoulder in a fireman's carry and strolled out the front door.

His teammates, scattered throughout the crowd at tonight's fundraiser art show, would appreciate the entertainment. Better still, the subsequent headlines would send his father's anal retentive campaign manager into convulsions. Wyatt imagined the bulging vein in his father's temple as he read the articles, and his smile was smug.

Shaking his head, he dismissed the tempting fantasy and resumed his search for the lady photographer with the sexy British accent. He owed Piper Darrow an apology, but even if that task didn't weigh on his shoulders, he wasn't going anywhere. At least for the next few hours. First, because the success of tonight's fundraiser benefiting Down syndrome research was important to him personally, and second, because dear old dad wasn't the only one riding his ass at the moment.

He frowned and sipped deeply. Thanks to a freak, off-season injury, the last month and a half had been a ball buster, and yesterday's lackluster performance hadn't helped matters. With the increased stakes this season, it was no surprise the Marauders' front office was playing hard ball. Forget the hundred-grand fine the team had imposed on him for disregarding the no dangerous shit clause in his contract. Caroline Wainwright had personally promised to hit him up for some real money if he didn't keep his nose clean and the press off her back.

A derisive snort flared his nostrils as he glanced around the packed room. As if that was possible. From the day the Marauders had taken a chance on him, a two-year, untried backup quarterback who had yet to play in a single game, the skeptical press had been on him like stink on shit.

In the seven years since, he'd proven his detractors wrong. Leading the Marauders to four Super Bowl games, he'd netted two league MVP titles and three rings in the process. And none of that mattered. A new season started every September—along with predictions of Wyatt Hunter's failure to live up to the hype surrounding him.

The collective doubt pissed him off, but was nothing new. Growing up under Richard Hunter's maniacal insistence on perfection, a much younger Wyatt had discovered the best way to deflect the constant criticism was to never let anyone, especially his father, see him sweat.

The key was to make everything he did look easy, even when it wasn't.

Football certainly wasn't. Not when a brand new crop of rookies showed up at camp every summer, determined to make their mark. The truth was, Wyatt worked as hard or harder than anyone in the league. He just did it with a lazy, fuck you smile on his face.

Consequently, he'd been tagged as a lucky slacker back in high school and the label had stuck. But hell, this was his tenth pro season. He knew the drill and the outside criticism only served to push him harder.

The incoming fire from those he considered friends was something else.

He grunted in frustration as his scanning gaze landed on one of those supposed friends. V, as everyone referred to the Marauders' PR wiz, stood on the far side of the gallery. Sam Fitzpatrick, her husband of six months and the team's new offensive coordinator, laughed at something she said and pressed a kiss to her brow. Wyatt scowled, then downed the remainder of his champagne in a healthy gulp.

"Damn, Wyatt. Are you still sniffing in that direction?" Wyatt flicked a sidelong glance at Tuck who'd slipped up beside him wearing a taunting sneer. "She married the man, buddy. It's time to move on."

"Fuck you." Wyatt flagged a passing waiter.

Tuck chuckled and eyed the couple across the room. "I don't blame you for being pissed. It's got to sting to know you let an old man steal her right out from under your nose."

"Sam is what?" Wyatt scoffed. "Two years older than you?"

"Three." Tuck shrugged and grinned.

"Then I wouldn't be calling him old, and he didn't steal V from me." Wyatt exchanged his empty glass for a fresh drink, then waited until the waiter walked away. "She's a friend. Nothing more."

"Is that why you spent the entirety of last season begging her to sleep with you?"

Wyatt snorted. "There was no begging involved and, technically, I only asked her out for real that first time."

"And she shot you down."

Tuck's eyes flashed with satisfaction, but Wyatt shrugged good-naturedly. "Like a clay pigeon, and it was the luckiest rejection I've ever received."

He'd gone on to have the best game of his career that night. Of course, being a superstitious son of a bitch, he'd asked her out again the next Sunday. Once again, she'd said no thanks, and the Marauders added another W to the win column. Unfortunately, his dick had done his thinking on week three. While on the road in New England, he'd been distracted by a brunette ad executive he'd met in the hotel bar, and had temporarily forgotten about his current lucky charm. The Marauders suffered a crushing loss that Sunday.

Throughout the rest of the season, his teammates had razzed the hell out of him, but a smart man didn't question what worked. Whether by phone or in person, he'd approached V every subsequent game day, even *after* she and Sam had become an item. Come February, the Marauders completed their season at nineteen and one. In the process, they'd bagged their second consecutive Super Bowl win and V had become that rarest of things, a female friend.

Wyatt scowled her way. "She's still pissed at me for getting hurt."

Tuck followed his gaze. "You scared her. Hell, you scared all of us."

Wyatt's chest surged on a harsh sigh. "Yeah, that wild-water rafting trip turned out to be a dumb ass idea, but shit. It was a couple bruised muscles. It's not like I severed my throwing arm."

As the team's PR consultant, diffusing the press firestorm over his off-season injury had fallen on V's shoulders. But hell. She was his friend. He'd expected her to understand and cut him some slack. Instead, she'd looked at him with disappointment in her eyes, going so far as to question his sanity, and worse, his commitment to his career *and* his teammates.

Weeks later, her accusation still stung.

Tuck shrugged. "It's Sam's first season with the pros. Her interest in the team's success just got personal. Besides, she can't help it. She's a woman. They carry a maternal gene that requires them to bitch bite a man if he does anything they consider dangerous." He grunted. "Especially if that something is fun."

Wyatt smiled at his friend's grumbling complaint. "Speaking from experience?"

Tuck swirled the wine in his glass. "You missed the Malones' barbeque last month so you didn't see, but Jake bought a sweet all-terrain vehicle to use around the farm. One thousand cubic inches of muscle and speed." Tuck hummed appreciatively deep in his throat. "CC took one look at it and said if I even considered getting one, she'd go straight to Caroline and narc me out."

Wyatt chuckled. Recently retired from the field, Jake Malone, the Marauders' record-breaking tight end, was no longer constrained by the clause that had gotten Wyatt into trouble. Tuck was, however, and it was obvious his wife was familiar with the contents of his contract.

Wyatt faked a heavy sigh. "Women. Can't live with 'em...."

"Can't kill 'em," Tuck finished for him, and they shared a grin.

"Ain't that the truth." Wyatt shook his head. "Between Caroline and V, my hide is full of bitch bites." Then there were his sister's pleas that he call a truce with their father. Christ. He rolled his shoulders. "I don't know what the problem is lately. It's like the females in my life have all gone nuts. If I was smart, I would seriously consider steering clear of the softer sex for a while."

Mackenzie Crowne

Bethany chose that moment to walk by. She sent him a smile sultry enough to leave a contrail of perfumed steam in her wake.

Tuck sucked air through his teeth. "Yeah, good luck with that, buddy."

Wyatt's answering grin widened as he caught sight of Tuck's wife across the room. Partially blocked from his view by an elderly couple, CC Tucker stood in front of a wall of black and white photographs. Spotting Wyatt, she dipped her head to the side and returned his grin, wiggling her fingers in a wave.

"Speaking of the softer sex. Your wife is looking..."

Wyatt froze with his glass an inch from his lips as the elderly couple moved on, revealing the woman at CC's side. The redhead's simply cut ebony gown was in keeping with tonight's black on black dress code. Her plaid silk scarf in bright blues and greens wasn't. However, the unexpected splash of color wasn't what made her stand out in the sea of black. Not for anyone who carried a Y chromosome, anyway.

Raised in the elite halls of society's one percenters, Wyatt recognized a debutante when he saw one. Her glossy auburn hair was slicked back in a severe twist at the back of her skull and her delicate facial features spoke of aristocratic roots. So did her precise bearing.

Chin held high, her hands were folded properly at her slim waist. Whoever she was, she radiated sophisticated elegance, but the modest cut and demure boat neck of her silk-blend gown did nothing to diminish the impact of the body it covered. He ran his gaze over luscious curves designed to bring a man to his knees, then lowered his glass and puckered his lips in a silent whistle.

Beside him, Tuck snickered. "I wondered how long it would take for Piper to catch your eye."

"Piper?" Wyatt whipped his head around to spear Tuck with a narrow-eyed stare. "The *redhead* is the lady photographer?"

He grinned and nodded. "In the flesh."

Wyatt turned and was struck again by Piper Darrow's flesh. The shy photographer was fucking gorgeous. He repeated his quick inspection of her curves before moving to her face. No hardship there. High cheekbones and full lips. Pale, flawless skin. He squinted, searching for the expected fallout from her broken nose and winced at the slight swelling marring the bridge. However, she'd done a masterful job of concealing any bruising beneath her cat-shaped eyes. Light in color, they were either blue or green. He couldn't tell from this distance, but he'd damn well be finding out.

Either by accident of fate or serendipity, she'd been instrumental yesterday in turning a sure defeat into a spectacular come-from-behind victory.

As soon as the post-game interviews were done, he'd set about learning her identity and tracking her down. He'd intended only to thank her by picking up her hospital tab, but she'd hung up before he could explain his reason for calling.

His fault for teasing her the way he had, and a lucky break as it turned out. The Marauders had apparently stepped in to take care of her medical expenses, leaving Wyatt to find some other way to make up for her broken nose. Now that he'd gotten a look at her... Anticipation thrummed in his veins as his mind supplied a few enticing possibilities.

According to his source in the front office, Piper would be heading home to England within a day or two of tonight's event. Unacceptable. He'd need a lot more time than that if he was going to thank her properly. With the season underway, non-business travel was temporarily out of the question until the team's bye in a couple of weeks. He wasn't free to follow her to her home turf, and preferred to seduce her on his, anyway. Which meant he'd have to convince her to extend her visit. After all, there were many forces in the world, and the one that had delivered the hot photographer into his was a force he didn't plan to ignore.

"Introduce me. I need to talk to her."

Tuck laughed and drew his attention. "I know that look."

"What look?"

"The look that says you've discovered your newest lucky charm."

Damned right, he had. Wyatt shrugged. "You've got to admit, the game took a miraculous turn immediately after she got hit."

Tuck's smile was smug. "Nothing miraculous there, buddy. Just the sweet combination of Grover's dirty hit, my superior speed, and your mediocre passing abilities."

"Blow me."

Tuck laughed, then shook his head. "Asking V out every week was one thing. What are you going to do? Convince Piper to let you break her nose every week for the rest of the season?"

Wyatt curled his lips in a toothy leer. "What? You don't think she'd agree?"

"Not a chance, asshole."

"You're probably right." Wyatt chuckled. "I'll just have to charm her into showing up on the sideline as my personal guest."

"For the next five months? That might be a problem. She's heading back to England in a couple of days."

Wyatt let his gaze linger on her face. "Not if I can help it."

"That's what I thought." Tuck heaved a happy sigh. "I hate to see you crash and burn, my friend."

"Why would I..." Disappointment washed through Wyatt as he spun his head back around. "Shit. She's married." He'd never been saddled with a bunch of self-inflicted restrictions when it came to women, but he did have a couple hard and fast rules. At the top of his list was no poaching.

"She's as single as they come."

Wyatt studied Tuck's provocative smile and winced. "Please tell me she's not another of your relatives." Wyatt wouldn't be surprised. The Tucker clan seemed to have an overactive *babe* gene. Since another of his unbreakable rules was to steer clear of his friends' female relatives, the Tucker women were off-limits.

Tuck shook his head and grinned. "No relation. CC and Piper met when they were kids. They're friends."

"Then what's the problem?" The level of relief gushing through Wyatt surprised him.

"Piper doesn't like athletes. And I mean, she *really* doesn't like them." A dimple popped in Tuck's cheek. "Present company excluded, of course."

Wyatt frowned. Well, shit. He'd attributed her coolness during their short phone conversation to shyness or a natural reserve but, apparently, something more personal was in play. A definite problem, but not an insurmountable one.

"Never mind. I'll introduce myself." He headed for the other side of the room.

Tuck hurried after him, laughing like an ass. "I've got a C-note that says she'll..."

Wyatt held up a hand. "I'm not betting with you on this one."

"Oh, ho. He's serious."

Wyatt snorted. Fuck yeah, he was. He didn't screw around when it came to winning games *or* hot redheads. He sent his friend a sidelong sneer. "How do you think CC will react when I tell her you tried to place a bet on her friend?"

Tuck's step briefly faltered before he caught up once more. He grumbled beneath his breath, "Low blow."

Wyatt smiled smugly and set a course for his gorgeous lucky charm. Reaching her proved impossible, however. Slowed by the press of bodies attending tonight's fundraiser, he spent the next three hours tracking her movements as he greeted the guests and dignitaries in attendance and glad-handed the deep-pocketed patrons. Much to his frustration, each time he managed to close in on her, she headed in the opposite direction. In fact, the one time he managed to make eye contact with her, she skittered into the crowd like a rabbit dodging the wolf.

When the evening finally came to a close, she was nowhere to be found. It was the damnedest thing but, apparently, Tuck was right. Wyatt's lucky charm had done her best to avoid him and, tonight at least, she'd succeeded.

Frustration jabbed him in the gut as he slipped out of the gallery through the loading bay at the back of the building. Behind the large window of the security office, the guard bumped his chin in greeting and cued the large rolling door. Wyatt waved and keyed the remote on his Aston Martin DB11. A deep-throated rumble echoed through the cavernous bay.

With a determined grin, he slid into the driver's seat, revved the engine, then merged into traffic on the busy avenue. His redheaded rabbit might have given him the slip tonight, but no self-respecting wolf would give up without a fight.

Chapter 3

"You're not playing down your injury so we won't worry, right?"

"I'm fine, Moira," Piper reassured as she had the last six times her friend and Delaney Manor's co-manager had called to check on her. Switching the phone to her left hand, she dabbed a drop of concealer on her fingertip and leaned toward the bathroom mirror. Just as the doctor had predicted, the only remaining evidence of her broken nose was a bit of tenderness and some minor swelling. The pale purple smudges beneath her eyes had thankfully faded enough that a fine layer of makeup easily hid the discoloration. "Seriously, I'm perfectly fine. You're worrying over a bit of nothing."

"Oh, pish posh. You'd say it was nothing even if your nose had fallen off your face."

Piper grinned and dropped the tube of makeup into her bag. In bra, panties, and thigh-high stockings, she padded back into the bedroom of the Tuckers' guest suite. "My nose is still attached, so stop fussing and tell me how things are there. Did Mr. Tidwell come by to fix the sticky door lock on the Rosewood suite before the Warrens arrived? And what of the delivery from Wellesley Farm? As I recall, Tilly was running low on jam for her breakfast scones."

Piper tossed the bag into her open suitcase and swept up her skirt. "Oh, and before I forget, one of Alice Remington's bridesmaids has yet to confirm her room for next week's bachelorette weekend. I meant to call and check in with her before I left, but it slipped my mind. Would you do me a huge favor and contact her today? Her number is in the reservations book."

Moira's laughter sounded in Piper's ear. "Relax, Mother Goose. You are supposed to be enjoying yourself there in the States, not fretting over what's happening here at the manor. Tilly and I *can* muddle through for a few days without you, you know."

Piper's sigh was guilty. "I know that. It's just..."

"It's just that you insist on taking everything onto your shoulders, even when the practice isn't necessary."

"That's not true." Piper stepped into her dark gray linen skirt.

"Oh, really? Then what were you doing on a ladder on Saturday, painting the carriage house shutters when you should have been well on your way to the airport?"

Piper jerked straight. "How did you..." She narrowed her eyes.

Angus, you old tattletale.

After sliding the skirt over her hips, she zipped and hooked the closure at her waist. Okay, so she'd cut her arrival at the airport nail-bitingly close, but that couldn't be helped. Angus, her mother's favorite cousin and the estate's long-time groundskeeper and handyman, was getting on in age and refused to accept there were some chores he should no longer be doing on his own.

She snatched her pale peach blouse from the mattress. "When I was putting my bag in the boot of the car, I spotted Angus working on the ground level shutters. I didn't want him tackling the second floor, okay? Besides, the painting only took me a few minutes." Thirty, actually. Which was why she'd nearly missed her plane. Tucking the phone between ear and shoulder, she worked the buttons on her fitted blouse, then smoothed the hem at her waist. "For heaven's sake, he's seventy-eight and suffers from vertigo. He has no business climbing a fifteen-foot ladder."

Moira's voice was full of easy humor. "Agreed, but if you'd bothered to ask before climbing the rungs yourself, you'd have known I'd made arrangements with one of the boys from town to help him with the ladder work."

Piper's shoulders drooped as some of the indignant starch leaked from them. "Well, bother."

A sigh drifted through the phone. "You know we love you and appreciate all you've done for us, especially since becoming a hotelier was the last thing you wanted."

"Oh, hush. Delaney Manor belongs to all of us and, really, turning the house into a B&B was our only viable option considering the circumstances." Piper dropped to the edge of the mattress and slipped her foot into her high heel. Bending at the waist, she dug around under the bed in search of the other.

"Not according to Abigail. To hear her tell it, the sale of Delaney Manor is inevitable."

Piper straightened and glared at the far wall. "My cousin is a greedy, elitist vulture, furious I've made her wait so long for her mother's half million pounds."

Piper swallowed. *And I have just three months to earn the last one hundred fifty of it. If I can't, scraping together enough money to feed us all at the end of the month will be the least of my worries.*

Moira snorted. "With a dash of luck and a lot of hard work, the B&B will be in the black one day very soon." The determination in her voice intensified. "Once it is, we'll pay her off and never have to deal with the snotty cow again. In the meantime, it's clear to anyone who knows you, there are things you'd rather be doing with your life than playing the proper baroness for our guests."

Piper flopped to her back to stare at the ceiling. How true that was. Although she'd coveted neither the title nor the responsibilities that came with it, her fate had been sealed centuries ago. In fulfillment of the original writ, granted to her grandmother eight times over, Piper became Lady Darrow, Baroness of Delaney, upon her mother's death, less than an hour after Piper's birth.

Flopping an arm over her eyes, she bit back a sigh. She'd gladly continue to play the role of proper baroness if it meant she could hold on to the manor, but smiling and posing for pictures with the strangers invading her home every week wouldn't be enough. Already reeling from her father's sudden death in a tragic car accident nearly three years past, she'd been shocked to learn the alarming truth of the estate's finances and horrified by the discovery of a long-forgotten stipulation in his will.

Although the title and lands had come to Piper through her mother, it had apparently been her father's modest fortune that had kept the manor afloat these last thirty years. Piper cringed at the funds wasted, especially on her behalf. How much had Da spent, raising her with extravagance to fill the hole left behind by her mother's death? Private schools, summers on the beach in Italy, riding lessons, not to mention flying her here and there with her friends while on breaks from university, or simply on a whim.

He'd spoiled her horribly. Selfishly, she'd let him and, now that he was gone, there was a price to pay. After covering the inheritance taxes, the estate had been in no position to satisfy the five-hundred-thousand pounds Da had long ago set aside for his only sister, Abigail's deceased mother, Claire. The forgotten stipulation might as well have been for five hundred million, and the three-year deadline to pay it, three days.

Not that Piper was destitute. She wasn't. The value of the five-hundred-acre estate on the eastern coast of northern England made her a very wealthy woman—on paper.

Land rich, she was cash poor, but selling off the estate to make good on the debt was out of the question. Four hundred years of tradition wasn't something Piper took lightly, and there was more than just herself to consider. With Da's passing, Piper was the last of her line, but Angus was true family, and Moira, and her mother, Tilly, were more family than staff. The estate was their home as much as Piper's. She had a responsibility to keep the familiar roof over all their heads.

So far, the fledgling B&B had managed to hold off their creditors and the rush of land developers circling the coastal property like wingtip-wearing birds of prey, but there wasn't a lot left over at the end of each month. What little was, Piper added to the small portfolio she'd built on the tiny trust her mother had left her. Unfortunately, the three-hundred-thousand-pound nest egg fell far short of covering Abigail's payoff, and time was running out.

Not wanting to worry them, Piper had kept the deadline included in Da's stipulation from Moira, Tilly, and Angus. With the end of the three-year grace period looming ever closer, Abigail had become increasingly demanding and pushy. The *someday* Moira predicted couldn't come soon enough.

The sigh Piper had been fighting broke free. "The title comes with..."

"Responsibilities," Moira spoke the word with her. "Yes, yes. So your father said many a time, but this isn't the seventeenth century, luv. In today's world, your title is little more than a romantic throwback to another time."

Piper frowned and sat up. "My *title* is the curiosity that has helped us fill the manor's guest suites for the past two and a half years."

"Maybe that was true at the beginning, but it's the manor and its grounds, and my superior skill at keeping our guests happy, that have grown our reputation."

"Is that so?" Piper slipped her foot into her second heel, stood, and turned to smooth the bedding.

Moira's laughter drifted through the phone. "Mum's scones might have something to do with it, too, but my point is we're doing perfectly fine, despite the baroness not being in residence. The pantry is stuffed with jam and Mr. and Mrs. Warren are snoring peacefully behind the decidedly unsticky lock of the Rosewood suite door. And I spoke to Alice Remington yesterday. It seems her tardy bridesmaid has been sacked from the bridal party for shagging the chief bridesmaid's boyfriend."

Piper snapped straight. "Oh my."

Moira snickered. "I know. Can you imagine? Anyway, Alice has already replaced the girl and paid for the new attendant's room. There's nothing for you to worry about here. Enjoy your last day in Manhattan. I can't believe you've spent the last two nights in Kevin Tucker's house. I am positively green with envy. Is he as tidy as he looks in those magazine ads?"

Piper coughed on a laugh. "He's married to CC."

"So?"

"So, she's my friend."

Moira snorted. "Right, and her husband is utterly peng."

Piper shook her head and laughed, but had to agree. Kevin Tucker was definitely hot.

The image of another big, blond hottie flashed in her mind, and she fought a shiver. As she'd discovered last night at the fundraiser, Tuck's good looks held a hint of bad boy, but the perfection of Wyatt Hunter's handsome face was far more dangerous to a woman's heart rate. She could just imagine Moira's reaction should she ever get a close look at the Marauders' uber-hot quarterback.

"Speaking of Tuck and CC, they're going to wonder what's keeping me. Give Tilly and Angus my love. I won't be arriving at the manor until late, so I'll see you in the morning."

They said their good-byes, and Piper tucked her phone in the pocket of her skirt, then headed downstairs to join her hosts. She wore an apologetic smile as she stepped from the hallway into the kitchen.

"I hope I haven't kept you waiting." The breath backed up in her throat as she halted abruptly.

****

Wyatt turned his head as Piper Darrow rounded the corner. Her gaze collided with his, and she skidded to a stop. So did his breathing. He'd told himself he'd imagined the weird blow to the chest when he'd spotted her across the gallery last night, but there it was again. Bam! A sucker punch to the ribs right below his heart.

He dragged a stealthy breath through his teeth as he devoured the sight of her up close and personal. Green. Her cat-shaped eyes were a vivid emerald, rimmed by a thick fringe of auburn lashes the same shade as the shiny russet curls tumbling over her shoulders.

As if she'd been hit by the same fist of attraction, she stared at him in wide-eyed silence. Heat unfurled in his gut as a sudden blush flared on her sharp cheekbones. Instinct insisted he move, take the three steps necessary to reach her. Cup her face in his hands and explore that first taste of her mouth in what he knew intuitively would be a sweet feasting.

He wasn't quick enough. Before he could act on the impulse, she blinked. Once, twice, three times in slow repetition. Her chest lifted on a sharp intake of breath and her gaze skittered away.

Disappointment rushed him in a full-out blitz, but he took solace in running his gaze over her sensible two-inch heels, shapely calves, proper knee-length skirt, and pale peach button-up blouse. She reeked of respectability and sophistication, and he went hard on a helpless surge of lust. He bit back a groan as his imagination fired on all cylinders.

The erotic images running through his head like a high-dollar porn were short-lived, however. Tuck cleared his throat, demanding Wyatt's attention. His friend wore a familiar shit-eating grin. As if he'd read Wyatt's mind, he quirked a knowing brow, but it was eleven-month-old Huey Tucker, propped on his daddy's right forearm, who killed Wyatt's wholly inappropriate fantasy involving a shy kindergarten teacher with dark red curls and a body made for sin.

"Piper. You haven't technically met Wyatt Hunter." CC wiped her hands on a towel. She shoved her way past Tuck to round the center island of their large kitchen. "I can't believe I spaced that Tuck had invited him to lunch this afternoon so they could watch some game tapes together."

Wyatt winced, but Tuck grinned unrepentantly at his wife's blatant lie. Smart woman that she was, CC hadn't bought their story for Wyatt's unexpected arrival less than two minutes ago. Apparently, she wasn't going to call out either of them on the bullshit excuse. Not now, anyway. But from the narrow-eyed glower she'd pierced Wyatt with a moment ago, she'd have plenty to say later if he didn't behave himself with her friend.

Tuck, on the other hand, had clearly placed his money on things going badly between Wyatt and Piper. After jerking him around when Wyatt had called an hour ago, desperate to find the shy artist before she left the country, Tuck had taken great pleasure in announcing Piper was, at that very moment, showering in the Tuckers' second floor guest suite. He'd then invited Wyatt to lunch with the stated purpose of being on hand to watch him crash and burn with their sexy houseguest.

"Ah." Piper glanced at Wyatt. A strained smile pulled at her full lips. "A pleasure to meet you in person, Mr. Hunter."

Wyatt cocked his head. "Wyatt, please. I hear Mr. Hunter and look around for my old man."

He waited for her to correct herself. Women like her lived by the rules, after all, and decorum demanded she acknowledge his comment. She didn't let him down, although the way her lips flattened said she wasn't pleased at the necessity.

"Very well. A pleasure to meet you, *Wyatt*."

She started to turn away, but he wasn't having that. "Does it still hurt?"

"Pardon me?"

Confused by the way she stiffened as well as the wariness in her eyes, he tapped a fingertip to the side of his nose.

"Oh." She relaxed visibly, the subtle tension in her shoulders easing. "As I explained the other night, the damage was minimal, but thank you for inquiring." She glanced away. "CC, I..."

"Where in England are you from? I spent a lot of time in London when I was a kid and I'm picking up an odd lilt to your accent."

Her gaze snapped back to him and something he couldn't quite figure flashed in her eyes. She covered whatever it was with a polite smile. "You're probably hearing a bit of the Scots. My people were originally from a small fishing village in Argyll."

"You're Scottish?"

She nodded and turned again. Nope, he wasn't finished yet. "I thought I recognized the highlands in some of your photographs at the fundraiser." Surprised pleasure filled the gaze that swung back to meet his, and he pressed forward. "You have quite an eye."

Beautiful, intriguing eyes a man would give his soul to be staring into as he climaxed.

"Thank you. That's very kind of you to say."

A riot of color bloomed on her cheeks and, for a moment, he was afraid he'd spoken aloud. He shoved a fist into the pocket of his jeans and shifted his feet. *Shit, Hunter, get your mind out from under her skirt before she notices your Johnson trying to drill its way through your zipper.*

"So, you live in the highlands?"

The suspicion in her eyes didn't make sense. With her looks, she had to be used to men wanting to find out all they could about her. Finally, she rolled her shoulders in a negligent shrug.

"No, but I did spend my childhood summers there. I live in a small village on the east coast of northern England, not far from the Scottish border."

CC handed little Huey a sippy cup. "As usual, Piper is being modest. She's the Lady..."

"Lady proprietor of a lovely B&B forty kilometers or so from Carlisle." The smile Piper turned on CC was overly bright.

Wyatt glanced between the two women. From the hesitant wrinkle of her brow, CC got the silent message her friend had just sent. Whatever that was.

He shook his head "I thought you were a photographer."

Another shrug. "Photography is my art, but changing bedding and booking holidays for happy travelers is how I pay the bills." Piper spun around, giving him her back. "CC, what can I do to help?"

Talk about having the proverbial door slammed in his face. He made the mistake of glancing at Tuck, who bared his teeth in a triumphant sneer. Wyatt knew better than to take his friend up on his challenge, but that didn't mean Tuck would ultimately claim victory on their non-bet. Wyatt would win over the shy photographer because, damn it, he hadn't been this attracted to a woman in…. Hell, he couldn't remember ever being this jacked up over a woman he'd just met and had yet to touch.

He shot Tuck a one-fingered salute. The asshole burst out laughing.

CC directed a sharp gaze at both men, then smiled at Piper. "If you wouldn't mind grabbing the wine, everything else is ready." CC bumped her chin toward the two bottles breathing on the counter.

"Yes, of course." Piper glanced around. "And the glasses?"

CC lifted the platter of sandwiches from the island. "They're already on the table outside. It's such a nice day I decided we should have our lunch on the patio. Tuck, can you open the door for me? And Wyatt, be a doll and bring out the pitcher of ice water? It's in the refrigerator."

Huey squealed with laughter as Tuck shifted the baby to his shoulder, hefting him like a sack of potatoes, and crossed to open the French doors for his wife. They disappeared outside and Wyatt turned to discover he stood between Piper and the wine. They performed an awkward shuffle of feet, each stepping in the same direction, then together in the opposite, and back again.

The fourth time they nearly collided, he paused and held up a hand. "If I'd known we'd be doing the cha-cha, I would have worn my dance shoes."

He was surprised by the genuine humor in her curved lips. A definite improvement over the cool dismissal he'd received from her so far. When she dropped her gaze to the floor, he expected her to skitter past him without a word. Instead, she studied his feet for a moment before looking up.

"Do they make dance shoes in size gigantic?"

A tiny wrinkle appeared between her eyes as if her question were sincere. She blinked again, the way she had earlier. Three distinct cat-like winks of her lashes. He found the quirk so endearing it was difficult not to close the distance and sweep her into his arms. His pulse rate spiked in anticipation, but he tamped down the dangerous urge. Kissing her senseless now would only doom the intimate plans he had in mind for the two of them.

He needed to tread lightly, but damn. Was her skin as soft as it appeared? Glancing toward the doorway where the Tuckers had disappeared, he grunted beneath his breath. He had Piper alone for the moment and wasn't about to waste the opportunity to move the chains a little farther downfield.

He called upon every ounce of patience he had in him and smiled. "I wear a size sixteen, and yeah, they make them. I've bought a couple of pairs over the years."

"Couple of pairs? Of *dance* shoes?" The wrinkle between her brows deepened as she stared at him. "You dance?"

He couldn't help grinning at the incredulity in her voice. "I doubt Julliard will be calling anytime soon, but yeah. I dance. Or, more precisely, I've taken lessons off and on since I was in college."

"Julliard?" There was that slow triple-blink again. "Ballet lessons?"

He chuckled. "Along with some ballroom. You'd be surprised at how efficient dance is at strengthening the core muscles."

She ran her gaze down his body, pausing on his feet, then back up again. "I apologize. It's just that you're a little…bulkier than the typical dancer."

He briefly glanced down at his body before looking up at her to tease, "Bulky? Is that a polite way of saying I'm fat?"

"Good Lord, not at all. Why, you're perfect." Embarrassment widened her eyes, and she shook her head. "That is… What I meant to say is, anyone who looks at you can see how very nicely muscular you are." A tiny whimper of distress sounded in her throat, and she slammed her eyelids shut. "Oh, bother. I'm going to stop speaking now."

He grinned. *Very nicely muscular?* Yeah, screw patience. He closed the unacceptable gap between them and slid his fingers beneath the loose cuff of her elbow-length sleeve. Just as he'd suspected, the softness of her skin put the brushed silk of her prim blouse to shame. She jolted, staggered slightly on her heels, and her eyes flew open.

He tightened his grip. "Steady there."

Her pupils dilated within a shrinking ring of emerald iris as she stared into his eyes. She mumbled beneath her breath. The only words he could make out sounded suspiciously like mojo and disaster. He rubbed his thumb along the silky soft skin of her inner elbow and was rewarded by her shiver.

The pulse point beneath his thumb had gone thready and matched her voice when she spoke. "They're waiting for the wine."

"They won't die of thirst." Using his grip on her elbow, he urged her closer. "No one's ever accused me of being perfect before."

The blush on her cheekbones intensified. "I tend to say the most absurdly inappropriate things when I'm nervous."

"I make you nervous?" He slipped his hand around her waist and eased her flush against his chest. She gasped at the contact, but he was pleased she didn't shove free and bolt for the doorway.

"Very much so." She tipped her head back to retain eye contact and surprised him by clutching his bicep with her right hand. "I probably shouldn't admit that."

"No, I'm glad you did. I like knowing I make you nervous." Like hell. Her admission was the best news he'd had in months.

His pulse wasn't exactly steady, either. He dipped his head until his lips were a breath above hers. If she didn't stop him in the next three seconds, there was a good chance he would doom to failure any possible chance he had with her, but he couldn't bring himself to care.

On the other hand, he'd never forced himself on a woman and fair play demanded he give her the last say on the matter. He dropped his voice to a husky whisper. "I'm going to kiss you."

Another whimper, but she didn't jerk from his hold. "I know, and that's an extremely bad idea."

He tightened his arms around her and brushed his lips along her cheekbone to her ear, then down until he could nibble her jaw line. She smelled of vanilla and woman. "I disagree. Tasting you is the best idea I've had all year."

"Maybe for you. I, on the other hand…" She slid her left hand up his chest and around the back of his neck.

He lifted his head to meet her hazy green gaze. "You what?"

"I am in *so* much trouble."

Before he could ask why, she rose on her toes and pressed her mouth to his.

Chapter 4

What the devil are you thinking?

Piper ignored the nagging voice screeching in her head and burrowed closer to the warmth of Wyatt's big body. Confident and supremely talented, he took full control of the kiss without hesitation, nibbling, sucking, and nipping at her lips before stabbing deep to swirl his tongue around hers.

His musky flavor permeated her taste buds and weakness flooded her limbs.

She wriggled closer and buried her fingers in his shaggy, blond hair. His deep groan of encouragement vibrated from his chest wall into hers, increasing the delicious friction of his solid pecs against her tightened nipples. A helpless moan of pleasure purred in her throat. She rose on her toes and returned the favor by sucking at his invading tongue.

Through the silk of her blouse, his wide-palmed hand warmed the skin at her waist. Every feminine nerve ending in her body poised in desperate anticipation as his fingers rode over her ribs until he'd replaced his chest with his palm. Cupping her breast, he flicked his thumb over the tip of her nipple, straining against the silk barrier of her blouse and bra.

Piper, pay attention! Been here, done this. Remember? With disastrous results.

She whimpered into his mouth as the nag in her head broke through the fog of desire to point out the obvious. Okay, yes. Getting involved with another playboy athlete would be the height of stupidity, but she wasn't naïve enough to let that happen again. Life was a harsh teacher, after all, and she was an excellent student.

The older, wiser Piper was firmly grounded in reality. Professionally, she did what was expected of her, of her title. What was right for Delaney Manor and Tilly, Moira, and Angus, not to mention the villagers who'd come to count on the infusion of cash brought to the area thanks to the stream of visitors to the B&B. And on the personal side, living like a nun was a price Piper willingly paid after that debacle with Cody Beckett.

But good Lord in heaven, she hadn't realized how much she'd missed the pleasure of a man's touch or the intimacy of his kiss.

Self-preservation demanded she call a halt to this madness immediately, but it had been ever so long since she'd been held intimately. Was it any wonder a simple kiss would sear the blood in her veins after her self-induced dry spell?

Wyatt shifted his head, taking the kiss deeper. Sharp pleasure pulsed through her, and the folds between her thighs swelled and heated.

Dry spell, me arse. Don't be daft, Piper. You're in the middle of an utter melt-down and the man's kiss is anything but simple.

Bloody hell. He tasted of sin and pleasure—a combination too delicious to resist.

Just a few more moments. CC and Tuck were right outside and she was catching a plane in several hours. It wasn't as if she were at risk of forgetting who she was or what her responsibilities entailed. Didn't she deserve a few sweet moments of the illicit pleasure found in the arms of an incredibly sexy man before facing her dismal reality once again?

She purred into his mouth. He slid his free hand to her bum and urged her into fuller contact with his body. Heady pleasure made her gasp at the hard evidence pressing against her mound and belly, telling her she wasn't alone in her madness. She didn't object when his hand left her bottom to slip beneath the hem of her skirt. Nor when his fingers trailed up the back of her thigh, then stilled at the bare skin just above the elastic lace leg-band holding her stocking in place.

Wyatt broke the kiss and lifted his head. She hung in his arms, staring into his eyes, hot with arousal.

His chest rose and fell like a bellows. "Damn, sweetheart. You are one hot surprise after another."

He dipped his head, but her short, sexy-as-all-hell reprieve was apparently over. Reality slapped her across the face in the form of childish giggles from outside.

She jolted and held her breath. He slammed his eyelids shut. A crushing disappointment squeezed her chest until she wanted to cry. Instead, she sent a silent thank-you to Huey Tucker for bringing her to her senses before her knickers ended up around her ankles.

Her inner nag was blessedly silent for a change. A miracle, that. Then again, with her body still throbbing, she didn't need to be reminded she had a dangerous weakness when it came to larger-than-life, warrior playboys. Counting herself lucky over the close call, she freed her fingers from the silky strands of Wyatt's hair.

His hands dropped to his sides as she stepped back. With the island behind her, she couldn't go far, and the proximity of his big body disturbed her more than she would've liked to admit. She momentarily got lost in the irresistible sight of his solid body and bit her bottom lip.

Nicely muscular was an understatement. Last night at the fundraiser, she'd been aware of little more than the mega wattage of his smile. Rattled, she'd been too busy avoiding him to take a good look, but it seemed his fitted tuxedo had blunted the strength of the body it covered. Not so, his street clothes. His black T-shirt molded to impossibly broad shoulders and well-defined pecs. Peeking from beneath the hem of one short sleeve, the edge of a tattoo was visible on his thickly muscled bicep. Faded jeans rode low on his trim hips. The material stretched tight at the thighs and...

She swiftly skipped past the clear ridge of the healthy erection that had been pressed against her like a steel lightning rod, dropping her gaze to the frayed denim resting atop the toes of his scuffed boots.

She cleared her throat. "Oh, dear. Did I say bad idea? I should have said disastrous."

"On the contrary." Bold as can be, he slid his hand over his crotch to adjust himself. "The temperature in here jumped a good fifty degrees the moment I touched you, and I wasn't the only one caught up in the flame."

Her insides reheated to near sizzling. With false bravado, she lifted her head. The dismissive hand she slashed through the air was meant as much for herself as it was for him. "That was simple chemistry."

A dimple appeared with his smile. He didn't have to step forward to cup her chin. She gritted her teeth against a helpless wave of pleasure as he brushed his thumb over her cheek. "You may be right, sweetheart, but chemistry this hot is too rare to ignore."

Obviously, he wasn't familiar with the concept of spontaneous combustion. She'd been burned once before, and by a flame much less scorching than that which had flared between them just now. A smart woman knew when to retreat and, if that didn't work... She'd run like hell.

"Be that as it may, what just happened won't be happening again." She twisted her head, freeing her chin from his fingers. He dropped his hand to his side once again.

"Then you shouldn't have kissed me like that." He dipped his chin and the husky need in his voice was reflected in his eyes. "That kind of thing gives a man ideas."

The breath stalled in her throat. Goosebumps broke out and danced over her skin.

Right. Time to run.

She stepped around him before she could do something she'd regret—like lose what was left of her mind and wrap herself around his gorgeous body like a clinging vine.

"Any ideas I might have given you will be short-lived. I'm boarding a plane back to the UK in a few hours."

"What if I asked you to stay?"

Positive she'd misheard him, she paused and slowly turned. Okay, so the kiss they'd shared was incredible. She was still weak-kneed from its effects and frustrated she couldn't do a thing about it. But asking her to stay? What kind of man would suggest a woman abandon her home and country because of one sizzling kiss?

He held up a hand. "It's not what you're thinking."

She plucked the wine bottles from the counter. "That's a relief. I would hate to think CC and Tuck had befriended a man barmy enough he runs around kissing strange woman and then asking them to relocate."

Back came the dimples, along with his deep chuckle. "Damn, even the way you toss out insults is a turn-on."

She stiffened as her frustration intensified. "I'm sure you're having a lovely time poking fun at me, but I'm being perfectly serious."

"So am I. Your sexy accent turns me on. And your eyes... Did you know they go all dark and mysterious, like a spitting cat, when your back gets up?" She opened her mouth, but he stepped forward before she could say a word. Propping his hands on the counter on each side of her hips, he caged her in. "You turn me on quicker and hotter than any woman I've ever met, but I'm not suggesting you relocate. Not permanently, anyway."

Caught between excitement over the possibility she affected him as he did her, and confusion over what he could possibly be suggesting, she clutched the wine bottles to her chest. "You're not making sense."

"I doubt it'll make a lot of sense to you once I've explained, but I'm hoping you'll hear me out before you say no."

Like a sneaky secret weapon, his smile was suddenly all hopeful anticipation and boyish charm. Prudency insisted she harden her heart against the irresistible pull, but that didn't stop her from being curious. She dipped her chin in a wary nod.

"I want to hire you."

She blinked. Of anything he could have said, a job offer was the last thing she expected. "Why... That's ridiculous. Besides, I already have a job."

"Yeah, but I'm willing to bet it doesn't pay anywhere near as well as I will."

She stared into his eyes, unsure if he was sincere or simply having a laugh at her expense. Lord knew, she needed every shilling she could pull in if she was going to save the manor, but...oh, bollocks. What was she thinking? Saving the manor would require a miraculous windfall, and nothing good could come of any association he might suggest. Best she catch her flight and not look back.

She opened her mouth to reject his offer out flat.

"As for what I'd be asking of you to earn that money, well, that's the part that might not make sense."

Curious in spite of herself, she lifted a wary brow. "Try me."

His lips tweaked in a wicked smile, and he leaned his upper body toward her. She held him off with two liters of Chardonnay to the chest. Obviously, he was having a go at her, and it bothered her she'd nearly fallen for his line. She knew better.

"Forget it." Slipping around him, she headed for the patio doors.

"Wait." He laughed and stopped her with a gentle hand to her elbow. "I'm not going to lie. You're a beautiful woman and getting you into my bed is definitely part of my short-term agenda."

Had she considered his boyish smile a secret weapon? It couldn't hold a candle to his sexy croon or the carnal intent in his sparkling grayish-green eyes. She clenched her teeth against the tingles of pleasure his bold admission elicited in her traitorous body. Damn the man. He simply didn't play fair.

As if he were reading her mind, he curled his lips in a wholly male grin. The gentle squeeze of his long fingers ended on a slow caress as he ran his hand down to her wrist, then released her. "Say the word and we're in a private suite at the Plaza, but our sleeping together has nothing to do with my job offer. What I want from you professionally is completely on the up and up."

If she were smart, she would shake her head and walk out the door, but she had to know. "What, exactly, would be required in this job?"

Satisfaction flashed in his eyes, and she could have sworn his shoulders relaxed marginally. "Well, now. There are a couple of things. First, seeing your photographs at the fundraiser last night got me thinking. We could raise a hell of a lot more money for Down syndrome research with one of those hunk of the month calendars, don't you think? I'm sure I could round up a year's worth of guys if you'd be willing to take the pictures."

He was kidding, right? "I..."

"And second, I need you to show up at the remaining Marauders games."

"To do what?"

He dragged a palm around the back of his neck, looking a bit sheepish. "Nothing, really. All you'd need to do is be at each of the games and stand on the sidelines."

But, of course. He wants to pay me to stand on the sideline. Why didn't I think of that? The man is out of his head.

A lifetime of proper behavior kept her from telling him what he could do with his asinine offer. She curved her lips in a bland smile and added an extra bite of sarcasm to her rejection. "No, thank you. If you'll recall, the last time I was on the sideline, I ended up with a broken nose."

"Which is exactly why I want to hire you."

Oh, for heaven's sake. She stared at him as several seconds ticked by. The sincerity in his eyes appeared real enough and he looked completely normal. Yet, American football was a very physical sport. Perhaps too many hits to the head left him a bit off.

"You really are quite mad, aren't you?" She shook her head and spun toward the door.

"Mad enough to pay twenty-five hundred per game, plus travel expenses. First Class, of course, and five-star lodging."

She stopped short and glanced over her shoulder.

He dipped his chin. "Since we came from behind to win last Sunday, right after you were hit with the ball, I'll include week one in the tally. If the season goes as expected, the Marauders won't be battling for a wildcard spot, but I'll throw that week in as a bonus. At nineteen games, that's," he angled his head to the side as if calculating, "forty-seven-five."

With her fingers going numb, she had to clutch the bottles tighter so she wouldn't drop them. Forty-seven thousand, five hundred dollars?

"I'll double it if we make it to the Super Bowl. That comes to ninety-five." He tossed his shoulders in a shrug. "Ah, hell. Let's make it an even one-hundred grand."

One-hundred-thousand? Dollars, not pounds! She swallowed hard and did a quick conversion calculation in her head. Good Lord, she'd be within twenty thousand pounds of paying off Abigail…

Her pulse shot toward the dangerous range, and she turned to face him fully. "Why in the world would you pay anyone that kind of money to stand on the sideline?"

The boyish smile returned. "Not just anyone. You, Piper. First, because I broke your nose and I owe you for that."

"Nonsense." She frowned. "I told you that's not necessary."

"It is to me, and second…" She cocked her head when he hesitated. "Because, thanks to you, we did come from behind to win the game."

"Thanks to me? I don't understand."

"Everything I've ever wanted is on the line this season. The Marauders are in a position to do what no other team has done in league history." His eyes glittered with expectancy. "With perseverance and a little luck, we'll take our third consecutive Super Bowl and permanently claim our place in the record books as the best pro team ever fielded. As team captain and quarterback, it's up to me to see we achieve that ultimate success. To do that, I have to stay healthy, and I need my good luck charm." A dimple winked in his easy smile. "That's you, sweetheart."

She stared at him, unblinking. Forget a bit off. He was a complete nutter who looked and sounded more like a teenager on steroids than a thirty-something captain of a professional sports outfit.

She shook her head. "Let me get this straight. I'm a human rabbit's foot?"

Humor twinkled in his eyes. "Go ahead and laugh, but we were on the brink of losing to a team we should have crushed Sunday until you showed up. Consider it an eccentricity if you like, but if something works, I stick with it."

"If you recall, I was also hit with a deflected ball."

A wince puckered his forehead. "You wouldn't be expected to repeat that part."

She snorted a helpless laugh. "I should hope not."

He shrugged good-naturedly. "I know this sounds crazy, but superstitions are pretty common amongst the ranks of professional sports. I'm not the only Marauder who recognized your injury as a turning point in play."

Of all the… He couldn't possibly be serious. She was about to suggest he see someone who could help talk him through his delusional crisis when he held up a hand.

"Don't knock the power of belief. It plays a crucial role in a person either successfully getting what they want or walking off the field a loser."

She smirked. "Yes, well, most people aren't nutty enough to spend one hundred-thousand dollars on a crazy superstition."

His grin was unrepentant. "True, but only because most people don't have an extra hundred grand lying around. Lucky for me, the Marauders pay extremely well. I've worked hard for every penny, and I've invested wisely. As a consequence, I have more money than I'll ever be able to spend. I choose to spend some of that money to get what I want." An intensity that hadn't been there before slipped into his eyes. "And I want you, Piper Darrow."

She swallowed as her body insisted on applying a purely personal meaning to his words. He held her gaze as the heat of a blush worked its way up her chest to her cheeks. Even considering his proposition was courting disaster, but damn, damn, damn! It was a shame, really. He was incredibly tidy, and one hundred thousand dollars…

Bugger. Taking advantage of a mad man would be completely unethical, not to mention just plain mean. She spoke the denial before she could foolishly leap off the cliff of her own demise. "I'm sorry, but I can't possibly accept. I'm afraid you're simply going to have to find yourself another rabbit's foot."

Chapter 5

"I beg your pardon?" Piper blinked at V Fitzpatrick.

The Marauders' PR specialist wore a hopeful expression. "The team will purchase the copyright for any photographs you produce. We'll also cover any expenses while you're here in addition to paying you very generously for your time."

The figure V quoted was half the amount Wyatt had offered Piper earlier this afternoon. Fifty thousand dollars wouldn't get her anywhere close to paying off Abigail, but…

Wait. Half the amount Wyatt had offered?

Suspicion slammed into Piper's mind, and she jolted.

"I'm sorry. Um…." She hesitated. The offers differed and V worked for the team, not Wyatt. It would be impolite to accuse the poor woman without good cause, but bloody hell. After having failed to get Piper to accept his bizarre job offer, had Wyatt made a call, pulling strings through the team? He was their quarterback, after all. They'd want him happy, but just how far would they go to make sure that happened?

Piper clenched the strap of her purse. "By any chance, did Mr. Hunter have anything to do with the team making me this offer?"

"Wyatt? No-o-o." Genuine confusion creased V's brow as she dragged out the word. "I personally approached Caroline and suggested we invite you on board for this project. She took one look at your photographs and agreed." V's eyes widened, and she stiffened as understanding dawned over her face. "Oh, hell. What has he done this time?"

This time? The woman clearly *expected* Wyatt to be in some sort of trouble, which didn't surprise Piper.

Good luck charm, me arse. The man obviously had more money than he knew what to do with and an imagination to match.

Piper clamped down on an unladylike snort that, combined with the unacceptable language running through her head, would have given

Tilly a case of the vapors. From V's response, it was clear Piper's knee-jerk suspicions were unwarranted. Though relieved on that score, she'd inadvertently opened a door she would prefer remained closed. Shifting in her seat, she searched for a way to steer the conversation away from a topic *she* wouldn't be comfortable discussing—like that searing kiss she'd shared with Wyatt several hours ago.

She settled on a flat-out denial. "Nothing. Forget I mentioned him."

"Nothing? Are you sure?" V studied her with squinted eyes. "That would be a first for Wyatt."

Bollocks. I should have kept my big mouth shut.

Piper took her own advice and said nothing.

V's smile was knowing. "I can't say I'm surprised. You're beautiful and you're a redhead. Two of Wyatt's favorite traits in a woman." The blush heating Piper's cheeks must have shown because V sighed. "Just as I thought. Let me guess. He invited you to run off with him for a romantic weekend in Bermuda?" She cocked her head. "No, that's wrong. He's got a game on Sunday and practice all week." Snapping her fingers, she nodded curtly. "I've got it. Dinner and drinks in a private suite at the Plaza." She arched an auburn brow. "How close am I?"

Piper's mouth dropped open. She snapped it shut. "Frighteningly so. The suite at the Plaza came up." She scowled. "*He* offered me a job, too."

Surprise flashed in V's eyes. "Really? What sort of job?"

Piper shifted uncomfortably. "He said he'd been thinking of doing a *hunk of the month* calendar to raise more money for Down syndrome research. He wanted me to take the photographs."

"I see." V's eyes darkened with understanding. "No wonder you asked if he'd had anything to do with our proposal."

Piper nodded, then shrugged. "The calendar turned out to be nothing more than an excuse to keep me in the States. When I declined, he all but admitted what he really wanted was for me to stand on the sideline for the Marauders' remaining games, and you wouldn't believe how much he was willing to pay me to do so. Apparently, he has a delusional belief that I was somehow responsible for last Sunday's win."

"Oh, shit." From the way V twisted her lips, she was fighting not to laugh. "You're this year's lucky charm."

"That's what he claimed." Piper stiffened as the rest of V's comment registered. "Wait. This year's? You mean there have been others?"

"A few. Myself included." The laugh she'd been fighting broke free, and she smoothed her palm over the tight twist of her hair. "I told you, he has a thing for redheads."

Piper pressed two fingertips to the pulse pounding in her temple. "Just as *I* thought. The man is barmy. Uh…crazy."

"Crazy like a fox." V picked up a gold pen from the desktop. "His motives for putting together that calendar might be suspect, but the idea has merit. Hmm." She fiddled with the pen, a shrewd glint in her eyes. "We'll get back to that. For now, let's focus on the offer already on the table. The moment I saw your exhibit last night, I knew you were the perfect choice for the still shots I want."

Flattered, yet more than a little bewildered, Piper twisted the strap of the purse in her lap. "You realize I don't take traditional portraits? My preference is candid shots, snapping that which catches my eye. Surely, there's a local photographer who would jump at the opportunity to work with the team."

"Several, without a doubt, but your candid eye is the reason I was anxious to speak with you before you left town." V slid the pen between her fingers. "Your photographs tell stories, Piper, which is precisely what I'm after. The one of Alick Graham was mesmerizing. I want that same quality telling the story of our 'Fab Five.'"

A rush of warmth surged through Piper. The photograph of Alick had sold last night for quite a tidy sum. Thrilled to contribute so handsomely to such a worthy cause, she was nonetheless a little sad to see the print go. And not just because she had a soft spot for Angus's rough and tumble, time-weathered twin. She'd looked through her lens at Alick, grinning as his sloop was tossed about by the choppy waters of Loch Fyne, and knew the shot would be a favorite even before the shutter had clicked. And she'd been right. Light, depth of field, and subject matter had come together in a stunning composition.

She shoved aside her professional pride to ask, "Fab Five?"

"If," V paused and held up her hand, "no, *when* the Marauders win the Super Bowl at the end of this season, sixteen current players will earn their fourth championship ring as Marauders. I'm not sure how much you know about American football, but that's quite an accomplishment. Caroline plans to make a big deal of the rare stat, which is the reason behind the production you'd be working on. The finished piece will be broadcast at the halftime show of the Marauders' last home game. Which, if all goes as expected, will be the conference championship."

V stilled her restless fingers. "The production will profile each of the sixteen ring bearers, and include the rest of the members from this season's team, but the focus will be on the five original members of the starting offensive line Caroline put together the year she purchased the Marauders.

She's looking to show her 'Fab Five,' as she calls them, not just from a professional perspective, but a personal one as well."

She tapped the pen against the desk's blotter. "Some candid shots of the men on the field are necessary but, mostly, we're interested in a more personal exposé. An intimate look into their private lives type of thing. Interspersed throughout your photographs will be interviews with each of the guys and videos of memorable plays." She dropped her chin and held Piper's gaze. "You're the expert. Based on what I've told you, will a week of full access to each of the five men be sufficient to get what we're looking for, or will you need more time?"

Piper's lips quirked in a helpless smile. "I would answer that, but I haven't said yes. Yet."

V chuckled. "Caught that, did you?"

"I have a master's degree in business. My favorite professor's number one rule of negotiation was, *'Draw the client in by calling on their expertise on a minor detail and you're halfway to making the deal.'*"

V grinned. "Your professor was right. It usually works."

"Yes, it does." Piper had used the tactic more than once while dealing with contractors hired to work at the manor. But her home wasn't her concern at the moment. The Marauders' job offer was, specifically, the identity of the men she'd be expected to photograph. "Who are the five?"

As if sensing victory, satisfaction gleamed in V's eyes. "Gabe Tillman, Jamal Knight, Mario Davis, Kevin Tucker, and," she opened her hands as if in apology, "Wyatt Hunter."

Piper ignored the uncomfortable tingle of adrenaline pulsing in her nerve endings. The others she could manage without an issue, but a week of full access to Wyatt Hunter? Bad idea, that.

"Before you say no, there a couple of things I'd like to explain. I know you have a car waiting downstairs to take you to the airport, but will you give me a few more minutes?"

Piper swallowed. Prudence insisted she shake V's hand and run as fast and as far from Wyatt Hunter's domain as she could get, but there was the matter of fifty-thousand dollars. Beyond closing the gap to finally shedding the specter of her cousin's shadow from her daily life, how lovely would it be to spend five guilt-free weeks focusing on her photography again instead of stressing over which Peter to rob in order to pay one of several Pauls?

A flush of anticipation she hadn't experienced in nearly three years shimmered through her veins. It stung, of course, to acknowledge a good portion of her excitement came from the thought of remaining in the States for a time—where a certain sexy athlete resided—but she didn't like to lie to herself. The cold truth was, she was attracted to Wyatt. What warm-blooded woman wouldn't be?

Nothing she could do about the helpless pull, but being aware of a problem was the first line of defense. If she dared to take the offered job, she'd simply have to keep up her guard and refuse to give in to that particular temptation.

She dragged in a deep breath to calm her racing pulse and, schooling her features into professional curiosity, she nodded.

V set aside the pen and folded her hands. "Let me preface what I have to say by admitting I consider Wyatt a close friend, and that *he*, specifically, is the reason I called you here this afternoon." She studied Piper's face. "From that blush flaming your cheeks a few minutes ago, you already know he's a charming devil."

The blush made a reappearance, warming Piper's cheeks, and V's easy laughter echoed through the room. "Trust me, you're not the first woman to respond to his irresistible appeal. He's a charmer, all right, a playboy of the first order, but he's also a gentleman in the best sense of the word. If you're not interested, all you need to do is tell him. Just understand, it's not in him to give up. Don't be surprised if he keeps asking, but don't stress it, either. He's not the kind of man to push a woman."

Yeah, but what if the woman was interested, despite not wanting to be? Piper smiled wanly. "That's good to know."

V nodded. "Bottom line, those of us lucky enough to know the real Wyatt know he's one of the most open and amiable men you'll ever meet." Her blue eyes softened as she smiled. "And, once you have, it's simply impossible to dislike him."

Piper wished she could disagree. She couldn't, however. Even knowing the Marauders' handsome quarterback was dangerous to her equilibrium, she'd been thoroughly charmed.

V rested her hands on her desk when Piper remained silent. "He's a genuinely good man, an extremely talented quarterback, and a natural leader. The players respect him and the front office can't argue with his consistent success on the field." A sardonic smile quirked her wide mouth. "That's not to say he's perfect. The good ol' boy persona he shows to the world can be downright annoying, and he has a rebel streak running through him that gets him into trouble far too often." She shook her head and laughed. "I swear, sometimes he acts more like a perpetual teenager than the grown man and successful athlete he is."

Piper couldn't disagree with that assessment, either. Hadn't she thought the same thing two hours ago? She frowned and grumbled beneath her breath. "He's Peter Pan with a grownup libido."

V's startled laughter was rich and full. "Oh, God, how perfect. He'd love that description." Her lips twisted in a crafty grin. "If you don't mind, I'm going to steal it."

Piper waved a hand. "Steal away."

"It's a deal." V's humor slowly faded. "He's also the only son of Richard Hunter."

Surprised by Wyatt's apparent relation to the prominent American politician many assumed would someday reside in the White House, Piper sat up straighter. "I hadn't made the connection."

V nodded soberly. "If it were up to Wyatt, no one would. From what I understand, his father and he don't get along, and never have." She studied Piper with keen eyes. "Unfortunately, his family's fame adds another layer of scrutiny to everything he does. With your background, you'd understand how trying that can make things at times."

"My background?" Piper tensed.

V smiled softly. "I chaired the art show, Baroness. I also Googled you when CC first mentioned including your work in the fundraiser."

"Ah." Embarrassment swamped Piper. She didn't have to imagine the headlines the Marauders' PR specialist had read.

V's lips flattened in distaste. "From what I can tell, Cody Beckett threw you under the bus to protect his own overblown ego. It's too bad we hadn't met back then. The press are little more than rabid vultures, but they can be useful tools if you know how to work them. By the time I'd finished with your ex-fiancé, no woman would have gone within an inch of him and he'd have had a hard time winning an endorsement selling used cars."

Piper choked on a laugh, but sobered quickly. "Who else besides you, CC, and Caroline know of my title?"

"No one that I know of. Caroline made it clear from the beginning that information wasn't to be shared."

Piper relaxed subtly. "I'd like to keep it that way, if you don't mind." She attempted a casual smile and failed. "As you said, with my background, I do understand. Which is why I don't use my title when traveling, but for rare instances. Being plain old Piper Darrow suits me and keeps things less…complicated, shall we say?"

V nodded even as her eyes softened with unexpected compassion. "Makes perfect sense. From what CC's told me, those headlines were nothing but lies."

Mackenzie Crowne

Proof of CC's support caused a tightening of Piper's throat. "Unfortunately, not everything was a lie. I am, indeed, in debt up to my knickers, or rather, the estate is, just as the papers claimed." She shrugged. The financial deadline looming over her head wasn't a topic she was willing to discuss. "The situation has improved slightly, thanks to the severe tightening of our belts and lots of hard work, but maintaining five hundred acres of prime real estate isn't cheap. Unless I'm willing to sell off my ancestral home, which I'm not, I'm technically broke and expect to remain so for the foreseeable future, if not the remainder of my life."

"Sacrificing your personal life to return home and run the family business doesn't sound like the actions of a gold-digger, Baroness."

True, but neither did one simply walk away from London's premiere football star unscathed. Cody's rabid fans at *The Daily Bugle* had no reason to question his claim that he'd dumped Piper upon discovering she was only with him for his money. After all, what woman would willingly give up a jet-setter life, including Cody Beckett, for the solitude of a country manor?

Like the unimaginative lemmings they are, the rest of London's tabloids gleefully repeated the *Bugle*'s Gold-Digging Baroness label, and the moniker had stuck. Temporarily, anyway. Apparently, pictures of a self-serving, man-trapping baroness doing nothing more scandalous than helping an old man muck out the barn didn't sell papers. The press had eventually moved on to juicier stories.

"Exactly how much did Wyatt offer to pay you for his calendar idea?"

Caught off guard by the quick change of subject, Piper blinked. "Um. He didn't, actually. The quote he gave me was for his *good luck charm* sideline appearances, which he promised to double to one hundred thousand if the Marauders made it to the Super Bowl."

V studied Piper in silence for several seconds. "That much money can do a lot of good things if a person spends it wisely."

Piper cleared her throat. "Without a doubt."

V nodded. "If I can convince you to work with me on the Fab Five project, would you object to accepting Wyatt's offer to produce the calendar he mentioned?"

"I..." *Oh, holy hell.*

"The more I think about it, the more I believe a fundraiser calendar would dovetail nicely with the various promotions the team has planned." A slight frown marred V's brow. "Of course, something like that would have to be approved by Caroline, but I can't see her objecting. Especially if Wyatt agrees to pick up the costs. It's only right he does, since the idea was his."

"Well, I..."

"As for your commission." A sly smile slowly curled the corners of V's mouth. "I think one hundred thousand sounds about right, don't you?"

Piper coughed. "I couldn't possibly..."

"Of course, you could." V waved an airy hand. "He opened this particular door, and it's not like he doesn't have the money. He was willing to shell it out to get what *he* wants. It'll do him good to have his tactics turned on their head for a change."

Piper drummed her fingertips on the clasp of her purse. "Not to mention you'd get what *you* want. That is the reason you're dangling the possibility of an extra chunk of cash in front of my nose, isn't it?"

V's grin was unrepentant. "Money is the root of all evil but, in this case, sweetening the pot a little is done with the purest of intentions. You need the cash. I need your skills. And Wyatt is willing to pay quite well to achieve his goals. If it makes you feel better, you could always indulge his superstitions by attending the games as he requested. Tying up your weekends for nearly five months is worth a bit of cash, wouldn't you say?" She didn't wait for an answer. "The way I see it, that's a win-win-win situation."

If only it were that simple. "A lovely sentiment until the press discovers I've hooked up with another professional athlete, and this time with the express purpose of monetary gain."

"Money you will earn in exchange for your photographs, Piper. There is no shame in doing an honest day's work, even for a member of the peerage."

Piper did snort this time, and was thankful Tilly wasn't around to witness her mortal sin. "Clearly, you've never had a brush with the European press."

V laughed softly. "No, I haven't, and thank God for that. The Americans are bad enough."

Piper sighed. "Why me? Why are you so insistent on me saying yes?"

V eased back in her chair. "May I speak candidly?"

"You mean you haven't been so far?"

V's laughter was light and genuine. "I do like you, Baroness, and that is one of the reasons I'd like to work with you. Another is your eye. I wasn't blowing smoke up your skirt when I said I liked your photographs. Simply put, they're stunning. But the most compelling reason you are perfect for our project is precisely because you *do* understand that added layer of scrutiny."

She straightened in her chair. "This project is designed to highlight the team and the Fab Five but, for me, it's all about Wyatt." She shook her head. "Unlike the rest of us, even you, apparently, he doesn't *have* the option to be plain old Wyatt Hunter. Ever. Between his family name and his high visibility position with the team, he's *always* in the spotlight."

Her lips pulled flat in aggravation. "His record speaks for itself, but a certain block of the sports press act like his accomplishments are due to little more than blind luck. Maybe it's that he was born with a silver spoon in his mouth, or they don't like his father's political philosophy. Personally, I think a lot of the flack he takes is due to plain old jealousy. But, whatever the source, too many members of the press seem to have a hard-on for him, and not in a good way. In the meantime, they treat other quarterbacks in the league, players whose stats don't come anywhere close to Wyatt's, like gods."

Her blue eyes glittered. "I can't tell you how much that pisses me off. He shrugs off the unwarranted criticism, claiming he doesn't give a shit what others think, but that's bull. He cares, more than he'll ever admit. And it's not just the press." She spoke through gritted teeth. "Early this summer, things got personal when his father was quoted in an article at *Eye on Sports*. In a supposedly offhand remark, Richard Hunter all but agreed with the interviewer when he questioned whether or not Wyatt had the mental fortitude to lead the team to the Super Bowl again this year."

A stab of sympathy pierced Piper's heart. The press may have gobbled up Cody's lies like red meat, but at least she'd had Moira, Tilly, and Angus in her corner. "What a wanker." Horrified at her rare *spoken* slip into the gutter, Piper gasped. "I beg your pardon. That was completely out of line."

V waved her off with a quick grin. "Don't apologize. As far as I'm concerned, wanker is the perfect description for a man who would say something like that about his son. Especially to a bottom feeder website like *Eye on Sports*." V's grin faded to a scowl. "After the interview was posted online, Wyatt disappeared for three days. When he resurfaced, he'd wrenched the muscles in his right shoulder. The idiot tried his hand at extreme white water rafting, injuring his throwing arm and nearly drowning in the process."

Twisting her lips in what looked to Piper like a guilty grimace, V shook her head. "He scared the hell out of me and I said some unforgiveable things to him. Things I didn't mean." She sighed and her shoulders sagged marginally. "I can't take the words back, but I can make it up to him by helping him beat the press and his...*wanker* father at their own game."

Piper bit her lip. "I'm afraid you've lost me."

"It's simple. The Marauders making it back to the Super Bowl this February is *the* biggest sports story in the history of the league. The eyes of the world are on us and will remain so as long as we have a chance of succeeding. Which means we'll have five months of intensified interest."

She cocked her head. "I wasn't bragging when I suggested I knew how to work the press. As a sports agent, I spent more than a decade making Jake Malone and others look better than they usually deserved. I did it by spinning the story I wanted printed. As frustrating as Wyatt can be at times, he's nothing like the caricature the vultures have created of him."

Her eyes flashed with a mix of anger and determination. "It's time I utilized my skills to put an end to their nonsense. You can help me do that with your incredible eye and your understanding of what it's like to be in the spotlight. Together, we'll do an end run around the press and present the fans of football with the funny, generous, talented and, yes, imperfect man Wyatt's teammates and friends know and care for."

Intensity gleamed in her eyes. "I'd be willing to pay half your fee up front, and I'm sure a similar arrangement could be made with Wyatt. That should free you up from some of the, shall we say, *financial concerns* you might have on the other side of the pond."

Embarrassed horror unfurled in Piper's chest. *God, CC, how much of my private life did you share with this woman?* She spoke through clenched teeth. "CC Tucker has a big mouth."

"No, what she has is a sweet disposition and a very pushy friend." A grimace creased V's brow. "Don't blame CC. It's my job to learn all I can about the people the Marauders choose to work with, and I'm very good at what I do. I'm also the epitome of discretion when the situation warrants. Nothing we've discussed today goes beyond the two of us. So, what do you say? Do we have a deal?"

Chapter 6

Piper carried a stack of clothes to the bed in her large bedroom, automatically avoiding the squeaky board at its center. From the time the manor was built in the seventeenth century, generations of Delaney children were cared for in this, the third-floor nursery. The suite of matching bedrooms with adjoining bath had been underutilized in modern times. However, the rooms were the perfect solution to house Piper and Moira once the B&B had opened and they'd given up their suites on the second floor to their guests.

Never a morning person, Piper had chosen the nursery's west bedroom where she wouldn't be disturbed by the rising sun. Placing the clothing into her suitcase, she straightened and looked through the mullioned windows of the room's French doors. A tiny bistro table and chairs took up most of the private widow's walk balcony. In the distance, afternoon sunlight glinted off the pond at the edge of the clearing. The reflection of the wooded grove beyond the water wavered as a crane danced its feet along the surface to land in a smooth glide.

Piper loved the tranquility of the manor's acres and would surely be ready to return after five weeks away. Not that she didn't enjoy the hustle and bustle of life in the city, but it wasn't home. Her Da used to say she'd been born under a wandering star, but had a homing bird's soul.

A spear of grief pierced her heart.

Travel had once been a big part of her life. She'd lived for the adventure of a new place, a new culture, a new sunset, which had been a big part of her attraction to Cody. If she'd been born under a wandering star, he was a nomad. Boredom inevitably set in if he spent more than a day or two in one place. She'd happily tagged along as he chased one sunset after the next, with biweekly stops at the manor to recalibrate her homing signal.

It wasn't until she'd received word of her father's death and had returned home to the manor for good that she'd realized how unappealing her life with Cody Beckett had actually been. In truth, giving up the man and his nomadic ways to save her beloved manor had been more of a relief than a hardship. She'd supposedly loved him but, if not for the fallout, thanks to his egotistical need to place the blame for their broken engagement on something or someone other than himself, parting ways with him would have been a mostly positive experience.

And what did that say about her? It wasn't as if she was incapable of loving another human being. Her love for Da had been boundless, and Tilly, Moira, and Angus each held an irrefutable piece of her heart. Still, she wondered if perhaps she was one of those people who were incapable of true romantic love.

The concept saddened her, but there were worse fates. Like spending her life locked in a loveless marriage or, God forbid, obtaining the first divorce of the Delaney line. Still, she wanted a family some day and would need a husband if she were to produce the next Baroness of Delaney, as was expected.

Besides, she enjoyed men too much to pull off spinster.

Her nipples puckered helplessly as the memory of Wyatt's kiss snuck into her head. She slid her palms over the tightened peaks. The pressure only made matters worse. With a grimace, she imagined the rumble of four hundred years of ancestors rolling over in their graves as she added Wyatt Hunter to her list of mistakes. Because, let's face it, the Marauders' sexy quarterback would no doubt provide a hot and heavy distraction for a time, but he was no more marriage material than Cody had been.

Dropping her hands to her sides, she returned to her packing. It was a shame, but if she'd learned nothing else from her time with Cody, it was that a simple life, lived with a simple man, was the way to go. Now, if she could just find him.

"Okay, luv. It's just me here, so fess up. What aren't you telling us?"

Jolted by the unexpected interruption, Piper pivoted her head to find Moira standing in the doorway of the common bath. "Whatever do you mean?"

Moira snorted and crossed her arms. "You look so melancholy I'm about to burst into tears."

The complaint was vintage Moira, and brought a smile to Piper's lips. She came up with the best excuse she could think of. "I was thinking of Da, and how much I'm going to miss you all and Delaney Manor while I'm gone."

Moira dropped her arms and approached the bed. Climbing onto the foot of the mattress, she wrapped an arm around the mahogany post in a cross-legged slouch. "I thought you were excited about the Marauders' job offer."

"I am." Piper smoothed her stack of silk blouses into her suitcase. "Good Lord, Moira. With the conversion rate, the job pays close to sixty-five thousand pounds. Combined with the three-hundred-fifty I have saved, I'll be within eighty-five thousand of getting Abigail off our backs once and for all." She picked up her favorite cream with bold florals bra and panties set and folded them neatly. Dipping her head, she tucked the fine lace into the case. "*And* if I play my cards right, there is a good chance I can pick up that much and more with a side project."

"What side project?" When Piper didn't answer immediately, Moira straightened from the post and bent low until she could see her face. "You're blushing, Piper." She let out a piercing squeal. "Oh my God. You met a guy!"

Piper winced at the sheer volume of the comment. Thank God the house was empty of guests for the day or Tilly would be sitting them both down to repeat her proper "Innkeeper Decorum" lecture. Shaking her head, Piper folded more of her lingerie into the bag.

"Technically, I met quite a few guys. You might not have known this, but American football teams are chock full of them."

Moira's scowl was pure exasperation. "Don't be cheeky. Who is he?"

Experience had taught Piper that keeping a secret from Moira was next to impossible. It could be done, of course, and had been, as with the deadline to pay off Abigail, but when it came to guys, Moira seemed to have a sixth sense. Somehow, she'd always known the moment a boy had caught Piper's eye.

Still, as guy crazy as Moira could be, she was surprisingly level-headed. She also loved Piper. Unlike those grave-rolling ancestors, Moira wouldn't judge if Piper were to temporarily forget she was supposed to be looking for a simple guy and take the Marauders' sexy quarterback up on his invitation to that private suite at the Plaza.

Sighing, she plunged in with both feet. "His name is Wyatt Hunter."

A grin creased Moira's freckled face. "I knew it!"

Piper smiled and shook her head. "Yes, well, it's not exactly what you think."

Moira wrenched forward to slide her cell phone from the back pocket of her jeans. She snorted as her thumbs raced over the screen. "That blush says differently."

Piper sighed. "Okay, maybe it is, but…. Oh, bother. Are you Googling him?"

The look Moira shot her said clearly, *Well, duh.*

Piper picked up her stack of linen slacks with an internal shrug. She wouldn't need to see the screen to know when Moira pulled up Wyatt's profile.

And… There it was. Her friend's audible gasp said it all.

Moira spoke without taking her eyes from the phone's screen. "Please tell me you lied about spending the weekend with the Tuckers and that you were actually shacked up with, and shagging, this sex god for the past forty-eight hours."

Piper laughed as she craned her neck to check out Wyatt's picture. Leave it to Moira to point out the obvious. Sex god was an apt description for the tanned face capped with unruly blond hair smiling on the screen.

"Sorry to disappoint you, dearest."

"I'm not the one who should be disappointed." Moira's strawberry-blond curls bounced as she shook her head. "He's positively edible." She slowly dragged her gaze up to meet Piper's. "Well, then, if you weren't having carnal knowledge of the sexy Yank, why the blush?"

"Because I'd really, *really* like to have carnal knowledge of this particular Yank." Piper squeezed her eyelids shut in a grimace.

"Way to go, Piper! And, might I say, it's about bloody time."

Her eyes popped open on a strangled laugh. "Of course, you'd say that, since he's lovely to look at, but..."

"Stupendously lovely."

She'd get no argument from Piper on that.

Moira sighed dramatically. "Outrageously peng."

Or that.

"He's fucking gorgeous," her friend proclaimed.

Piper coughed on a laugh, and shot a glance at the open doorway.

Moira waved her off. "Not to worry, Baroness. Mum is in the village having lunch with the DW's."

Piper relaxed and turned back. The Dowager Wannabes, as Tilly and her friends referred to themselves, met once a month and the luncheon rarely lasted less than four hours. Piper eyed the phone in Moira's hand. "You're quite right about Wyatt Hunter. He's all that and more."

"I have the feeling there is a but coming."

Piper smirked. "*But* he's also a professional athlete, which puts him clearly in the off-limits column. At least for me."

Moira cocked her head. "Why is that?" At Piper's bland stare, Moira narrowed her eyes to slits. "Oh, come on. You can't be serious."

"I most certainly can. The last thing I need is some nosey reporter announcing to the world that The Gold-Digging Baroness has set her sights on another unsuspecting jock." She slashed her hand through the air. "No, from now on, I'm looking for an unassuming man. Preferably one from the country with no particular wealth to muddy the waters."

Moira rolled her eyes and affected an upper crust whine. "Yes, those poor, vulnerable multi-millionaires. Why, they're like babes in the wood, having absolutely no defense against scheming predators like the Baroness of Delaney." She blew a raspberry through puckered lips.

Piper chuckled. "That is exactly the type of thing the headlines will say, and you know it."

Moira shook her head. "So, what you're saying is, not only did that wanker, Cody, feed you to the wolves for not selling out your home and friends so that you could follow him around the world—like the rest of his lovers, I might add—you're now going to let his memory put limitations on the men you're allowed to see?"

Piper frowned at the reminder she hadn't been the only woman warming Cody's bed, despite the ring he'd placed on her finger. "It's not like that."

"Isn't it?"

"Okay, maybe it is, but it took nearly six months for the fervor to die down and people to finally begin booking the rooms instead of setting up camp at the end of the drive to get their bloody pictures." And Piper knew only too well, they didn't have another six months to waste if they were going to keep the manor. "We're making a solid go of the B&B, Moira, but there is still Abigail's bequeathment to consider. Until she's paid in full, we can't afford another scandal."

The reality check dulled much of Moira's indignation. "What about this side job you mentioned? You said it would give you more than enough to cover Abigail's inheritance."

"It should." Piper swallowed. "If I take it."

"Why wouldn't you?"

"Because the job was offered by Wyatt Hunter, and there's a very good chance its only purpose was to get me to sleep with him."

"You poor thing." Her lips curled in a sly smirk. "I'd be happy to volunteer in your place."

Piper sent her a sidelong glance. "This situation is nothing to joke about."

"Who's joking?" Moira snickered, then held up her hands when Piper huffed and returned to yank open another drawer of her dresser. "I'm sorry, luv. What's the side job?"

Piper continued to pack clothing into her suitcase as she filled her friend in on what had happened in the Tuckers' kitchen. Moira's eyes went dreamy, and she fanned herself as she listened to Piper's retelling of the kiss she and Wyatt had shared. She laughed at the lucky charm reference, and her brows shot to her hairline at the amount of money he'd offered. Her mouth twisted in thought at how V Fitzpatrick had suggested Piper turn the tables on a man V supposedly considered a friend.

"You're right," Moira proclaimed when Piper finished. "It's obvious he was throwing out options, hoping something would stick in order to keep you in Manhattan."

And, as V predicted, he wouldn't pull back on his seduction attempts. Considering how quickly Piper had fallen into their sizzling kiss, how long would she be able to hold out? She wouldn't, and therein lay the problem.

She slumped onto the mattress with a sigh. "Added to what the Marauders will be paying me, the money he offered would make all the difference in the world, but I don't dare take him up on it."

Disappointment clouded Moira's eyes. "Why not?"

Piper flopped onto her back. "You've seen his picture. Believe me, he's even more intense in person." She dropped her arm to her side and pivoted her head to meet Moira's waiting gaze. "He's gorgeous, charming, and funny, too."

"Ugh." Moira slapped a hand to her chest. "Triple whammy."

Piper snorted, half laugh, half whimper. "I held him off after that kiss because I had a plane to catch, but it wasn't easy. Do you know long it's been since I've had sex? Forget sex. Since a man has kissed me?"

"Two years, ten months, and fourteen days?" Moira supplied deadpan.

A laugh this time. "Close enough. The thing is, Moira, I've never been so quickly attracted to a man. Or so strongly. Not even Cody." Beyond his over-the-top sexiness and larger-than-life personality, Wyatt Hunter had an uncanny ability to make Piper laugh. Even when she didn't want to. A dangerous combination, that. She screwed up her mouth in a grimace as she considered the truth of that statement, then shrugged. "Especially not Cody. And Wyatt made it clear he's in the same leaky boat when it comes to our apparent, mutual attraction. If he makes even the slightest push toward the bedroom, I won't last longer than it takes to fall into the nearest bed."

Moira blinked, and from the way she jammed her lips together, she was trying not to laugh. "You say that like it's a bad thing."

Piper groaned and slung her arm over her eyes.

The mattress bumped as Moira resettled against the post. "Let's think this through, shall we?" A pause, then, "You like him, right? Right?" She prompted when Piper didn't reply.

"Right. I think. Or maybe I'm completely blinded by lust."

"I'm marking that down as a yes." A rustle of the bedding as Moira folded her legs beneath her. "And he likes you. Obviously, or he wouldn't have bothered working so hard to come up with ways to keep you in Manhattan."

The image of Wyatt adjusting his erection through his jeans flashed in Piper's mind and she slid the arm from her eyes. "I can confirm without a doubt, lust is in play for him as well."

Moira nodded succinctly. "Okay, two yeses." She cocked her head. "This V person, his friend, she said the calendar thing was a good idea, right?"

"Well..."

"These are yes or no questions, luv. Don't overthink them."

Piper snickered and propped herself up on her elbows. "V said the calendar idea would dovetail nicely with the..." Moira squinted a warning, and Piper cleared her throat. "Um, yes."

"Good, and she thinks you should charge him the full one hundred thousand he originally offered."

Piper nodded and sat up. A glance at the clock, and she shoved to her feet. Whether or not she took Wyatt up on his offer, she'd made a deal with V. Her return flight to Manhattan was leaving in four hours and she'd yet to finish packing. She crossed to her closet as Moira drummed her fingers on her knee.

"And Wyatt was willing to pay you that much to simply show up at his games?"

"Yes." Piper selected several more blouses and matching skirts, and hung them over her arm. On a whim, she tugged another pair of jeans from a hanger and returned to the bed to stuff the entire pile into her suitcase.

"Bugger. Why doesn't this type of thing ever happen to me?" Piper smiled and arched a brow, and Moira nodded. "Right. V wants you to make his calendar. I'm assuming he would pose for it?"

"That was the impression he gave." Piper flipped the cover of the case shut.

"Who else, do you think? His fellow players, I would imagine, especially those he considers friends." She hummed appreciatively. "You did say he and Tuck were friends, right?"

Piper laughed and tugged on the suitcase's zipper.

"Seriously. If you need an assistant, I'm your girl." Moira waved a hand at Piper's smirk. "Fine. Here's my conclusion. With you doing his calendar, V gets what she wants, and you'll get his money. Which, of course, is what *you* want. The only one not getting everything on their agenda is Wyatt, since he ultimately wants you on the sideline at his games as well as in his bed." She nodded briskly. "The way I see it, the only fair way to handle this is to make a deal with him."

Piper muscled her bag from the mattress and onto the floor. "On which? The sideline or the bed?"

"Both, if you're smart." Moira's grin was sharp.

Piper rolled her eyes. "I meant what I said about keeping to unassuming, non-famous guys from now on. They're ever so much less trouble."

"That sounds lovely, if you can find one who looks like Wyatt Hunter." Piper couldn't help her snorted laugh.

Moira shrugged. "Whether or not you sleep with him is up to you, but isn't it time you started living your life again? I'm not saying you should run off and marry the man. Well, unless you want to." She bit her bottom lip. "Considering his profession..."

"Not to mention his reputation for dating a new woman every week," Piper added.

Moira nodded. "Yes, well, a quick jaunt to Vegas would probably be a bad idea, but God, luv. For nearly three years, you've put everything on hold to take care of everyone but yourself. You deserve one last fling full of good, old-fashioned, rock-your-world sex with a fucking gorgeous guy before you come home and find your simple man."

"When you put it that way..."

They shared a grin, then Moira pinned her with a knowing stare. "On the business end, I know you, and your honorable gene will give you fits if you do what this V person suggests without reciprocating. Give Wyatt Hunter what he wants. Do a fabulous job shooting his calendar and offer to attend those games, too. With as much money as he'll be forking over, you can afford a few transatlantic crossings."

The faint sound of crunching gravel outside interrupted Piper's consideration of all Moira had said, and she stepped to the window. She cursed beneath her breath and jerked to the side, not wanting to be seen as Abigail parked her tiny red sports coupe next to Piper's ten-year-old SUV.

She spun around and hurried to snatch her coat from the chair before grabbing the handle of her suitcase. "Did Tilly take the manor's station wagon to the village?"

"No, Agnes Coulter collected her. Why?"

"My dear cousin is here and I'd rather not see her until I have her check in my hand."

Chapter 7

Sweat soaked the neckline of Wyatt's sleeveless shirt and beaded on his brow. Male grunts competed with metal meeting metal and gritty rock 'n' roll as he pushed through the rep. He blew through his teeth and his triceps bunched, then stretched. Having received the all clear on his shoulder, he'd increased his workout level to where he'd been before his careless injury. The return to normal, here in the busy team gym, anyway, felt good.

Pretty much everywhere else, life sucked balls.

The family meeting his father had called could mean only one thing. Dear Old Dad had decided the time had come to throw his hat in the ring in his bid for the presidency. Wyatt pushed the bar toward the ceiling with gritted teeth. Nearly two years of angry phone calls and lectures on the concepts of family unity, political correctness, and positive optics, would stretch into another eight once the election had been won. And it would be. Richard Hunter didn't lose.

Wyatt's shoulder muscles contracted and released as he maintained a steady pace with the bar. Jesus. Talk about a clusterfuck. He was surprised Megan hadn't already shown up on his doorstep. His sister would no doubt be frantic to plan damage control.

A bead of sweat slid past his temple and into his hairline. Mentally shoving aside the imminent and unavoidable fallout from his father's political race, he attempted to clear his mind. He gritted his teeth when the image of cat-shaped emerald eyes filled the void.

He lowered the bar to hover above his chest before straightening his arms once again. Piper Darrow had been gone three days and he'd yet to come up with a viable plan to bring her back.

And the dirty dream she'd starred in last night wasn't helping.

"That's eleven." Gabe Tillman stood behind the bench at Wyatt's head, acting as his spotter.

Flat on his back with his legs spread wide, Wyatt cursed beneath his breath as a vision of russet curls sliding over his naked thighs snuck into his head. With half the Marauders' offensive line surrounding him, a hard-on would be damned inconvenient, but that didn't matter. Recall of the dream continued and his cock twitched as dream Piper lifted her head and looked him dead in the eye. She fluttered her lashes in that adorable three-blink quirk and curled her lips in an I'm-going-to-suck-you-off-now smile.

Christ.

He barely suppressed a groan and grunted through the next rep. Although some in the press would argue the claim, he'd never had trouble keeping his head in the game. Neither had he ever failed to shake a woman from his mind. Since clapping eyes on Piper, he'd had a problem with both.

Why that was, he hadn't a clue, but he was damn well going to find out. He had no choice. Although he'd like to, he couldn't, in good conscience, blame the uneasiness he'd been suffering on his lucky charm refusing to cooperate. He was the first to admit he was a superstitious bastard, but he wasn't so far gone he allowed himself to be led by circumstances.

When it came to his lucky charms, *he* made the rules or tweaked them to fit until he got his way. Piper was an ocean away, but a phone call before each game would do the trick professionally. Personally? Yeah, a phone call wouldn't satisfy that part of his agenda.

He wanted her close enough to touch. Now. Not three weeks from now when the Marauders had a bye week and he was free to follow her to England.

How else was he to discover what it was about her that wouldn't leave him alone? He flexed his fingers on the bar. Not that he was looking for long-term from the sexy photographer. Fuck no. She was hot as hell, but she was just a woman and there were plenty of them out there. Sure, he planned to settle down one day. Do the whole family thing. He liked kids and wanted a few of his own, but there was plenty of time for that. Later. Once he'd achieved his goals on the field.

An image of Piper's sultry smile flashed in his head, and he grunted. Damn it, the sexy photographer was fucking with his head, and there was too much at stake to ignore the potential fallout.

"That's fifteen," Gabe said from above. "Three more for a full four sets."

At the next station, spotting Jamal Knight in his workout, Mario Davis turned his head. "Four sets? You're off light duty?"

"Light duty." Jamal snorted and paused between reps. "Anyone with eyes could see his shoulder has been fine for two weeks. The team docs were playing it safe."

Straddling a third bench, Tuck snickered and his eyes flashed with a teasing glint. "Wyatt's not worried about his shoulder. It's another body part that's giving him trouble. Ain't that right, buddy?"

Wyatt ignored him, clenching his teeth through the last two reps.

"Which means there's a woman." Jamal rolled his head to the side. "Who is she?"

"And does she have a sister?" Gabe grinned down at Wyatt, unfazed by his irritated glower.

"I want in, if she does." Jamal eased the bar into the brackets, then flopped his arms onto his stomach.

Mario leaned on the bar to study Jamal from above. "What happened to the Italian babe with the southern accent and killer ass?"

Jamal sighed. "She rang the death knell."

"Ah, hell. She asked you to meet her mamma?"

An exaggerated shudder wracked Jamal's body. "*And* her daddy."

"Fuck, yeah." Gabe shook his head. "Total deal breaker."

Mario laughed, then turned to eye Wyatt. "So? Who is she?"

"His new lucky charm." Tuck bared his teeth in a happy leer. "Remember the lady photographer with the broken nose?"

Wyatt would have told Tuck to get bent, but was interrupted by Mario's almost reverent sigh. "Piper, right? I met her at the fundraiser the other night. Shit. That woman is *fine*."

His last rep completed, Wyatt resettled the bar and sat up. He pinned Mario in place with a squinted scowl. "Did your fiancée meet her, too?"

Mario grinned and shrugged. Jamal and Gabe chuckled, but it was Tuck's full-throated laughter that scraped along Wyatt's strained nerve endings.

"He's bent out of shape because he failed to seal the deal with the fine photographer. She went back to England a few days ago."

Wyatt met Tuck's taunt with a toothy leer. "It ain't over 'til the fat lady sings, asshole."

Tuck chuckled and shook his head. "I'll up that C-note to a thousand that she's already started humming."

"You, ah, might want to rethink that bet, Tuck."

A question creased Tuck's brow as Gabe jerked his chin toward the gym doors.

Wyatt followed his gaze, and his pulse rate skyrocketed to stroke range. Piper Darrow glided across the gym's rubber matting like a stunning apparition. At her side was V Fitzpatrick, stalking toward them with her usual purposeful stride.

Green eyes, brighter than an Irish countryside, brushed over Wyatt before flitting away to pause on each of his teammates. Every sinew and muscle in his body clenched in almost painful anticipation as he slowly rose to his feet. He didn't have a clue what was happening or why, but he wasn't about to look a gift horse in the mouth. She was here, and he meant to keep her around at least until he'd figured out how to break the funky spell she'd cast over him and eject her from his head.

"Good. You're all here." V came to a stop and cast her gaze around to encompass Mario, Jamal, and Gabe. "Gentlemen, if you haven't met her yet, this is Piper Darrow."

Much to Wyatt's frustration, Piper continued to avoid his gaze. She shook hands with each of his teammates. He looked on silently as she accepted Tuck's kiss on her cheek.

He shot Wyatt a challenging grin before turning back to her. "What are you doing back in town? And does CC know you're here?"

The cool mask she'd worn while greeting the rest of the guys softened into a smile, but V beat her with an explanation. "I was lucky enough to convince Piper to work with us on the Fab Five project. We spoke to CC a few minutes ago and she gave the green light to start with you, Tuck. Beginning tomorrow morning."

Well, shit. Wyatt had the urge to smack his forehead. He should have thought of Caroline's video project himself, instead of tossing out his clichéd calendar idea. He'd have to come up with some way to thank V for succeeding where he had failed but, for the moment, he wanted Piper's emerald eyes on him.

"How long will you be in town?"

This time, he was prepared for the punch to the gut when she slid her gaze to his. From the way she'd been avoiding looking at him, he'd expected nerves. Instead, the green depths of her eyes held a light he hadn't seen in them before. Maybe it was wishful thinking, but it looked to him like the light of challenge. Fuck, yeah. Whatever she had in mind, he was all in.

"I'm scheduled to be in Manhattan for the next five weeks. After that…" She shrugged. "Well, it depends."

Five weeks wouldn't cover the season, but it gave him some room to work. He snatched a towel from the back of the chair beside the bench. "Depends on what?"

"Not what. Who." It happened so quickly, he wasn't sure, but his cock twitched, insisting she'd given his body a fast once-over before she met his gaze again and smiled. "That depends on you, actually."

Heat lashed across his lower belly. "Well, now, sweetheart. I sure do like the sound of that."

And there were the nerves he'd expected, along with a blush.

"Oh, ho, Tuck. Looks like you lose your..." Mario stopped short on a grunt, followed by male snickers.

Wyatt didn't turn to find out which of his friends had tossed the elbow and prevented Mario from sticking his foot in his mouth. Again. Most likely, Tuck had done the honors this time, since he'd be on the receiving end of his wife's anger should CC learn he was placing bets on her friend.

V ran her gaze over the group. "We've booked Piper to spend up to a week with each of you to get the photos we're after. Tuck is covered, but I'm expecting the rest of you to swing by my office sometime in the next forty-eight hours so we can work out the schedule." She pinned Gabe with a warning stare. "Don't make me come looking for you, Tillman."

"Yes, ma'am." Gabe held up both hands in surrender.

Turning her head, she looked at Wyatt and bared her teeth in the smile he'd watched her use to make even the toughest of players nervous. He fought a grin and slung his towel around the back of his neck. The tactic wouldn't work on him. She might still be angry with him over that rafting shit, but he knew her too well to be intimidated by her hard-ass lady-agent glare.

She pointed a finger at his nose. "I need to see *you* in my office ASAP."

He shifted his gaze back to Piper, where he wanted it. She swallowed, and he couldn't help but wonder at the return of her nerves. "Now works for me."

"Take a shower first, big guy." V smirked, her eyes full of satisfaction. "We'll meet you upstairs once I've finished giving Piper the nickel tour."

* * * *

Wyatt paused in the doorway of V's sixth floor office, his gaze landing unerringly on Piper's profile. She stood beside the floral couch he'd occupied often over the past year. The rapt pleasure on her face as she listened to Jason Goodwell, head of the Marauders' marketing department, would have lit up Times Square.

"And the note she hits at the end." Jason's chest swelled on a heaving sigh. "It's a thing of beauty, I tell you."

"I will definitely make a point to see it while I'm in town."

"If you need a date, I'd love to see it again. In the meantime, if you have any questions or need anything, business *or* pleasure, give me a call."

The urge to land his fist in the guy's face, despite knowing full well Jason batted for the other team, took Wyatt by surprise. Shit. What the hell was that all about? He didn't get jealous. Ever. And especially over a woman he'd yet to take to bed. Maybe he was coming down with something, a bug, or virus of some kind. Whatever it was, he needed the cure, and fast.

"There you are."

V drew his attention and he cursed beneath his breath at her smug smile. She was up to something. He just didn't know what.

She waved him in. "Shut the door and have a seat."

He hesitated with his hand on the knob. In all the times he'd come to V's office, she'd never requested he shut the door. Not such a strange thing, really. While they were both on the Marauders' payroll, the two of them had never had actual business before. The Fab Five project was technically team business but, for some reason, he suddenly felt the way he had in third grade when he'd been called to the principal's office for stealing a kiss from Sheri Johnson.

He shot a darting glance at Piper.

That depends on you, actually.

Well, shit. Despite her heated reaction to his kiss the other day, had she complained to management over what had taken place in the Tuckers' kitchen? Uneasiness pricked the hair on the back of his neck, until she turned her head and met his gaze. Her tentative smile put him at ease and tied him in knots at the same time.

"Wyatt." V rolled her eyes when he didn't move.

Tugging the door closed behind him, he strode to the single wingback chair to the right of V's desk. Piper and Jason settled on the couch.

V crossed her arms on her desktop and studied Wyatt. "This hunk of the month calendar Piper mentioned? Were you thinking 'amateur production whipped up in the garage' or will you be handing her photos off to actual professionals to produce the final product?"

Oh, shit. He jerked his gaze to Piper. Her tentativeness from earlier was long gone. And the light of challenge in her eyes? Yeah, like blinking neon. The little red rabbit had done an end run around him, calling in reinforcements to verify his job offer was legit.

Damned if he didn't find that sexy as hell.

He attempted to keep the anticipatory grin off his face, but failed. "Change your mind?"

"As I said downstairs, that depends on you."

She shifted on the couch, crossing her legs, and he was momentarily distracted by the flash of toned calves and the memory of silky soft skin above a stretchy, lace garter. He lifted his gaze and, staring into her emerald eyes full of self-confident satisfaction, the gnawing tension in his gut eased for the first time in days.

He flashed his most winning smile. "I'm in."

"That's nice," V drummed her nails on her desktop, "but you never answered *my* question."

Wyatt dragged his gaze from Piper to look at V. From the phrasing of her question, she knew damn well he'd thrown out the idea on a whim, and the smirk in her eyes said she was enjoying calling his bluff. He thought fast. If they were actually going to do this thing, the Down Syndrome Research Foundation was the logical vehicle.

"I'm thinking DSRF will jump at the chance to be involved, since any funds raised would go to them. They also have an excellent marketing department."

He bared his teeth in a thought-you-had-me grin. V shook her head, but it was clear from the quirking of her lips she was impressed and didn't want to show it. He was more than a little impressed himself. Hell, he'd made his bullshit ploy to get Piper into bed sound like the real deal. At the same time, he'd nearly managed to pull the first smile from V since he'd returned from the Colorado River with his throwing arm in a sling.

Not bad. Not bad at all.

"Obviously, you've yet to nail down the particulars." All trace of humor vanished from V's face as she glanced between him and Piper with a no-nonsense stare. "Until the two of you work out the details and sign a contract, this is all conjecture. But, as it appears both of you are in favor of proceeding, there are a few specifics I'd like to throw out there."

She waited until they'd both given their assent, then addressed him directly. "I'm assuming the initial funding will come from you, personally?"

Wyatt nodded, wondering where she was going with her line of questioning.

"That being the case, and contingent upon DSRF coming onboard, Caroline has authorized a ten-thousand-dollar donation. She'll bump it up to twenty-five if you agree to use Marauders players only."

"Marauder of the Month." Jason hummed. "Has a ring to it."

V smiled and met Wyatt's gaze once more. "Of course, she would require the courtesy of final approval before the calendar goes into production."

Wyatt propped his ankle across the opposite knee. "Tell her to double her donation to fifty and she has a deal."

V didn't blink an eye at the demand. "I can't see her objecting to that." She shifted her gaze to Jason. "Piper and I have tentatively agreed to meet each Friday afternoon so I can see a sampling of what she's gotten for the Fab Five project and to deal with any issues that might arise. Will that work for you?"

"Perfectly."

V nodded and stood. Jason and Piper did as well. Wyatt sliced his gaze between them as he slowly rose to his feet.

Jason stuck out his hand to Piper. "Nice meeting you. I'm looking forward to our working together."

"As am I, and it was a pleasure meeting you as well."

"Wyatt." Jason acknowledged him with a dip of his chin, then tucked the binder he carried under one arm and headed for the door. Piper stayed where she was.

V plucked her jacket from the back of her chair and rounded her desk to stop in front of Wyatt. "I heard the doctor cleared you for a full workout today."

He nodded. V Fitzpatrick didn't often show signs of uncertainty, but the hard-as-nails agent turned PR wiz was suddenly nowhere to be found. In her place was the woman he'd come to know as a friend.

Guilt clouded her eyes. "I'm glad. I hated seeing you hurt."

Wyatt frowned. "V..."

Rising on her toes, she pressed her cheek to his and spoke softly enough only he heard. "I'm sorry for the things I said, and I'm going to make it up to you." She kissed his cheek, stepped back, and slid her arm into one sleeve of her jacket.

Surprised by the unexpected apology, he wasn't sure what to say. "Are we going somewhere?"

"I'm meeting Sam downstairs." She tugged the jacket up the other arm and adjusted the collar. "And you are taking Piper to dinner. The two of you have terms to negotiate and some major details to work out."

Chapter 8

Wyatt assisted Piper from his swanky sports car and guided her toward the doors of a building on the Upper West Side. A valet slid into the driver's seat as she eyed the building's white brick exterior. There was no sign she could see, but then, that wasn't so odd. During her engagement to Cody, they'd visited Manhattan often. On at least two occasions, they'd dined in five-star restaurants tucked away in non-descript locations. When she'd commented on the lack of advertisement out front, he'd laughed as if she'd said something funny.

Apparently, the finest of restaurants didn't require signage. Exclusive clientele were well aware of both the establishment's address and who to contact to reserve a table.

Clearly, Wyatt was part of that exclusive crowd. After settling her in the passenger seat of his fancy automobile, he'd made a call on his cell phone, informing whomever had answered that he and a guest would be arriving within twenty minutes. After a moment's pause, he'd ended the short conversation with "*Surprise us.*"

A uniformed doorman appeared, seemingly out of nowhere. He had the look of ex-military. Barrel-chested but trim, he moved with precision, his bearing proud as if coming to attention had long been a habit. Beneath the flat top cut of his silver hair, his dark-eyed gaze met Wyatt's as he swung the door wide at their approach.

"Good evening, Mr. Hunter. Miss." He recognized Piper with a curt nod. She responded with a polite smile.

"Good evening, Morris." Wyatt slid his hand to the small of her back and led her inside. "Anything interesting happening?"

"As a matter of fact…" The doorman's sober gaze briefly flicked to Piper, then away.

"It's okay, Morris. Is there a problem?"

"No problem, sir. Misses Tonya and Amanda arrived ten minutes ago. Miss Megan was close behind. They're waiting for you upstairs."

A slight hesitation, then Wyatt nodded, and Piper bit her bottom lip. Having decided to take him up on his dual job offers, she was still wavering on the fling Moira had suggested, but was definitely considering it. *If* she could work up the nerve to broach the subject, *and* he agreed to her conditions, that was. But this…. Sitting down to dinner with three of Wyatt's apparent harem wasn't how she envisioned this evening going.

She shot a wary glance heavenward. Was someone up there trying to tell her something?

Battling a returning case of nerves, she pretended an interest in the empty seating area off to their right. Subtle wealth was evident in the two long, gunmetal gray leather couches separated by a black granite coffee table. White marble floors gleamed beneath the glow of subtle track lighting. The only color was provided by six enormous rubber plants. Like living pillars, they lined the walls in large, evenly spaced chrome pots.

She startled as Wyatt urged her toward a bank of elevators on the far wall. Producing a key from the breast pocket of his leather bomber jacket, he inserted it in a lock beside the lift farthest to the left and twisted his wrist. The doors opened, and she blinked.

Bloody hell. Had she thought exclusive? The man had his own key to the restaurant. Then again, he was a Hunter as well as a highly-paid athlete. He probably owned the building.

Returning the key to his pocket, he escorted her inside the lift's car and turned to face Morris beyond the doors in the lobby. She ventured a peek at Wyatt's face. Perhaps it was a trick of the light, but a rare tension tightened his features as he cued the single white button next to an identical red one.

"How's your mom doing, Morris?"

A grin transformed the doorman's sober face. "She's taken herself a boyfriend, sir. A younger man. He's seventy-nine and a half."

Wyatt chuckled as the doors slid closed. The car began its ascent and they both spoke at once.

"Maybe we should forget tonight and meet at the complex tomorrow."

"Megan is my sister. Tonya is her best friend. Amanda is five."

Far more relieved than she should be, Piper turned and met his watchful gaze. They spoke in tandem a second time.

"Why the hell would we forget tonight?"

"Your sister and her friend?"

Wyatt frowned. "I have a fairly good idea what my sister wants and the conversation won't take long." He jabbed the red button. The car lurched to a stop, and he turned to face her. "You and I, on the other hand, have a lot to talk about." He stepped forward and she backed up until her shoulder blades brushed the car's walls. "Like why you kissed me as if you couldn't get enough, then left the country an hour later." Bracing a hand on the paneling beside her head, he dipped his until she could make out the individual grayish striations in his green irises. "And why you've decided to come back."

Oh my. She was a woman who appreciated candor and honest speaking, but...

She cleared her throat. "I hardly think questions of that nature are appropriate for mixed company."

One corner of his mouth lifted in a smile. He looked left, then right, encompassing the entirety of the small space before facing her again. "Well, now, duchess, it looks like we're all alone for the moment, so feel free to answer."

She stiffened. *Duchess?* "I'm not a...." She lifted her chin to demand, "Why ever would you refer to me as a duchess?"

He grinned and shook his head. "Because you sure as hell go on like one." His grin widened, and he tucked his curled fingers beneath her chin to close her gaping mouth. "That wasn't an insult, *duchess*." Silent laughter danced in his eyes. "You've got that whole...upper crust enunciation thing going, all softened by a sexy Scottish burr. I get hard every time you open your mouth."

Bugger. He's the devil, Piper. Run and save yer arse. Now, while ye still have a fightin' chance.

She blinked, a bit too turned on to pay heed to the nag in her head. Still, someone had to keep the situation from spiraling out of control. Otherwise, there was a good chance she'd gain that carnal knowledge she yearned for right here in this three-by-three box.

She dragged in a calming breath. "I wish you wouldn't do that."

Twin dimples bracketed his mouth. "Do what? Speak the truth?"

Ha! 'Tis true he makes ye wet with his words and voice alone. The devil, I tell ya.

Truer words were never spoken, but she wouldn't be sharing *that* with Mr. Sexy Talk Quarterback. Not while riding in a lift about to join his sister and her friends in a restaurant full of people. She grabbed hold of the diversion as if it were a lifeline in a storm-tossed sea. "I'm sure your sister and friends are wondering where you are."

Reaching past him, she poked the red button. Nothing happened. She jabbed the white one and heaved a sigh of relief when the car jolted into motion.

He shook his head, but only smiled as the car climbed to its unknown destination. The doors whooshed open, and he held out his hand, indicating she should precede him. She took one step and froze.

Arching her neck, she glanced at him over her shoulder. "Why does this restaurant have a decidedly residential feel?"

He coughed as if he were fighting laughter. "Maybe because it's not a restaurant. Welcome to my home, Piper."

"Bollocks." Her eyes widened at the escaped curse, and she whipped her head around to face what was obviously a lovely, *private*, foyer.

She grimaced inwardly, but the blinding reminder that Wyatt Hunter played on an entirely different plane than most men was a good thing. If she ultimately decided to extend her association with him into the personal realm—and the way her limbs went weak whenever he was near left little doubt of which way she was leaning—there could be no more assuming. Carnal knowledge of the man was one thing, risking her heart was another. Spelling everything out so there could be no misunderstandings down the road was priority one in their pending negotiations.

A childish squeal sounded from somewhere in the distance. He wrapped his arms around her from behind, one across her upper chest, the other spanning her belly, and spoke into her ear. "Would you do me a favor?"

She nodded, her gaze focused on the end of the long hall off the foyer.

"Promise me anything you see or hear in the next few minutes will go nowhere."

She tensed as V's comments about his family name and the high visibility spotlight he lived in echoed in her head. Empathy tightened her throat. "It disturbs me that you feel you need to make that request in your own home. You shouldn't have to." She nodded briskly. "You have my word."

He was silent for a moment even as his chest swelled against her back with his deep breath. "Thanks. One more thing." He rubbed his lips across her cheek in a soft kiss. "Try not to say too much until I've dealt with my sister or we'll *both* be embarrassed."

Her eyes widened as he followed up his request with a subtle thrust of his hips against her bottom, delivering a hard reminder of his suggestive claim in the lift.

"Unkie White. Unkie White!"

After a brief squeeze, Wyatt dropped his arms and stepped around her to catch the hurtling ball of energy charging down the hallway. The little girl shrieked with laughter as he swung her high in the air before settling her against his chest and stomach. She wrapped her legs around his waist, and Piper gained a sudden understanding of his interest in Down syndrome research. Clearly afflicted with the physical abnormalities associated with the disorder, the girl's broad facial features were lit by a gummy smile as she cupped his jaw in chubby hands.

"I missed you." She jerked her head back and forth in a rough nose rub. "To the moon. And. *Back*," she finished with intense resolve.

He grinned and dug his fingertips into her ribs until she shrieked with laughter. "I missed you, too, Mandy Candy."

The sudden clenching of Piper's heart was as painful as it was unexpected. She'd only known Wyatt a few days and had spent much less time with him than that, yet she'd seen enough to know he was aware of the power infused in his smile. Sharp or cunning, innocent or suggestive, he wielded the weapon of his curled lips with precision to achieve his goals. But none of the smiles she'd witnessed so far could have prepared her for the complete and undeniable joy on his face at this precise moment.

Love looked devastatingly beautiful on Wyatt Hunter.

"She's pwetty."

He turned to Piper. "Yes, she is. Her name is Piper."

"Pipah. Pipah." Innocent concentration tightened the girl's round face as she formed the sound with her lips.

"That's right. And this," he adjusted the child until she rested on his hip, "is Mandy."

Piper smiled. "It's a pleasure to meet you, Mandy."

"Mandy Candy," she corrected, her pudgy cheeks nearly eclipsing her eyes with her grin.

"You've created a monster, Wyatt."

Piper turned to face the two women who had quietly followed Mandy down the hall. Both were blondes. One petite, the other tall. The shorter of the two shook her head.

"She insists her teacher print her name that way on all her papers." The smile she turned on Piper was open and friendly. She held out her hand. "I'm Tonya West. Amanda is mine."

Piper shook Tonya's hand and murmured a greeting as she flicked a gaze toward the other woman. The tall blonde was obviously Wyatt's sister. The eerily similar facial features and bone structure were unmistakable. Piper's gaze landed back on Wyatt. Mandy had greeted him with her version of uncle, and then there were the eyes. Green irises flecked with gray. Anyone looking at them would assume they were related.

"I'm Megan, Wyatt's sister." She was beautiful, as one would expect of Wyatt's sibling, but her greeting was far cooler than Tonya's had been and the tug of her lips appeared strained. "Tonya and I have been friends

for years. When Amanda came along, we became roommates as well."
Megan's soft laugh held what sounded to Piper like the edge of panic. "My
brother horned in as he usually does to snag the label of honorary Unkie."

"Unkie White!" Mandy bounced in his arms.

Piper smiled wanly, unsure of the purpose behind Megan Hunter's
detailed explanation of their various associations, and uncomfortable in
the face of the woman's obvious nerves.

"Um," Megan twisted her fingers together at the waist of her linen
slacks. "I hope you don't mind if I steal Wyatt for a few moments." The
look she gave her brother was almost pleading. "We have some urgent
family business to discuss."

Wyatt sighed, but lowered Mandy to her feet. He patted the seat of her
pink pants and she skipped into the living area to the left of the foyer. Clearly
comfortable in his home, she opened a drawer on the coffee table, retrieved
a remote, and aimed it at the incredibly large flat screen TV on the wall.

He straightened and turned to Piper. "Do you mind? This won't take long."

"Of course not."

Still, he hesitated. "The food I ordered should be here in a few minutes.
I'll be back before it arrives." He glanced around, ignoring his sister as
she cleared her throat. "Tonya, would you mind fetching Piper a glass of
wine?" He turned back. "Or if you'd prefer, a cocktail?"

"Wyatt." Megan demanded his attention.

Beyond uncomfortable, Piper forced a smile. His sister was becoming
more agitated by the moment. "I'm fine, thank you. Go. I'm sure Tonya
and I can manage a few minutes without you."

He hesitated another moment, then pinned Tonya with a narrow-eyed
stare that would have frightened puppies. "Don't let her leave. If she's not
here when I get back, I'm blaming you."

****

"Are you insane? Introducing that woman to Amanda?" Megan accused
the moment he shut his bedroom door behind him.

"That woman is my guest, and this *is* my home, in case you forgot."
Wyatt shrugged out of his jacket, tossing it onto the couch in the corner.
"If you don't want Mandy exposed to strangers, then you shouldn't show
up without calling first."

Megan's shoulders dropped. "I know. I'm sorry, it's just that..."

"You're in panic mode."

"Of course, I'm panicking." She slumped onto the tufted ottoman at
the foot of his bed. "He's running, Wyatt. Which means we'll all be under

the microscope, even more than usual. We can't afford any mistakes at this late date."

"We?" He crossed his arms and held her in place with a stern stare. "If you'll recall, I advised from the beginning that telling him the truth was the best call."

And for years, she'd ignored his continued predictions that not only was making herself invaluable to their father a waste of time and effort, her masochistic self-punishment would eventually blow up in her face. Now it was too late. In this age of opposition research, it was only a matter of time before Mandy's true parentage was discovered. The moment that happened, neither her personal sacrifices nor the long hours Megan had put into helping their father get where he was would amount to jack shit.

And not simply because Dad would consider her illegitimate daughter an unacceptable blight on the family portrait, which was one of her major fears. The bastard would see Mandy as exactly that, but was too skilled a politician not to recognize the potential upside to being the grandparent of a disabled child. No, Megan's unforgivable sin would be in creating a situation whereby Richard Hunter was forced to spin a surprise story of this magnitude at the very moment he was set to grab hold of his ultimate victory.

Wyatt sighed and shook his head. "Don't kid yourself, Meg. That microscope we've grown up under is a cheap kid's toy compared to the KGB style anal probes that are about to be launched. The minute Dad's press announcement is over, his primary competition will be all over us like stink on shit. If they aren't already. And *their* research machines are nothing compared to what he'll face in the general election."

She groaned, squeezed her eyes shut, and dropped her chin to her chest.

Rolling his eyes heavenward, Wyatt slid onto the bench and wrapped an arm around her. "Tell him, Meg. The longer you wait, the worse it'll be."

The harshness of her laugh bounced her shoulders. "I can't." Her eyes gleamed with resolve in her sidelong glance. "You, of all people, know what it's like to live in the reflective glare of Daddy's shadow. I can't do that to my little girl. I won't. Not willingly." She burrowed closer to his chest the way she had when she'd been little herself and needed her big brother to chase away the monsters. "If the truth comes out, I'll deal with Daddy's wrath, but if there is a chance Amanda can live her life free of the public eye, I have to give it to her."

He hugged her close, not at all surprised by her response. As much as he'd disagreed with her decision to keep Mandy a secret from the world, he understood, and had never doubted her love for her daughter.

"If you haven't come to brainstorm with me on how to break the news to Dad, what are you doing here? I figured he'd have you working triple time to ramp up for his big announcement."

She sniffed and straightened away from his chest. "He sent me to fetch you because you never returned Walter's calls."

Wyatt snorted. His father's campaign manager had left five voicemails in the past twenty-four hours, each one more insistent in tone. "You mean his summonses."

Familiar humor eased some of the starkness in her eyes. "Don't blame Walter. He's just following Daddy's directives."

"Nothing changes." As a boy, he'd often imagined the loyal Walter Crowley as Igor to his father's Dr. Frankenstein. "I can hear Walter now." Affecting an eastern European accent, Wyatt waggled his brows. "Yes, master."

Megan grinned and poked him in the ribs with her elbow. "Daddy said, and I quote, 'Tell that stubborn brother of yours to get his ass home. I expect to see him standing right beside you at my news conference. It's not every day a man's daddy announces his intention to run for the White House.'"

Wyatt lifted a wry brow. "Well, at least he referred to me as a man this time and not a boy."

Megan winced. "It's important to him, Wyatt."

"Yeah, I don't exactly consider that a compelling argument." A quick squeeze of her shoulders, and he stood. "In case you've forgotten, the season has started, and I've got a couple of other irons in the fire as well."

Megan stood with a smirk. "No doubt the redhead waiting for you in the living room is the hottest one."

He laughed. "You know me so well. And speaking of Piper…"

Megan held up a hand. "Okay, I'll get out of your hair as soon as you promise to show up on Monday." He opened his mouth to refuse, but she brushed by him and stalked toward the closed door. "After all, I came all this way to ask you to do me this tiny little favor, *and* I brought Mandy along—at no small risk, I might add—just so you could see her. So, dear brother." She opened the door and glanced over her shoulder. "Can I expect you at my side in Oklahoma City on Monday at eight AM sharp?" Uncertainty momentarily clouded her eyes. "I'm going to need your moral support."

He frowned, but there was never any doubt he'd say yes. Which was the reason Dad had sent her. "Only for you."

Relief brightened her smile. "I love you, too."

Chapter 9

"Sorry about that." Wyatt found Piper in the kitchen, sipping a glass of golden wine. As he'd promised, his conversation with Megan had been short and sweet, but he'd had a hell of a time convincing Mandy she should return to the hotel with Megan and Tonya rather than spend the night with him. "Mandy must be tired from the flight. She doesn't often have meltdowns like that."

"She definitely seems attached to you. And vice-versa."

He grunted and tore open the bag of Chinese takeout Morris had delivered during the chaos. If, or until, the truth of Mandy's parentage was revealed, the less said the better. The need for secrecy bothered Wyatt, however, especially since Piper seemed to have connected with his niece in the short time he'd been speaking to Megan.

He eyed the haphazard braid behind Piper's right ear and grinned. "She wants to be a hairdresser when she grows up."

Smiling, she touched her fingertips to the knotted twists of her hair. "She's the reason for your interest in the Down Syndrome Research Foundation."

With a nod, he plucked two dishes from a cabinet. "Actually, she's the reason *behind* the DSRF. I wrote the check for its inception a week after she was born."

The mild confusion crossing her face tangled a ball of nerves in his gut. Cursing beneath his breath, he spun away to open the silverware drawer.

What happened to the less said the better, dumbass?

He selected a fistful of knives, forks, and spoons, and returned to the island where Piper had opened most of the containers. "Speaking of raising funds, we've got some terms to negotiate."

She spooned beef and broccoli onto her plate. "Yes, we do."

He slid onto the stool across from hers. "Before we start, I have a question."

She set aside the carton and selected the shrimp lo mein from the remaining dishes before meeting his gaze. "What would that be?"

"Why *did* you come back?" She arched a brow, and he was quick to clarify the reason for his curiosity. "Not that I'm complaining, mind you, but you made it pretty damned clear you thought I was nuts."

She paused with her fork hovering over the open carton. "Technically, I still think you're full-on barmy." A single dimple popped in her cheek and her emerald eyes twinkled with laughter. "But I've been assured your money is quite spendable."

He didn't have a fucking clue what barmy was, but if accusing him of being so made her smile like that, he'd gladly become the king of *Barmyville*. He poured himself a glass of wine. "So, you came back for the money?"

He'd rather she'd come back for his body, but she was here. Sitting in his kitchen. He wasn't one to look a gift horse in the mouth.

She paused in scooping the Chinese noodles and shrimp onto her plate and cocked her head. "Even we *duchesses* are occasionally in need of coin."

"Touché." He chuckled, then sipped at the chilled chardonnay. "If you don't mind my asking, what's V paying you for the Marauders' deal?"

Piper set aside the carton and picked up her fork. "Fifty thousand dollars, plus expenses, and the copyright purchase of all the photographs I produce."

He whistled between his teeth. "Not bad money for five weeks of work."

She nodded her agreement, and satisfaction gleamed in her eyes. "Added to the one hundred thousand you'll be paying me, you can understand why I came back."

He dipped his chin and leaned in to tease her. "Yeah, duchess, now that I'm thinking about it, that amount is pretty high. Especially since the profits go to charity."

She didn't blink an eye. "Sorry, that figure is non-negotiable. I'll require half up front with the remainder due upon completion of the photographs, which is the same arrangement I made with V on the Fab Five project."

He bit back a grin and leaned toward her with his elbows on the granite countertop. "That's all well and good for V, but if you recall, the one hundred thousand dollars was contingent upon your physical attendance at all twenty of my games this season."

She mirrored his position, leaning in. Challenge glittered in her eyes. "Which I'm willing to do, *if* you agree to your originally quoted figure, *plus* cover any additional travel expenses I've incurred once I'm back in England and have to return to follow you around the States."

He straightened with a jolt. "Hold on. Are you screwing with my head? You're willing to show up at the games?"

He'd all but given up on that happening, which sucked. Sharing a bed with her would be impossible from the other side of the Atlantic, but then, sleeping with her wasn't a requirement of her lucky charm status. Neither, technically, was her attendance at his games when a weekly phone call would've covered it, but he wasn't about to admit that now.

Having her on his turf, live and in person, was worth a hell of a lot more to him than a lousy hundred K.

Her lips flattened in a prim line. "It's the least I can do, considering you're paying me a fortune. And, I assure you, I have never *screwed* with anyone's head."

He choked on a laugh. Jesus, with the exception of that *bollocks* slip, the woman spoke like Queen Elizabeth's spinster cousin. The contradiction of Piper's upper crust speech and made-for-sin body, not to mention the way she'd kissed him… He shook his head. He'd bet his Aston Martin she hadn't learned *that* skill at some dusty boarding school. Fuck, yeah. The enticing paradox of her was a definite head screw.

He grinned. "Then you should try it sometime. You have a natural talent for it." She slowly straightened on her stool and he held up his hand. "You've got yourself a deal. One hundred thousand plus any travel expenses to get you to and from the games after you've finished the calendar and returned to England." And since it appeared this was his lucky day, and she was in such a generous mood… "One more thing. About that suite at the Plaza…"

Blink, blink, blink.

Just when he thought his heart was going to explode, she sniffed. "Now, you're just being greedy."

Well, hell-o, duchess. She hadn't said no.

With a shrug, he picked up the carton of beef and broccoli and dumped the remainder onto his rice. "I want what I want."

Cool as can be, she spread a napkin over her lap as if they were dining at the Ritz and he hadn't just propositioned her.

Fucking sexy as hell.

She wagged her fork in the air. "Maybe so, but you get what you pay for. It so happens, I'm not for sale."

He opened his mouth to point out she'd just jacked him for one hundred grand to take twelve pictures, but thought better of it. He had the next five weeks to change her mind.

She slipped a fat shrimp between her lips and his mouth watered. Cocking her head, she studied him as she chewed. "Before I decide *if* I'll be sleeping with you, there are a few stipulations you'll need to agree to."

He choked on his wine and wiped the back of his hand over his lips. If he expected her to blush and stammer on about spouting absurdly inappropriate comments when nervous, he was mistaken. She met and held his gaze with a purpose in her eyes he wasn't sure he understood, but wasn't about to question.

"Like?"

"First, we'll be working together on both the Fab Five project and your calendar. Ideally, I'd prefer to remain anonymous in those endeavors, but I'm aware that might not be possible. I will, therefore, settle for your agreement to keep my identity to yourself unless absolutely necessary."

She looked so adorably serious, he couldn't resist teasing her. "Why don't you want your name getting out there? You're not a felon or anything, right? Escapee from a federal penitentiary?"

Her lips turned down at the corners, and she ignored his ridiculous questions. "However, I insist that any personal association between the two of us remain strictly private." She lowered the hand holding the fork to rest on the countertop. "On this, I'm firm. No offense meant, but I have no desire to have my name tangled with yours romantically."

Well, shit. That was a first. Most women went out of their way to have their names associated with his, but then, most women weren't Piper Darrow. He rolled one shoulder in a negligent shrug. "None taken."

She dipped her chin in a curt nod. "And second, any expenses associated with our," she waggled her fork in the air, "*fling*, will be split down the middle."

Humor creased his brow. "You want to go Dutch?"

"Yes, I do. Business is one thing. I'm performing a service by taking the photographs you need and you're paying handsomely for them, but I won't have anyone accusing me of using a personal relationship with you for monetary gain. When you and I do check into that suite at the Plaza, I'll be paying half."

He frowned and studied the hard gleam of intensity in her eyes. *Why would anyone accuse her of using him? What the hell was she talking about?*

"If you have a problem with that, we can just forget the whole thing."

No way in hell was that happening. "Nope. Dutch works for me." He lowered his wineglass to the counter. "But, you know, there's a king-sized bed on the other side of that wall that won't cost either of us a dime."

Her emerald gaze followed the jerk of his chin in the general direction of his bedroom. The nerves he'd expected had shown up by the time she looked back but, he had to hand it to her, nervous or not, she didn't back down.

"I'm sure there is, but the *when* I mentioned isn't today."

He could live with that, as long as there *was* a when.

"And third…"

Of course, there was a third stipulation.

"I want it understood from the beginning, when we sleep together, I expect no strings or obligations. Neither should you. My only condition is that you show me the respect of curtailing other relationships while we're together. I'll be returning to England in five weeks and if this…thing between us should last that long, it ends there. If that's a problem for you, let me know now and we'll keep our relationship on a purely business footing."

Was she fucking kidding? A five-week, all-access pass to her body, backed up by a no-strings-attached promise? He eased back on his stool with a shake of his head. "Duchess, you may be the most perfect woman ever born."

She smiled and the remaining tension eased from her shoulders. "It's imperative to me that we walk away from any association, be it personal or business, on a friendly note." She stabbed another shrimp. "And speaking of business, did you want to attempt to have the calendar finished for a late fall release, or will you wait and put it out next year?"

He was slow to drag his mind from the bedroom back into the boardroom. When he did, his stomach plummeted. His calendar idea had been a shot in the dark. A vehicle designed to keep Piper in town. He hadn't given the specifics of such an enterprise a thought, but he was now.

V's taunting smile earlier in her office flashed in his mind, and he cursed beneath his breath.

He'd been set up by a pro. V knew him better than just about anyone. She would have known exactly what he'd been after with his bogus job offer. She'd called his bluff and he didn't know whether to thank her or strangle her. After that surprising apology, thanking her seemed right. But considering he now had to convince eleven of his friends to pose for hunk pictures—taken by a woman who would soon be sharing his bed—he was leaning toward strangle.

He cleared his throat and forced himself to recall Piper's question. Right. The calendar release.

"With the hype surrounding this season, we'd be guaranteed bigger sales come January and leading up to the Super Bowl. I'd rather get it out there sooner than later, but will that be possible with the Marauders' project tying you up for the next five weeks?"

She finished chewing and swallowed. "V and I discussed that possibility."

He'd just bet they had. Definitely strangle.

Piper spun Chinese noodles around the tines of her fork like pasta. "Since the team is paying me a flat rate, she has no problem with my working concurrently on the calendar. If all the models for your project are Marauders, I'll be working with some of them for the Fab Five production already."

She lifted the fork to her lips. "If you'll let me know what you want in the individual shots, I'll get them while I'm working with the particular models for V's project. The rest of the men can be photographed on an off day of your choosing."

He'd have to convince them to say yes first. If he couldn't, his entire deal with Piper would go up in smoke. The knots in his gut twisted tighter. "You're the photographer. Shouldn't you know what shots will work?"

She arched a brow. "The production you're asking for will require a bit more than snapping a few pictures and posting them together in a spiral binder. Theme first, then we'll work on the content." She'd lost him, and her sigh said she knew it. "We'll work that out later."

That sounded like an excellent idea to him.

"In the meantime, I can expedite the review process Caroline requested by including the calendar pictures in my Friday meetings with V and Jason. That way, I can have all the copy ready for you in five weeks. It'll be up to you and the foundation's marketing department to put the finished product together in time for a year-end release."

"Sounds very efficient." And boring. He rose to his feet.

She glanced up and shrugged. "I'm a professional."

"You're beautiful."

She didn't move a muscle as he rounded the island toward her with a single-minded intent. "When isn't now, Wyatt."

"I know." He stopped before her.

"Then, what are you doing?"

"Sealing our deal."

"Oh." She switched her fork to her left hand and presented her right for him to shake.

He wrapped his fingers around hers and tugged her from her stool.

She stumbled into his chest, blinked, and the breathy way she said his name was an invitation he couldn't resist. He'd meant the kiss to be no more than a quick meeting of their lips. A brush of skin to skin, close enough to assure himself the heady scent of her hadn't been a figment of his imagination. To remind himself the razzing of his teammates and V's smug satisfaction were a small price to pay compared to the pleasure of holding Piper in his arms.

He'd intended to settle for a taste today, knowing the full meal would soon be his but, as she curled into him, his mind shut down and every good intention fled. Releasing her fingers, he slid his hand around her back and over the sweet curve of her ass. Firm and full, her cheek filled his palm.

Her whimper of pleasure urged him on, as did her beaded nipples stabbing at his chest wall through the silk of her blouse. He plunged deep with his tongue, projecting the need of his body to be buried hard and fast in her hot channel. She squirmed closer and, as she sucked at his tongue, he feared the top of his head would blow off.

With a helpless groan, he curled his arm around her waist and tucked her closer, hissing at the press of her mound against his growing erection. He shifted his head, adjusting his mouth on hers. Sliding his hand down the curve of her hip to the hem of her skirt, he curled his fingers beneath the material and up the silky column of her thigh. Past the stretchy lace of her stockings to even silkier skin, then farther, to the damp silk at the juncture of her thighs.

She gasped into his mouth as he burrowed his fingers beneath the elastic edge of her panties and sought the sultry heat beneath. He slid his fingertips through the curls shielding the path to paradise to her slick and swollen folds. A delicate shiver raced over her and she bucked against his caressing hand. Once. Twice. On a third violent tremble of her body, she broke apart in his arms and the cry on her lips was his name.

Crushing her to him, he held her close, fingering her through the latent spasms to prolong her pleasure. His cock was a pillar of granite and his fingers were drenched with her essence when she finally lifted her head from his chest.

Hazy with pleasure, her gaze met his, and she breathed his name.

"Shhh." He pressed a kiss to her forehead as he withdrew his hand from beneath her skirt. Because he couldn't help himself, and wanted her to know it, he brought his hand to his lips. Inserting his middle finger into his mouth, he tasted her as he stared into her eyes.

Her pretty mouth rounded in a silent gasp, and the flush riding her cheeks deepened. Repeating the process with his index finger, he fought his own shudder and dragged in a haggard breath. Dropping his forehead to rest against hers, he came as close to begging as he ever had.

"Just say when, Piper. And say it soon. I want you so badly, I'm not sure how much longer I can wait."

Chapter 10

Twenty-four hours later, with half the funds for both the Marauders and Wyatt's projects pending approval in her private account, Piper clicked the shutter, focusing on Tuck's face. With an eye for composition, she'd skirted the patio of the Tuckers' sprawling Long Island home in order to capture the line of trees at his back edging the green lawn. Their colorful fall foliage created a natural backdrop that would make the photos pop.

There. She snapped off several shots in quick succession, capturing the handsome wide receiver's pure joy as the molded plastic swing raced toward him on its forward arc, and his infant son squealed his excitement. Tight at first, Tuck had loosened up as the day passed, as if he'd forgotten her presence.

"Tuck! Dear God. Not so high," CC admonished from behind Piper.

She glanced over her shoulder as CC exited the French doors leading from the kitchen.

"He loves it. Don't cha, big guy." Tuck grinned and gave the swing a hearty push. Huey shrieked his agreement.

Piper winced and snapped a few more shots as the swing reached its backward zenith, hovering for a fraction of a second with the delighted eleven-month-old stretched out perpendicular to the lawn. She made a mental note to keep these last few photos private, for Tuck and CC's viewing alone. Made public, the damning pictures could potentially end up as evidence once the authorities launched their child endangerment investigation.

"I'll be completely gray before I'm thirty-one," CC grumbled.

Piper lowered her camera and turned. "That's eleven months from now and you don't have a single gray."

CC handed Piper a glass of wine, then shot a glance toward her husband and son. "With those two, it will take a lot less than a year." She bit back a gasp and held out her arms. "Bring him here, Tuck, before he throws up."

Piper laughed and lined up CC in her lens. "I thought you said you'd be working in the gallery studio until five."

"It's five-thirty. I ran by the grocer on my way home to pick up some wine and juice. Kris and the rest of the Gridiron Girls are joining us for dinner."

"There goes the neighborhood," Tuck called as he unbuckled Huey from his swing.

CC huffed at his teasing slight to her friends. The Gridiron Girls, as the five friends referred to themselves, included CC and her cousin, Kris, who had married Tuck's brother, Tim, last year. V Fitzpatrick was also part of the group, but Piper had yet to meet the last two women. According to CC, Gracie Malone, wife of the Marauders' retired, record-breaking tight end turned broadcaster, was the apparent leader of the group. Then there was Jessi Tucker-Grayson, Tuck's country music superstar cousin.

Piper lowered the camera. "Oh, CC. I wish you wouldn't go to such trouble. I'm here to work, not to be wined and dined."

"It's no trouble, and it's the least I can do since you insist on staying at a hotel instead of here with us." CC waved her off. "Anyway, the girls wanted to meet you."

Tuck approached and wrapped CC in a one-armed hug. Piper stealthily raised her camera to document the heated kiss he bestowed on his wife before handing her their son. They shared a private smile, and a pang of envy tugged at a spot just below Piper's heart. Would she ever know the type of passionate and joyous relationship her friend had found with her handsome player husband? If, by some miracle, Piper found the simple man whose vague image hovered in her mind, was she even capable of the deep and lasting love required to build a happy life and family? After Cody, she'd come to believe she wasn't and the possibility left a lingering sadness behind.

She shook aside the melancholy as Tuck shot a glance at the house. "I think I'll make myself scarce before the horde arrives."

CC nuzzled her baby boy's cheek. "Weenie. I don't expect them for a few minutes yet."

"Good. Gives me a decent head start." Swatting her behind, he headed for the house.

"You're just trying to get out of helping with dinner preparations," she called to his back.

He laughed as he disappeared inside.

"I'll help," Piper offered. "What do you need?"

CC shook her head. "Nothing, actually. A little Italian place in the center of town delivers. The food will be here in a half hour." She waved a hand toward the patio table, indicating Piper should sit, then joined her. Arranging Huey on her lap, she pinned Piper with squinted eyes. "Which gives me plenty of time to find out why you arrived here this morning looking like you hadn't slept a wink."

Piper winced. "That's probably because I didn't."

"Why not?" Concern flashed in CC's Irish-green eyes. "What's happened?"

"I've miscalculated, CC. Badly." Piper bit her bottom lip. "Since you obviously told V Fitzpatrick about it, you remember the stipulation Da had in his will."

CC's nose wrinkled with her guilty grimace. "I didn't give V any actual details. She simply asked if I thought you would be open to taking the photographs for her project. I remembered you mentioning you owed your cousin her inheritance and told V I thought you could use the money." Her eyes filled with apology. "I'm sorry, Piper. I was just trying to help."

Piper sighed. "I know you were, and what you told V was the truth. I do need the money. Desperately." She shook her head. "What I didn't tell you was just how *much* the estate owes Abigail or that I'm under a rapidly approaching deadline to pay it."

Worry wrinkled CC's brow. "If you're short, we could…"

"Oh, dearest. No." Horrified, Piper leaned forward to press a hand to CC's arm. "I appreciate the offer, but it's not necessary. Between the money the Marauders are paying me and the," she dropped her gaze to fiddle with the zoom button on her camera, "um, project I've agreed to work on for Wyatt Hunter, I'll have plenty of cash on hand to settle with Abigail before the New Year's Eve deadline."

"Hold on." Piper glanced up as CC tugged her pearl necklace from Huey's chubby fist. "You're working on a project with Wyatt?"

Piper nodded.

"What type of project?"

"It's sort of a… Well, it's a…" Piper twisted the camera strap around her fingers, then tugged them free once more. "I'm shooting a hunk of the month calendar including him and eleven of his teammates."

"Of course, you are." CC burst out laughing and shook her head. "This was his suggestion, I take it."

"Yes, as a matter of fact, and he's paying me a fortune to do it."

CC's laughter choked off and her brows shot to her hairline. "Define fortune."

Piper arched a satisfied brow. "Enough to allow me to pay off the debt to my cousin when it's all said and done."

CC blinked, but then cocked her head. "You said his teammates, right? Who are the other eleven?"

"You know, I don't know the answer to that, yet." She hadn't thought to ask for that detail during their negotiations. Then again, discussing details was difficult while sucking on a man's tongue. She groaned inwardly.

"That's probably because Wyatt hasn't asked the guys yet. If he had, Tuck would have known and had a blast ragging on Wyatt about the project before volunteering for a month himself, of course." CC snickered. "But you said you'd miscalculated. How, exactly?"

Dragged back to the original point of the conversation, Piper frowned in self-disgust. "By letting my libido get out in front of my head."

"Oh, *reee-ally?*" CC pinned her with an anticipatory stare.

"I let him kiss me." Piper cringed as the understated mistruth left her lips. "Twice! The first one I actually *initiated*. In your kitchen."

"You slut, you!" CC grinned. "And the second?"

Piper blew a windy sigh. Twenty-four hours later, she was still teetering on the edge of meltdown just remembering it. "*He* initiated the second kiss and it was entirely too intense to be labeled a simple brush of lips."

"Well, well." CC fanned her face, making Piper cough on a laugh.

"I'm telling you, locking lips with him was a complete and utter miscalculation on my part." She'd climaxed, for heaven's sake. Fully clothed and standing on her feet, she'd come in Wyatt Hunter's kitchen with no more stimulation than his kiss and the flick of his fingers. The man was a danger she couldn't afford.

She groaned and slapped a hand to her forehead.

"Oh, please." CC bounced Huey in her lap. "He's single and gorgeous. So are you, and he's obviously interested. Why do you think he showed up for lunch last week?" She smirked. "That excuse he and Tuck came up with that Wyatt was here to watch game tapes was laughable."

"Game tapes?"

CC snorted. "Exactly. He showed up for one reason." She pointed a finger at Piper's nose. "You. I wondered what went on between the two of you before you came outside with the wine. *And* I noticed neither of you were bleeding, or even limping." She grinned. "So much for your bad mojo with athletes theory."

"Yes, well, you didn't let me finish. I also tentatively agreed to sleep with him for the next five weeks, so there's still plenty of time on the clock for disaster to strike."

CC laughed and placed her wineglass out of Huey's reach. "Neither of you are attached, so I still don't see the problem."

Piper sipped her wine before answering. "The problem is, I didn't think this through properly." But after he'd rocked her with a standing orgasm, she'd done plenty of soul searching throughout the sleepless night. "In the cold light of day, I fear sleeping with him would be a mistake on multiple levels." She gulped the remainder of her glass as the image of his face smiling at Mandy shimmered in her mind. "On a personal level, the more I see of Wyatt, the more I understand he's not just an incredibly sexy man. He's also a nice guy."

"Yeah, I can see how sleeping with a nice guy would be a problem."

Piper choked back a laugh at her friend's sarcasm. "The problem is, I'm a pushover for a nice guy, and when he comes in a package like Wyatt's?" She rested her free hand over her heart, not surprised to find it thumping erratically. "If I go forward with this, I fear I won't be going home with my heart intact when it ends."

CC struggled to hold on to her wriggling son as he spotted a squirrel on a nearby tree. "Going into this relationship assuming it's going to end might be the bigger mistake." She shook her head. "Wyatt isn't Cody. He might just surprise you. The fact is, you're right. He *is* a nice guy."

"He's also a player and a womanizer, who, I might add, agreed wholeheartedly with the temporary arrangement I suggested. In five weeks, I'll return to England and, no pun intended, he'll return to playing the field."

The smirk tweaking CC's lips made Piper nervous. "Maybe so, but Wyatt wouldn't be the first womanizing player to end his playboy ways thanks to a temporary arrangement." She pressed a kiss to Huey's cheek. "Trust me. I know. Tuck and I planned to go our separate ways after such an arrangement, and well." Her eyes flashed with utter happiness. "You get my point."

Piper swallowed. "The situation between Wyatt and me is completely different than what happened with you and Tuck. Why, anyone can see the two of you were made for one another. Plus, you lived in the same city when you met. I live and *work* on another continent. Wyatt plays football for a living, and throws around money like it grows in his garden."

Her shoulders heaved on a sigh. "I have responsibilities in England, CC. I no longer have Da looking after things for me while I fly around the world like a carefree heiress. Not that I ever was one, as it turns out. Da spent every last shilling of his family's money to keep Delaney Manor from being sold off. I owe it to him to assure that doesn't happen now that he's gone."

She shook her head. "The truth is, I'm broke. I *have* to work. At the same time, there are people counting on my good stewardship of Delaney Manor for their livelihoods."

Mackenzie Crowne

"Who's handling the stewardship of the manor right now?"

Piper squinted at CC's smirk. "You're missing the point."

"Which is?"

"My life and Wyatt's are worlds apart and I *need* the money I've been promised here. Sleeping with him could jeopardize everything, considering our professional connection." Piper grimaced. "Setting aside the calendar, I'm supposed to work with him on V's Fab Five project. What do you think she'll say if she finds out the two of us have become lovers?"

"I'd say, as long as you produce the quality shots I'm after, who you sleep with is none of my business."

Piper whipped her head around and bit down a groan at discovering V approaching the table.

Good Lord. If it weren't for bad *luck, I'd have none at all.*

Behind V, Kris and two visibly pregnant women exited the house from the kitchen. The Marauders' PR consultant stopped beside the table and helped herself to CC's half full glass of wine.

Sipping briefly, V offered Piper an easy smile. "Of course, if you hurt him, you die."

Piper's mouth dropped open and she blinked.

"Piper!"

Relieved by Kris's timely interruption, Piper rose to her feet to hug CC's cousin. "Good Lord, Kris, it's been ages."

"Yes, it has." Kris arched back to stab her with an accusing glare. "I can't believe you were in town last week and I didn't get to see you."

"You were in Cincinnati," CC pointed out with a shake of her head.

"That's no excuse. I'd have come back early had I known Piper was going to be in town."

"It's not Piper's fault," V supplied with a smirk. "We kept her pretty busy while she was here."

CC rose to make introductions. "Ladies, this is Piper Darrow. Piper, Gracie Malone and Jessi Tucker-Grayson."

Piper returned the women's smiles. "It's lovely to meet you both."

"Same here." With the exception of her prominent baby bump, Jessi, a petite redhead, looked exactly as she had on her latest CD.

Gracie held out her arms to Huey. The tall blonde laughed as he abandoned his mother in a fearless leap. "We're sorry for barging in on you your first full day in town, but we couldn't wait to meet you. Not after CC told us all about the trouble the three of you got into as children in Italy."

As if on cue, Piper and CC spoke as one, "It was all Kris's fault."

Their gazes met and they laughed. Kris shot them both a raspberry just as she had done when they were kids.

"Kris's ability to cause trouble is one of her best traits." A dimple accompanied Gracie's soft laughter and she turned to V. "So, who is it Piper is going to hurt, and why will she be dying for it?"

Piper blinked, lost.

V sent her a sidelong glance. "Wyatt has set his sights on Piper and she's decided to give him a run for his money."

"Literally," CC added.

Piper bit back a groan.

"She's his new lucky charm," V announced with a grin.

Gracie turned to Piper. "Oh, do tell."

"Good for you, Piper. Wyatt Hunter is so hot," Jessi proclaimed.

"I…" More than a bit overwhelmed at having her personal life discussed by strangers, Piper decided silence was her safest bet.

Gracie gently bumped Jessi's hip with hers. "Don't let Max hear you say that."

"She can do no wrong in Max's eyes, these days." Kris grinned. "Now that he knows his *son* will be arriving soon."

"Oh, Jessi." Gracie's eyes went misty. "A boy. When did you find out? And how is Max taking the news?"

"Yesterday." Jessi smiled dreamily. "He's over the moon excited, which is an improvement on the green-around-the-gills look he wore for the first trimester."

Piper added her polite smile to the laughter from the other women, until Gracie turned to study her with an arched brow. The rest of the Gridiron Girls followed suit.

"So, Piper," Gracie tapped a fingertip to her chin, "how are you planning to give Wyatt a run for his money?"

"Oh, I…"

"And what can we do to help?"

Chapter 11

Week two of the Marauders' season dawned crisp and bright with a gentle breeze that carried the scent of sunshine and early fall. A perfect day for football, according to those in the know.

Piper hadn't spoken to Wyatt since he'd dropped her off at her hotel after that panty-melting kiss in his kitchen. Consequently, she'd yet to tell him she'd changed her mind about their fling. Which might actually be a good thing, considering the way she kept wavering back and forth. As she'd explained to CC, V, and the Gridiron Girls, a "strictly professional" arrangement with Wyatt would be best for everyone involved.

Her head agreed with that sound and logical plan. But, bugger it all, how was a woman to cling to sound logic with the memory of Wyatt Hunter sucking the essence of her orgasm from his fingers while his eyes blazed with arousal?

A sensual shudder shook her as she slid from the limo that had delivered her to the Marauders' sports complex for this afternoon's game. How to broach the subject of renegotiation was the problem. After all, an extra fifty-six thousand pounds sat in her account as of yesterday. The bulk of which had come from him in the form of his half-up-front payment. Thus far, he'd been true to his word, yet here she was, planning to alter the arrangement they'd agreed upon after the fact. Guilt insisted she renegotiate the payment she would receive as well.

She didn't have a lot of wiggle room, not if she was going to pay off Abigail in time, and tying compensation to sex or, in this case, the lack thereof, left Piper feeling slightly icky. Still, fair play demanded she make some kind of gesture.

The money was all she had.

She hadn't left herself a lot of extra time, arriving at the stadium just before kickoff. After presenting her credentials to the security office personnel, she was escorted onto a private lift that delivered her directly to a tunnel leading to the field. As she stepped into the sunlight flooding the Marauders' sideline, it took a moment for her eyes to adjust. Once they had, she spotted Wyatt.

Muscular body displayed to perfection in white uniform pants and Marauders' blue and gold jersey, he stood a dozen or so feet away. As Dallas kicked off to start the game, Wyatt and a dark-haired man studied the tablet in the man's hands.

As if sensing her presence, Wyatt lifted his head and glanced her way. The hair on her arms prickled as their gazes clashed. Several heartbeats passed as he ran his eyes down her body, then up to pause first on her chest, then on the hat pulled low over her brow. His gaze dropped to meet hers, and she squelched the urge to fidget beneath his questioning smile.

For sure, the *I Heart NY* ball cap she'd picked up in a shop around the corner from her hotel was far from her usual, sophisticated style. So was the oversized sweatshirt printed with *Oops... Did I roll my eyes out loud?* Which made them perfect. Combined with the work denims she'd brought from home and the trainers she'd found in yet another store, she looked nothing like the Baroness Delaney.

Not that she expected the European tabloids to have a presence at an American sporting event, but neither did she plan to be recognized. Four more caps, a half dozen printed sweatshirts, and several new pairs of jeans hung in her hotel closet, and would throw off anyone looking while she was here in the States.

With a slight shake of his head, Wyatt tugged on his helmet. And, bloody hell, she had no business going woozy over the wicked grin and sexy wink he shot at her before loping onto the field.

Turning away, she met the smile of the adorably charming young man who had been the first to come to her aid last week after being hit by Wyatt's tipped pass. She rushed to repeat her gratitude for his kindness, and he waved her off, introducing himself as Kip Walker. In his third year at university, the handsome young athlete played tight end for Boston College, but his team was the Marauders. On every Sunday he could manage, he volunteered as water boy, making the round trip by train between Boston and Manhattan for Marauders' home games.

Tall and muscular, he fit right in with the mammoth warriors crowding the home team bench. The players' respect and affection for him was clear to see, in particular, Wyatt's. And those sentiments obviously went both ways. Whenever the Marauders' quarterback stepped from the field, the team's most loyal volunteer was there with a cup or towel, or anything else Wyatt might need.

Otherwise, Kip remained at Piper's side throughout the afternoon. After raising a brow at her sweatshirt, he returned from the locker room at halftime with a Marauders' hoodie. He grinned at her cocked brow, but then crossed his arms and waited until she'd changed into the bright blue garment sporting the team emblem.

For more than three hours, she snapped her photographs while attending American Football 101. With million dollar dimples and a clear love of the sport, Kip explained the fundamentals of the game along with some of the team's statistical achievements he considered important. Words like catch ratio, reception percentage, and rushing attempts made little sense to her, but his enthusiasm was impossible to resist.

And if she'd worried her bad mojo would show its ugly head, she needn't have. A repeat of last Sunday's accident wasn't likely with Kip hovering like some kind of self-appointed guardian angel. Several times he stepped between her and potential danger when the play ventured too close.

On one such occasion, a Marauders' receiver and his defender barreled toward the sideline in her direction. Before she could react, Kip scooped her up and spun her clear of the approaching mayhem. Setting her on her feet once again, he shrugged at her arched brow, white teeth flashing in his unapologetic grin.

She laughed and shook her head. Certain men should come with a warning label. With his solid build, midnight-black hair, laughing blue eyes, and naturally protective instincts, Kip was one of them. He'd said he was majoring in statistics, but he'd clearly already achieved a PhD in charm. Probably while he was still in the cradle.

Late in the fourth quarter, he raced onto the field with his water bottles during a break in the action he labeled the two-minute warning. Piper zoomed in on the Marauders players gathered loosely at the center of the field. Brushing over Tuck, she paused on Wyatt where he spoke to another of the men. The wooziness returned as his dimples made an appearance in his trademark grin.

She briefly glanced at the scoreboard. With the clock winding down, Wyatt and his teammates were clobbering Dallas, which might have something to do with his good humor. Except that, even in the first quarter, when the visiting team had taken an early lead, Wyatt's enjoyment of the game had been evident.

He loved what he was doing and it showed.

Piper gritted her teeth. How unfair was it that, shadowed by his helmet and beaded with sweat, his handsome face was even more appealing than usual and the curve of his lips sexier?

A whistle blew, ending the official time out. With a sigh, she readjusted her focus to the man she was *supposed* to be watching. The men broke their huddle with a clap of hands. They approached the line of scrimmage and she snapped a shot of Tuck.

"I almost didn't recognize you."

Piper glanced to her right before refocusing on the field. "Which is precisely the point of the disguise."

V sighed softly. "I guess I'd be a little paranoid, too, if I were in your shoes."

Piper adjusted the zoom. "I doubt any of those vultures you mentioned care about me after all this time, but…" She shrugged.

"Better safe than sorry?" V offered.

"Something like that."

A moment of silence, then, "How's it going?"

"Rather well, actually."

On the field, Wyatt called the snap. Bodies crashed together as Piper followed Tuck's movement with her lens. She pressed and held the shutter button. The camera whined as it captured Tuck's mid-air catch in burst mode.

The fans roared their appreciation. V added her encouragement, verbally cheering Tuck on as he added several more yards to the play before being forced out of bounds by a defender. He crashed to the ground, then immediately rolled to his feet. Impressed, Piper kept shooting. Even with her limited knowledge of the game, she recognized sheer athletic ability when she saw it.

Once he'd rejoined his teammates, she lowered her arms and turned to meet V's gaze. "He's quite talented, isn't he?"

A brisk nod. "He's headed for the hall of fame, as are a couple of his teammates currently on the field."

Piper slid her gaze back to the men gathering around Wyatt. "He's also incredibly photogenic."

"Who? Tuck or Wyatt?"

Piper's jaw sagged as she whipped her head around. Oh, bother. "V, I…"

"Yes, I heard you the other night. You truly believe a strictly business relationship between," she paused and glanced around at the milling players, coaches, and staff before meeting Piper's wary gaze, "the *two parties* involved is in your best interest."

Piper heaved a sigh, but her relief was premature.

"However, knowing the other party as I do, you can expect your decision to be challenged." She smiled softly at Piper's frown. "From your comment when I arrived at CC and Tuck's, I assume your feelings on this matter are due to a desire to avoid a professional conflict with the team. Or am I mistaken? Is there more to it than that?"

Piper stared at her. "I should think avoiding a professional conflict would be enough."

"Sure, if you have a personal issue along those lines." V glanced toward the red zone where the men were lined up. "But, please be clear...."

The stadium vibrated with frantic cheers and Piper turned back to the field. Her gaze landed unerringly on Wyatt, scrambling to his feet from beneath two huge defenders. His helmet and faceguard couldn't disguise the pure exhilaration on his face as he hurried toward the end zone to join in the celebration of Tuck's latest touchdown.

A warm glow heated her chest as she brought the camera back to her eye.

"As I was saying," V spoke at her side. "Please be clear that neither myself nor anyone associated with the franchise have a problem with what you and," she cleared her throat, "*the other party* do with your private time. As long as it doesn't affect your working together."

Piper slowly turned her head. "Oh, Lord. I really wish you'd kept that detail to yourself."

"Less temptation?" V's smile was as perceptive as her question.

Piper choked back a groaning whimper and nodded.

"Would it surprise you to learn I was in a similar situation not long ago?" V jerked her chin toward the tall dark-haired man Wyatt had sought out on the sideline throughout the game. The same man he'd been speaking to when Piper first arrived. "That's the team's offensive coordinator. His name is Sam Fitzpatrick."

Piper turned back and blinked. "Your husband?"

V nodded and the affection in her eyes as they followed Sam was impossible to miss. "We knew each other before he came to work for the team near the end of last season. We were married less than two months later. Ask me sometime how successful he and I were at keeping things between us *strictly business*."

Piper choked on an inner wince. *Nothing like demolishing the strongest of my self-erected barricades designed to keep me out of Wyatt's bed.*

V chuckled and held out her hand.

"What's this?" Piper shoved aside her crumbling hope of resisting the irresistible, and accepted the sheet of paper.

"It's Wyatt's list of models for his calendar."

Piper unfolded the sheet and read the names. "Well, he certainly works fast, doesn't he?"

V squinted, her smile sly. "Apparently so."

Piper didn't bother rolling her eyes at the not-so-subtle innuendo. The blush heating her chest and rising to her neck and face said it all.

V laughed softly. "Like I told you, the players respect and like Wyatt." She grinned. "He'd have no trouble finding volunteers for his project. But I would have loved to have been a fly on the wall when he told them what he wanted. I'm sure he took a ration of shit before they said yes."

Piper dropped her gaze to scan the list. Tuck's name was there. If CC was correct in her prediction, that ration of shit had definitely come Wyatt's way.

"One more thing."

Piper glanced up, and the apology in V's eyes brought an instant chill to Piper's skin.

Bloody hell. What now?

"I know you're slated to be with Tuck this week, but there's been a… development that requires a change of schedule."

She nodded warily, sure she wasn't going to like whatever V had to say.

"Wyatt needs to leave tonight for Oklahoma City. His father is holding an early press announcement tomorrow morning, which can mean only one thing. Richard Hunter is announcing his run for the presidency."

Piper held her breath, but it didn't do her any good.

Face stoic, V heaved a sigh. "I realize something this big isn't what you signed on for, but we respectfully request you to go with Wyatt to document the event."

Piper's stomach plummeted. So much for her clever disguise. And she'd been worried about being recognized among the thousands of people attending an American football game? Good God. She should have run when she'd had the chance.

Bollocks. I hate when my inner nag is right.

* * * *

Piper's cell phone rang less than a minute after she'd arrived back at her hotel room. Checking the screen, she breathed deep to calm the heavy thudding of her heart and answered Wyatt's call.

"Piper Darrow."

"Hiya, duchess. You looked beautiful today." She hadn't a clue how to respond. Not that it mattered. He went on before she could. "You left the complex before I could thank you properly for today's win."

She cursed the instant blush heating her cheeks and cleared her throat. "Statistically, the Marauders' lopsided victory was practically a given. I doubt my presence made a bit of difference."

"Statistically?" A deep chuckle, then, "A photographer, B&B owner, *and* a sports statistician?"

She smiled. "Hardly. The statistical information came courtesy of Kip Walker. Someone from the organization really should look at him more closely. His talent for numbers and recognizing successful patterns in the matchups of different lines is being wasted."

"Believe me, someone is looking at him. Several someones, in fact." Affection and humor competed in Wyatt's tone. "Sounds like the kid's picked up another disciple."

"Fan, actually." She shrugged out of her jacket and tossed it across the bed. "Most of what he said went straight over my head," she admitted with a laugh. "But he is so adorable in his intensity. I was utterly charmed."

"Yeah, he's adorable, all right." Wyatt paused as if he'd adjusted his phone from one ear to the other. "V said she spoke to you about traveling to Oklahoma City with me tonight?"

"Yes, she did." Reminded of what lay ahead, Piper eased to the edge of the bed and toed off her trainers. "What time is the flight?"

"Three hours. Will that give you enough time to be ready?"

For which? Attending your father's press announcement? Or spending the night in your bed in some hotel? How a woman was supposed to prepare herself for either of those scenarios, she hadn't a clue, but she would bloody well be finding out.

Everything had changed. Once his father made his announcement tomorrow, Wyatt would be under more scrutiny than ever before. As closely as they would be working together, someone was bound to take notice of her, but that was business, as V had said. Piper would deal with any fallout from her professional relationship with Wyatt, but their personal dealings were another matter.

A five-week fling between them was no longer an option. As soon as they arrived at their hotel in Oklahoma City, they'd be tackling those renegotiations she'd been considering. She no longer had a choice. If she and the Marauders' sexy quarterback were to have their "when," it was tonight or never.

She swallowed the nerves bubbling up in her belly like a geyser. "I can be ready if I get off the phone and start packing."

He said nothing for an extended moment, then sighed. "I'm sorry about this, duchess. I know the last thing you want is to be caught up in the limelight tomorrow's event will provide but, if you'll trust me, I'll see to it your name isn't part of the conversation."

Her throat tightened that he'd recognize her anxiety over the matter without her having to remind him. "I appreciate that."

"If it were up to me, neither of us would be going, but I understand why the team feels tomorrow should be documented."

"So do I," she admitted softly.

Another pause, then, "I sent the itinerary over by courier."

Piper frowned at the envelope on the small entry table. She'd scanned it in the lift. "It was waiting for me at the desk when I arrived. I didn't see any seating assignments for the flight."

"We'll handle that when we board."

"That's fine, but I'd prefer we be seated in different rows. I'd rather not advertise that we're traveling together."

He chuckled at the demand, until she pointed out maintaining her anonymity had been part of their deal. "I'll swing by your hotel in an hour to pick you up."

"That won't be necessary. I'll meet you at the airport."

His low laughter stroked her in places that had been dormant for several years. "Have it your way, duchess. The information on the gate location is included in the itinerary. Don't be late."

Though she'd left herself plenty of time, she had some difficulty locating the gate in the corporate terminal at LaGuardia. A helpful airport employee eventually directed her to an unmarked door at the far end of the building. Upon entering the posh waiting room, Piper worried she'd read the information incorrectly—until a uniformed employee greeted her.

The thin blonde wore a welcoming smile. "Good afternoon, Miss Duchess. If you'll follow me, Mr. Hunter is waiting for you on board."

Miss Duchess? Piper choked, turning her laugh into a cough. *Oh, you're a clever bounder, aren't you?*

Shaking her head, she clamped down on the helpless grin that threatened and followed the woman past several well-appointed seating areas, complete with four welcoming couches, a half-dozen recliners separated by privacy walls, and a full bar. Exiting the building, they traveled down a jet bridge that opened onto the tarmac. A large SUV with heavily tinted windows waited outside. The driver's door opened as they approached, and a bulky man in a dark suit, looking more like a bodyguard than a chauffeur, greeted her.

"If you're ready, Miss Duchess?" He held out his hand for her carryon bag. *Oh, for heaven's sake.*

She did grin this time, couldn't help herself, and handed over her bag. He opened the back door and she slid inside. She'd barely had time to appreciate the fine leather seats and interior before the vehicle stopped and the door opened once more. Placing her fingers into the chauffeur's large hand, she was assisted from the vehicle, then blinked at the small streamlined jet idling on the tarmac in front of her.

"Miss?" Mr. Bodyguard-Chauffeur turned to address her when she remained where she was instead of following him to the stairs at the rear of the plane.

He held out his hand and she hurried forward, preceding him up the steps. She stopped short just inside the door, and he tucked her carryon into a small closet to her right.

"Enjoy your flight, miss," he said before leaving her alone.

She glanced around and had to lock her jaw to keep her mouth from dropping open. Had she thought the private waiting area posh? Good Lord! The jet was glitzier than a lot of the five-star hotels she'd visited back when she'd had the wherewithal to do so.

"Right on time," Wyatt announced, and she jumped.

He moved toward her from the front of the plane and she lifted her chin. "I promised I would be." She pinned him with a squint. "Really? Miss *Duchess*?"

His dimples flashed with his grin. "I'm keeping your name to myself unless absolutely necessary…as requested."

She pressed her lips together to squelch her threatening laughter, but failed. "You consider yourself quite clever, I'm sure."

He bumped his brows in a jaunty waggle, then stood idle as she surveyed the high-end materials and furnishings in the private jet's long, narrow fuselage. She ran her fingertips over the glossy teak-wood table fronted by four large captain's chairs, then tested the springs of the wide couch with a couple presses of her hand.

She straightened and eyed him in a sidelong glance. "Swanky."

He chuckled. "Glad you like it. It folds out into a king-sized bed."

Her gaze jerked back to the couch as a flash fire of heat warmed her from the inside out. Bloody hell. She hadn't expected sleeping with Wyatt would grant her entrance into the mile-high club, but…. She eyed the dozen empty seats lining the fuselage.

Well, bother. She might be determined to get Wyatt Hunter naked before the night was done, but sex with an audience wasn't her style.

"We've been cleared for takeoff, Wyatt."

A disembodied male voice spoke from above. She lifted her gaze to the ceiling and searched for the invisible speakers. There were none that she could discern.

Wyatt pivoted and walked several feet away. He cued a button on a console beside a second couch at the very front of the plane. "Ready when you are, Curtis." He turned to face her. If the heat in his eyes was any indication, he knew the exact direction in which her mind had been traveling—and approved.

His smile came slow. "Have a seat and buckle up."

Swallowing, she glanced around at the various options. "Where?"

He propped his hands on his hips and held her gaze. "Wherever you want."

"Oh." She blinked. "There are no other passengers?"

"Not tonight. Tonight, it's just you and me."

She shifted her gaze between him and the closed door of the cockpit, then on to the couch. When she met his gaze once more, his eyes were fired with male interest, but he didn't say a word.

It was just as well. If she was only to have one night with him, she didn't want it limited by a takeoff and landing. She searched about for a neutral topic. "I didn't see any markings on the outside. Does the plane belong to the Marauders?"

"Nope."

"A charter?" Cody had been a gold star client of a London-based charter service.

Wyatt shook his head.

She chewed her bottom lip. "I don't suppose a wealthy friend was kind enough to lend it to you?"

His widening smile spoke volumes.

"Of course. You own your own plane. What was I thinking?"

With a self-derisive smirk, she slid into the closest seat and pushed the seatbelt's components together until they locked. He paused at her side and she glanced up, but had no time to prepare as he bent over her and covered her mouth with his. An increasingly familiar weakness flooded her limbs, and she thrilled at his lovely exploration. A gentle nip, a teasing suckle, the quick thrust of his tongue, and then... She bit down on a whimper of disappointment when he straightened away from her.

The satisfaction in his smile was in direct contrast to the heated arousal darkening his eyes. He turned toward the back of the plane, and she fought the urge to fan herself. Good Lord, the man knew what he was about in the kissing department, and the bounder knew it. Craning her neck, she followed his movements as he continued beyond the open seat to her left and chose a seat two rows back from her. The engines revved and the plane began to move.

She shifted her gaze to the empty seat separating them and back, then rolled her lips together against a laugh. "Let me guess. Separate rows?"

Silent laughter sparkled in his eyes as he nodded. "Your wish is my command, duchess."

Chapter 12

Piper blinked through the rails of the tall wrought iron gate. A large Victorian-style home sat at the end of a curving drive. To the right of the house, attached by a covered breezeway, was a huge five-bay garage.

So much for checking into a hotel for the evening. Obviously, with Wyatt, making assumptions was a foolish endeavor.

"Is this your father's home?"

Dear Lord, please say no. Please. *Say no.*

"Nope."

The breath she held released in a rush. *Thank you, God!*

Wyatt punched numbers into a security panel mounted in a column of the massive brick wall surrounding the property. "My father lives in the governor's mansion, which is where his press announcement will be held in the morning." The gate swung open, and he drove the SUV that had awaited them upon arrival at the airport in Oklahoma City around the curve of the drive. "This is Megan's place."

Bugger! Spending the night at Megan's wasn't much better than if they were to check in at the governor's mansion. The odds were slim Megan Hunter would approve of the two of them sharing a bed in her home.

Piper swallowed as he thumbed the screen of his phone and the far left garage door slid open. "Are you sure a hotel wouldn't be a better choice? I'm not blind, Wyatt. Your sister was none too pleased to meet me the other night."

"My sister's attitude had nothing to do with you. Now that she's had a few days to process Dad's announcement, she'll be a lot less stressed." He guided the SUV into the empty bay. "Besides, hotels have staff." Shifting into park, he cut the engine. The *cheep cheep* of crickets in the distance was the only sound as he turned to meet her gaze in the glow of the dashboard lights. "Staff with Facebook and Instagram accounts. The press will be expecting me to show up in town. It'll be easier to keep your name quiet if there aren't pictures of the two of us checking into the Colcord Hotel downtown."

"Good point." And one she should have considered herself, but damn. It looked as if Karma had spoken. Their "when" wasn't to be. Unless... She tossed out one last appeal and hoped Karma had a romantic side.

"Still, maybe we should chance it. It's, um, rather late to be arriving at someone's home unannounced, don't you think?"

"They're expecting us. In fact, I'll bet you a thousand dollars my sister is frantically pacing the floor, afraid I won't show."

With a deflated sigh, she nodded and unclipped her seatbelt. He stopped her from reaching for the door handle by cupping her shoulder in his palm. "Hey. You wouldn't be here if I thought your presence would be an issue. It'll be fine. I promise."

"I know. It's just..."

"Just what? Talk to me, duchess."

Now or never, Piper. If you want your one night with him, you're going to have to spell it out.

She swallowed. "Well, you see, it's..." She lowered her gaze to her hands. "I've been thinking, and... Well, after tomorrow, things will change."

His hand dropped from her shoulder. "You can count on it."

Her gaze jerked to the rigid line of his jaw as he stared through the windshield at the wall of the garage. Caught up with what Richard Hunter's announcement would mean to her and her romantic plans, she hadn't truly considered how drastic the change would be for Wyatt on a personal level. She, of all people, knew what it was like to be chased down by reporters hungry for a story, but her nightmare with the press had been relatively short-lived. Wyatt had dealt with the hunger his whole life but, starting tomorrow, the feeding frenzy would be taken to a whole new level.

She slid her hand over the tightened muscles of his forearm and squeezed. "I'm sorry, Wyatt. I know this can't be easy for you. Any of it."

"Comes with the territory." He turned his head and, with a toss of his shoulder, the tension slid from his face. He lifted his hand and cupped her jaw. "You said you've been thinking? About us, I hope."

His boyish smile eased some of *her* tension, but not enough.

"Actually, *we* are exactly what I've been thinking about and, the thing is, with the intensified scrutiny that's about to be unleashed..."

He brushed his thumb over her cheek when she stumbled to a stop. "Did I tell you how beautiful you were the other day when you came in my arms?"

Damp heat. Fire licking at her core.

"Wyatt, you shouldn't say things like that." Was that her voice? All breathy and soft?

He shifted, bending to nuzzle the spot where her neck and collarbone met. "Why not?"

She cleared her throat. "Because it doesn't help me remember what I'm trying to say."

"Am I making you hot?" He breathed against her skin, lips nibbling the tender tendon leading to her ear.

She arched her neck to give him better access. "I'm burning."

"Then I am too helping." He chuckled quietly. "Burning's good." He gently closed his teeth on her earlobe and she gasped. Leaving a trail of sipping kisses over her cheek, his warm breath bathed her lips as his mouth hovered above hers. "What are you trying to say, duchess?"

If he kissed her now, she'd be doomed. Her brain would be mush and she'd never say what needed to be said. Trouble was, she was already too far gone to recall the specifics of her renegotiation. All she could think was one word. It spilled from her lips like a plea.

"When."

Everything ceased. The cheeping of the crickets. Her heartbeat. The blood pumping through her veins. But, mostly, the heavy rush and pull of his breath across her face.

He stared at her as the moment stretched. "Did you say...*when*?"

She'd deal with renegotiations later. All she could manage was a nod.

His kiss was hard and swift. Before she'd even gotten the taste of him he'd pulled back. "You sure know how to grab a man's attention, duchess." His grin was blinding. "Let's go." With one more quick kiss, he left her swaying in her seat as he opened his door.

The dome light flashed on and jerked her mind back from hazyville. "Wait. What about your sister?"

"Shit." He paused halfway out the door, then shook his head. "With a little luck, she'll be asleep."

He slid from the vehicle and she followed suit.

Asleep? Now who wasn't thinking clearly? Not two minutes ago, he'd bet her a thousand dollars his sister would be pacing the floors.

Plucking both of their overnight bags from the back seat, he directed her toward a door. It opened onto the breezeway, leading to a small, lattice-enclosed patio off the back of the house. She slowed her steps as they approached a set of French doors. Light came from somewhere inside.

He swore beneath his breath, but produced a key and let them inside. Gripping her elbow, he prodded her forward, ushering her through a cozy den to the doorway of a large country kitchen. He tugged her to a stop and she couldn't suppress her charmed sigh. Traditional materials mixed with old to produce a warm and welcoming room. Exposed ceiling beams, dark granite countertops, and a long, rustic wood table offset the cream cabinets and stainless appliances.

Recessed lighting illuminated the large island at the center of the room where an older woman perched on one of four stools. She sat with her back to them, sipping from a teacup. Plump and round, she wore a thick white robe with bright red cherries on the collar and belt. Her black hair was generously streaked with gray and twisted in a loose braid running down her back. A thin cord ran from the small black device at her elbow to the buds inserted in her ears.

Shrugging the strap of his carryon from his shoulder, Wyatt quietly placed their bags on the counter to their left. Cupping Piper's cheek, he lifted her face to brush a soft kiss across her mouth. He straightened, winked, and pressed a fingertip to his lips.

He'd taken the two long strides needed to reach the island before Piper realized what he was about. She opened her mouth, but was too late to stop him from startling the poor woman. Bending at the waist, he pressed a kiss to her neck, then straightened away before her flailing arms could do any damage.

A lightning fast spate of what Piper recognized as Spanish filled the air as the woman jolted. Yanking the buds from her ears, she twisted her head around, then spun to face him on the stool. She slapped a hand to her ample chest and the emotion in her wide, dark eyes ran the gamut from fear, to admonishment, to relief, before morphing into excited pleasure.

"Wyatt," she said in a thickly accented voice. "Meg, she says you come, but I don't believe her."

Pure affection gleamed in his eyes. "Rosa, my love. You know I could never stay away from you."

"Ha." She poked him in the chest with a stiff finger. "Six months, you don't come home to visit your love, Rosa." Her dark-eyed gaze skipped beyond him to land on Piper. "And I see why." She faced him again with raised brows and a delighted smile. *"Muy bonita, mijo."*

With a laugh, he turned and draped an arm around Rosa's shoulders. "Piper Darrow, this is Rosa Fuentes. I've been in love with her since I was four years old and she took on the job of head monkey keeper at the Hunter Zoo."

Rosa jabbed an elbow into his side, eliciting a grunt and a grin.

"Okay. Nanny."

Rosa sniffed. "Ach. Don't listen to him, Piper. This one, he is a," her forehead wrinkled in thought, "how do you say, rascal?"

Piper laughed and shot Wyatt a she's-got-you-pegged smirk. "Rascal sounds about perfect."

"Smartass." His squinted warning couldn't hide his pleasure as he looked at Rosa. "Where's Meg? I expected her to be waiting out at the gate."

"She is upstairs with Miss Mandy. Our *bebe* is not feeling well."

Concern flashed in his eyes. "What's wrong with her? Has her doctor been called?"

"Sí, mijo."

He shot a quick glance at the ceiling. "And?"

"For now, it is a simple cold," Rosa was quick to reassure, "but you know how she is. She wants her mama when she is sick."

Wyatt's gaze briefly flicked Piper's way. "How *is* Tonya? Is she ill, too?"

Rosa's eyes widened and the horror in them made the hairs on Piper's arms stand on end. Wyatt's old nanny was quick to answer his question. "Oh, Tonya, she is fine. She is just worried about the *bebe* like the rest of us."

"Good." The glance he turned Piper's way was strained and oddly detached. "I'd like to check in on Mandy. I won't be more than a few minutes."

"Of course." Piper nodded.

He smiled, but the concern hadn't leaked from his eyes as he turned to Rosa. "I'd planned to put Piper in the yellow bedroom. Would you mind showing her up?"

"Not at all, *mijo*." She made a shooing motion with her hands. "Go. I take care of *tu señora*."

Without a word, he pivoted toward the other end of the kitchen. Piper frowned as he opened an inner door and stepped inside what looked to her like a pantry, then was gone. She glanced at Rosa to find her smiling.

"The house is old with many surprising passages." She indicated the closet where Wyatt had disappeared. "In days past, the servants used the stairs leading to the third floor. Meg and Tonya's apartments are there now. Wyatt's rooms are on the second floor."

Wyatt's rooms?

Rosa shuffled to the counter and picked up Piper and Wyatt's bags.

"Oh, please." Piper held out her hand. "Let me help."

Rosa smiled and handed over Piper's small bag, then led her out of the kitchen and down a hallway toward the front of the house. In the foyer, to the right of a gorgeous beveled glass front door, Rosa turned to climb the wide staircase with Piper at her heels. At the second floor landing, the steps curved and continued to the third floor.

To the left was a large formal living room. The hallway on their right ran to the back of the house and had four doors. Rosa stopped in front of the first one and stood to the side to let Piper enter.

A sigh escaped as she glanced around the large bedroom decorated with a definite feminine flair in pale yellow with cream and blue accents. In keeping with the décor of the rest of the house, Victorian period pieces dotted the room and complemented the focal, hand-carved canopied bed that would have been at home in any well-to-do, mid-nineteenth century English bedroom.

"How lovely." Piper ran her fingertips over a wingback chair covered in a Flights of Fancy pattern of cotton silk.

"*Sí*. You like?"

"Very much so." Piper turned to Rosa.

The older woman nodded and followed her inside, then crossed to open a door on the far right wall. "When Wyatt buys this house, I tell him, you pay too much for these things." She entered the adjoining room and reappeared a moment later, minus Wyatt's bag. "But he says, no. I want nice."

When Wyatt *bought the house?*

Rosa shrugged and, indicating the opposite side of the room, she gave Piper a quick tour of the generous en-suite bath, pointing out where the spare towels and toiletries were to be found. Piper eyed several toothbrushes still in their packages in the vanity drawer, then turned to glance across the distance to the open door of the adjoining room where Rosa had left Wyatt's bag.

"Does Wyatt often have guests who arrive in need of toiletries?"

She regretted the catty sounding words the second they left her lips, but it was too late to slap her hand over her mouth. She briefly squeezed her eyes shut. "Never mind. Please. Don't answer that. I have no right to ask such a thing."

Rosa patted her arm and her delighted laughter was the last reaction Piper expected. "When a woman has feelings for a man, *querida*, she has every right to ask."

"But I don't," Piper was quick to defend, "have feelings, that is." She laughed weakly. "Not that I don't care for him, it's just that he and I are... you see, we're..."

Rosa smiled serenely, but a question creased her brow.

"Oh, bother. I think I may have given you the wrong impression. Wyatt and I are just business associates."

"Ahh," Rosa drew out. "I help you unpack, *sí*?"

"That really isn't necessary. I don't have very much. Just a change of... Oh, all right." Rosa slid the overnight bag from Piper's loosened fingers.

She watched, slightly amused, as the older woman placed the bag on the mattress and tugged open the zipper.

"I tell you this," Rosa said over her shoulder. "For many years, I care for Wyatt." She removed the slacks and blazer Piper had packed for tomorrow's press announcement and laid them aside with the matching brimmed, newsboy cap. "I know *mijo* as the boy *and* the man. The women, they love him. They can't help it. He is *muy hermoso*." She glanced up from her task. "Er…handsome, and charming, too, no?"

Piper nodded because she couldn't argue Rosa's point—and it bothered her tremendously that the stab of jealousy she'd experienced over those toothbrushes was back.

Rosa dug into the bag once more and frowned. She held up the plain black ball cap and sweatshirt Piper had shoved to the bottom of the bag—just in case. Turning, the older woman ran a skeptical gaze over the chic slacks, blouse, and sweater Piper had worn on the plane. With a shake of her head, Rosa added the hat to the pile on the mattress.

"But, this," she swung an arm indicating the room and beyond, "this is his home, *querida*. His family is here. Meg and Mandy, they are his heart. Tonya, too," she quickly added. "Never once does he bring a woman here. So, I thinking, who is this lady *mijo* brings with him on such a special night?"

She reached into the bag one last time, retrieving Piper's small toiletry case and the short silk sleep shirt she'd included at the last minute, and turned to study her with a penetrating gaze. "Then, I see the way he looks at you and how you look back, and I know. This one." She waggled a finger in Piper's direction. "She is special."

Piper bit back a horrified whimper. Obviously, Rosa was something of a romantic, mistaking attraction for something deeper, but those hungry reporters would be circling starting tomorrow. If Piper was looking at Wyatt in a way that drew attention, she had to know.

"I'm not sure what you mean. Look back at him how? How do I look at him?"

"Like he is *the* one, *querida*."

Oh, bloody hell, no.

Chapter 13

Nine hours later, Piper swallowed against her nerves as she waited in the short queue at the west entrance to the governor's mansion. According to Wyatt's early morning phone call, her name had been added to the list of attendees for his father's press announcement. The car Wyatt had sent to deliver her across town had arrived promptly at seven-thirty and would be waiting to take her back to his house when the event was over. He'd meet her there once he was free.

Sounding tired, he'd apologized again for abandoning her last night. She'd brushed his apology off with a reminder his family came first. And he definitely considered Mandy family, just as Rosa had said. What had begun as a quick visit to the little girl's third floor bedroom had ended in a night spent pacing the floor of the local hospital emergency room with Tonya and Meg. A diagnosis of a respiratory infection was a concern for all of them, but Mandy was apparently doing much better this morning.

He'd ended the call with a promise to find the time for their "when" soon. She'd answered with a noncommittal reply. As far as she was concerned, Karma had spoken loud and clear. It was a shame, but their chance had passed. No doubt, he would argue they could find a way to keep their fling private but, from the look of the circus at the end of the mansion's driveway, that would be impossible.

"Name and ID."

Piper blinked up at the man holding a clipboard in his beefy hand. Wyatt had warned her she would face several layers of security, and the Cro-Magnon specimen studying her as if she were a potential threat was apparently the first line of defense. From what she could see, no other layers were necessary. Easily topping six-foot-five, the man's height alone was enough to intimidate. The narrowed, distrustful eyes, yard-wide shoulders, and muscles straining the seams of his dark suit were overkill.

She held out her passport. "Piper Darrow."

After checking his clipboard against her name, he shifted his intense gaze from her face to her passport picture and back, then he eyed her billed cap. "Please remove the hat, Miss Darrow."

"Of course."

Grateful for the large satellite trucks blocking her from the view of the cameras at the end of the drive, she slid the cap from her head and presented it to the guard. Not a single emotion crossed his face as he stared at the tight knot of her auburn hair for several seconds, then flipped the cap over. After checking the lining and bill, he handed it back along with her passport.

"Thank you, ma'am. If you'll place your bag on the table and step through the detector, you'll be directed from there." He didn't wait for her response before addressing the next in line. "Name and ID."

Once Piper's camera bag had been thoroughly searched and she'd received a secondary wanding from a female guard, she was directed down the hallway toward the front of the mansion where the press announcement was to be held. She removed the smaller of her cameras from her case as she walked, stopping here and there to snap photographs. Stanchions roped off several rooms of the historic building, but others were open to viewing, like the grand ballroom and a small but charming library.

"Ladies and gentlemen, if you'll proceed to the foyer, we're about to begin."

Piper turned her head at the young man's announcement, then followed the others streaming toward the front of the house. Compared to the huge crowd outside, the attendance inside was paltry. Maybe thirty people filled the foyer, but from what Wyatt had said, attendance was by invitation only.

She had to hand it to Richard Hunter. The man obviously knew the value of controlling his universe. The grand ballroom would have allowed for a much larger audience, but the elegant entryway with its stunning spiral staircase leading to the upper floors of the mansion was a much more striking backdrop.

A podium carrying the Oklahoma official state seal stood empty at its base. She noted there wasn't a single chair in sight. Obviously, the governor didn't mind a fidgety audience. That, or he planned to keep his announcement brief. Either way, it seemed he also knew how to make an entrance.

Wishing to remain as unobtrusive as possible, she tucked into a corner at the back of the crowd. Through her lens, she observed not just the building's impressive architecture, but the people who had been invited to such an event. As a British citizen, most of the faces were strangers to her, but she did recognize a few. Like the former, flamboyant Attorney General of the United States and his Hollywood starlet wife.

The chatter of conversation suddenly quieted beneath the whirl of cameras. Piper aimed her lens at the second floor landing from which Richard Hunter descended. In his late sixties, he was still a handsome man with a commanding presence impossible to ignore.

A half dozen people followed in his wake, including Wyatt and Megan. The governor stopped behind the podium and began to speak. His words were lost on Piper, however, as she captured father and son together in her lens.

Similar in coloring and stature, the familial connection was impossible to miss. Tall and muscular, Richard Hunter's shoulders weren't quite as broad as his son's, but they were close. His grayish-green eyes were an identical shade to Wyatt's. Glossy, dirty blond hair, sprinkled with gray, carried the same waves evident in his son's longer, shaggy cut and the hint of a cleft shadowed both their chins. However, where Richard Hunter's eyes and practiced smile gleamed with anticipation, the studied lack of emotion on Wyatt's handsome face made him appear sober and tense.

A far cry from his usual, easy humor and relaxed attitude, the difference in his appearance was striking to witness. She wondered if anyone else noticed the stiffness of Wyatt's shoulders or the lines of strain bracketing his lips.

Startled by how badly she wanted to smooth them until they were gone, she reminded herself she was here to do a job. Focusing on his face, she found the right composition with the governor slightly blurred in the foreground. As she snapped the shot, Wyatt's intense gaze found her through her lens. She lowered the camera. The moment stretched as they stared at one another. His features softened slightly. Not a smile, exactly, just an easing of the tension tightening his mouth, and emotion prickled the back of her nose and throat.

At the podium, his father introduced him and his sister, Megan. Wyatt looked away, breaking the silent connection. For the next ten minutes, Piper did the job for which she'd been hired, photographing the others standing behind the governor, and capturing candid shots of his audience as well. As Richard Hunter concluded his remarks by announcing his intention to seek the presidency of the United States, Wyatt shifted on the stairs behind him, momentarily exposing him and his sister to Piper's lens.

She snapped a shot as Megan leaned into her brother's side. Without looking her way, Wyatt closed his wide-palmed hand around her much smaller one, and squeezed. Around them, the candidate and his staff accepted the applause of the crowd with a sort of joyful anticipation. Piper aimed her shutter at the candidate's children, standing stiffly in the midst of the celebration as if in solidarity against an unknown enemy, and the prickling at the back of her nose returned.

This time, she lost the battle with the threatening tears. As the applause and shouts of congratulations continued, she dipped her head and slid from the room.

Inside the car, she tugged the bill of her cap low on her forehead and pretended to dig through her camera bag as the driver maneuvered the vehicle through the throng still staked out at the end of the driveway. A half mile from the governor's mansion, she gave up the pretense, dropping her head back against the rest and shutting her eyes.

Thank God Karma had stepped in to deny her and Wyatt their "when." Obviously, the good guy part of him had already weakened her reserve enough that she was tearing up over his protective nature for his sister. Good Lord. How much worse would it have been if she'd succumbed to her greedy attraction for him instead of just contemplating it? Sex with Wyatt Hunter would be a disaster. She'd been fooling herself, believing she could sleep with him, then walk away at the end of their fling with some lovely memories and a whistle on her lips.

She would never be able to pull off that lie. From here on in, she'd need to guard her mind and heart more effectively.

*	*	*	*

Wyatt swirled the inch of whiskey in the glass Meg had handed him and considered downing it. As requested, he'd done his familial duty. So why was he twiddling his thumbs in his father's private den when this was the last place he wanted to be?

If not for Meg, he'd relish telling his father's campaign manager to go fuck himself before stalking out.

Wyatt glanced her way and she offered him a grateful smile. Jesus. How the hell was she was holding up? The speed with which this latest infection had hit Mandy scared the shit out of him. He was still reeling.

"Who is Piper Darrow?"

Ah, shit.

He offered Walter Crowley a tight smile. "No one you need to be concerned about."

Richard Hunter's long-time henchman eased back in the winged-back chair opposite the couch where Wyatt sat. In a familiar nervous twitch, the older man tapped the file he carried on the knee he had crossed over the other. "From today on, *anyone* connected to the campaign is a concern."

Wyatt downed his glass, after all. Hissing at the burn, he spoke through clenched teeth. "She has nothing to do with the campaign."

Walter's cool gray gaze remained steady. "Then what was she doing here?"

"The woman in the ball cap?"

Wyatt cursed beneath his breath, but didn't bother to turn as his father spoke from the doorway. Obviously, Piper was the reason he was still here. He'd fucked up adding her name to the attendee's list at the last minute. He should have known it would raise red flags for Walter but, after last night, he hadn't been thinking straight.

"Her name is Piper Darrow." Walter stood and pulled a sheet of paper from his file. He handed it to Richard as he passed by. While Wyatt's father rounded his desk and sat, Walter turned to Wyatt. "She took a lot of pictures."

"Miss Darrow took a lot of pictures because it's her job, Walter." Meg spoke before Wyatt could. Squeezing his shoulder, she stepped around the couch to sit at his side. "She's a photographer hired by the Marauders for a promotional spot they're putting together."

"Then your brother should have presented her credentials instead of listing her as a guest."

"What credentials would those be?" Wyatt eyed the older man with a steely stare. "She's a photographer. Not a member of the press."

Jesus, if he could kick his own ass, he would. With everything that had happened in the last twelve hours, he should have put Piper on his plane and sent her back to Manhattan. Away from his family, Dad's announcement, and Walter's paranoid radar.

She was an intelligent woman and the car he'd ordered had delivered her through the same gauntlet he'd run at the end of the driveway when he'd arrived from the hospital. For a woman who wanted nothing to do with the limelight, today's chaos must have felt like something out of a nightmare, and she had to know it would only get worse in the coming weeks.

He'd caught her hesitation and her subtle evasion when they'd spoken earlier. She was going to slam the brakes on any personal association between them. Unfortunately, he couldn't allow that. While he couldn't blame her for being scared, neither was he willing to walk away from the unprecedented pull between them. Not until it had run its course.

He had his work cut out for him if he was going to calm her fears enough to convince her they *could* work something out between them. If she discovered *Igor* was asking questions about her when Wyatt had promised he'd keep her name out of things… Fuck that. She couldn't know anything about the campaign's interest in her because, if she did, he could kiss any chance he had of seeing her naked good-bye.

"Have Jennings run a background check on her."

"Bullshit." Wyatt whipped his head around to glare at his father. "I want her left alone."

"That's not your call."

"Like hell, it isn't." Wyatt slammed his empty glass to the coffee table in front of him. "Your sycophants and volunteers may be willing to let you invade their privacy, but Piper has nothing to do with you *or* your campaign. The only reason she was here today was because I brought her. Stay the fuck out of her life."

"You made her a part of *my* life by bringing her here."

Richard dropped the paper Walter had handed him onto the desktop and leaned back in his desk chair. Even from a distance of six feet and upside down, Wyatt recognized Piper in the photo. Security had obviously snapped the picture. Half in profile and minus the cap she'd been wearing, her dark auburn hair gleamed in the sunlight outside the west portico.

"A background check isn't necessary, Dad." Meg shifted on the couch to face Richard. "She really is working for the Marauders."

"Another redhead. At least you're consistent." Richard ignored her to pin Wyatt with a disappointed scowl. "I'd hoped the significance of what happened this morning would open your eyes to how badly you're wasting your life."

Wyatt snorted. *He'd* hoped that with his father riding high after his announcement, they'd be able to avoid yet another of their endless verbal skirmishes. Obviously not. "I made twenty-four million last year. I'm wasting my life?"

"There is more to life than money, Wyatt."

"Says the man who inherited one hundred million from his mother."

"Half of which you'll inherit when I'm gone." Richard smirked. "But that doesn't excuse you from chasing women and playing games for a living instead of using the mind the good Lord gave you to make the world a better place."

Wyatt scoffed a laugh and shoved to his feet. "Yeah, well, at least the women I chase aren't subjected to background checks because I see enemies wherever I look. No thanks. You can keep your version of a better world." He shot Meg an apologetic glance, then paused beside Walter on his way out the door. "The next time he wants to put on a dog and pony show, count me out."

"Wyatt."

He ignored his sister's call and stalked into the hall. One of his father's many assistants jumped out of his way as Wyatt turned the corner and took the stairs to the ground floor two at a time. Frustration ate at his gut and the urge to punch something was as strong as it had been all those times growing up, when his father had looked down his nose at one of Wyatt's friends, then had the kid's parents investigated.

Why the fuck anyone would work so hard to build a career where every living soul was a potential enemy, Wyatt had never understood, but that was Dad. A paranoid, narcissistic bully who believed he alone could right the wrongs of the world and had no problem resorting to scorched-earth tactics to deal with anyone he perceived to be in his way. If he wanted Piper investigated, she would be, and God help her if Jennings found anything the old man didn't like.

"Wyatt. Wait."

He glanced over his shoulder. Meg hurried down the stairs after him and linked her arm with his to slow his pace.

"Jesus, he never changes."

"Shh." She glanced around at the empty hallway.

He snorted and shot a glare over his shoulder at the staircase before pinning her with an annoyed scowl. He'd never understood Megan's unwavering loyalty to their father, particularly in the face of his heavy-handed interference in their lives, and never would. Calling her out on her lack of sibling support, however, wouldn't change a thing and would leave them both feeling guilty in the end.

With a shake of his head, he looked away. "He's got bigger problems than some volunteer overhearing me. If the citizens of this country ever discover what an asshole he is, his political career is over."

She squeezed his arm. "I'll do what I can to charm Jennings into giving me an advance copy of whatever he finds."

Fucking great. His chest heaved on a frustrated sigh. "I'd rather you convince Dad to back off where Piper is concerned."

Her steps slowed, and she tugged him to a stop to study his face. "You really like this woman."

He slid free of her hold to jam his fingers through his hair. "I don't know. Maybe." He snorted and dropped his hand to his side. "Fuck. I can't seem to help myself. There's something about her."

Meg smiled softly. "She is a redhead and she's beautiful."

"Thanks, Dad," he replied, deadpan.

She grinned, but then sobered. "I'll do what I can, Wyatt, but you know Dad."

Yes, he did. Which was why he left the governor's mansion with his guts tied in knots.

Chapter 14

Shortly after Piper left the governor's mansion, Wyatt called to say he'd been detained and didn't think he'd be back at his home before the line of thunderstorms moving into the area closed the airport. With their return to Manhattan delayed, Piper spent the next hour wandering the expansive grounds surrounding Wyatt's house. As late as it was in the season, she was surprised by the lush greenery, and charmed by the small pond at the back of the property.

The family of mallards nesting in the reeds along its bank reminded her of home. As she photographed mama duck with her babies, a sense of hope she hadn't experienced in much too long a time wrapped around her heart like a bittersweet silver lining. She and Wyatt Hunter may never come together on a personal level, but their professional association meant her debt to Abigail would soon be paid. Delaney Manor was safe.

Eventually chased inside by the first bolt of lightning, Piper climbed the stairs to the second floor to catalogue the space Wyatt had claimed as his own. In the yellow bedroom where she'd spent the night, she paused at the connecting door to the master bedroom. She swung the door wide and stepped inside.

A huge antique king's bed dominated the large room decorated in a more masculine burgundy and cream. The piece was of museum quality, featuring solid wood craftsmanship and hand carved designs on the thick posts and paneled top. She eyed the matching nightstands and dresser and arched a brow.

Both this and the yellow bedroom were gorgeous, but they were almost too perfect. Like they'd been staged. And a bit on the stuffy side. She far preferred the more casual style he'd incorporated in his Manhattan condo. If it were up to her, she would fill this room with simplistic pieces. Nothing too feminine, of course. Wyatt was a large man and would require furniture that fit, but… She squeezed her eyes shut and groaned.

You've gone daft, girl. Daydreaming about furniture with the devil's body in mind. Do the job for which ye were hired, collect the remainder of yer money, and go home!

A half hour and close to one hundred photos later, she entered the kitchen. A distant rumble of thunder announced the storm was finally moving off. Rosa stood at the stove stirring a large pot. Piper snapped several pictures before lowering her camera.

"Something smells delicious."

Rosa turned her head and smiled. "I make meatball soup for lunch. The meatballs and vegetables, they are too heavy for the *bebe* until she is better, but the broth, it is good for her."

"Mandy's home?" Wyatt had mentioned stopping by the hospital to check on her, but Piper assumed the girl had been admitted for a few days.

"*Sí*. She is much better today. Wyatt, he bring her and her mama home." Tapping the slotted spoon on the rim of the pot, Rosa set it aside and wiped her hands on the small towel tucked into the waist of her skirt. "He says you leave soon, but first, you have lunch, no?"

"Lunch sounds lovely." Piper glanced around. "Where is he?"

Retrieving several bowls from a cabinet, Rosa bumped her chin toward the end of the kitchen. "In the den. You tell him I serve lunch in five minutes."

Piper smiled and nodded her assent, then approached the den on hesitant feet. The sooner she told him she'd changed her mind about their fling, the better. For both of them. She needed the matter settled. Once it was, there would be less chance she would fall victim to tempting daydreams. Besides, stringing him along wasn't right.

She owed him the truth, but here in his home with his family around him wasn't the place for that conversation. If she could just keep the disappointment off her face until they were alone at forty thousand feet…

She paused in the doorway, and automatically lifted the camera to snap several shots. Expecting Tonya West, Piper was surprised to find Megan tucked to Wyatt's side on the tufted loveseat, his arm slung around her shoulders. In her lap was Mandy, wrapped in a pink blanket, her face pale, but smiling. The little girl's gray-green eyes were full of pleasure as she turned the thick, cardboard page in the book Wyatt held. He dipped his head and finished reading the story.

"The end," Mandy announced, and brother and sister shared a grin over her head.

Promise me anything you see or hear in the next few minutes will go nowhere.

The breath stalled in Piper's lungs as Wyatt's request echoed in her ears. Like tumblers in a lock sliding into place, a suspicion she hadn't been aware of clicked into certainty. She lowered the camera with shaking hands and stared at their three dirty-blond heads.

She wants her mama when she is sick.

Piper's heart galloped in her chest.

Tonya had said, *"Amanda is mine. Not, Amanda is my daughter."*

Piper swallowed the sudden rush of nausea burning its way up from her belly. Megan's nervous and unsolicited explanation the other evening in Wyatt's condo suddenly made perfect sense, and the implications were horrifyingly enormous. Wyatt hadn't needed to horn in on anything to claim the label of uncle with Mandy. He came by the relation naturally. His Mandy Candy wasn't a West. She was a Hunter.

Oh, bloody hell.

"Pipah. Pipah!"

Piper blinked at Mandy's shouted greeting, and shifted her gaze between brother and sister. "I'm so sorry. I didn't mean to intrude."

The warmth in Wyatt's eyes nearly made her cry. He set the book aside. "You aren't intruding. Couldn't even if you wanted to."

Bugger it. If you only knew.

"My brother's right." Megan slid from beneath his arm and stood. "Wyatt and I were just giving Tonya a few minutes to shower, since she's been at the hospital all night."

Piper hoped her new understanding didn't show in her eyes as she met Megan's gaze. "I just came in to let Wyatt know Rosa has lunch ready."

"Soup," Mandy pronounced.

"Yes, your favorite soup." Megan's smile was strained as she held out her arms to Wyatt. "I'll take her. Tonya should be down in a few."

Wyatt stood and handed Mandy over, but didn't immediately follow his sister and niece from the room. Tucking a crooked finger beneath Piper's chin, he lifted her face for his inspection. His brows slid together.

"You okay?"

Any answer she gave him affirming his question would be a lie. She settled for a half-truth. "Just tired, I guess."

In a flash, she was in his arms, and she was surprised to find his heartbeat against her breasts as unsteady as hers surely was. He rested his chin on the top of her head and sighed. "The last eighteen hours sucked."

Because she couldn't disagree, she nodded against his chest.

His arms contracted as he tucked her even closer. "But if you'll trust me, I'll make it up to you later."

It was her turn to sigh. "Wyatt, I..."

"I know what you're going to say, but you're wrong."

Releasing her from his hold, he pulled back enough to lower his head so he could kiss her. In less than half a moment her limbs had gone weak and the temperature in the room had jumped by half a degrees. When he finally broke the connection, she was in dire need of a fan and his grin said he knew exactly what he'd just done to her.

"That's right, duchess. Don't say a word. We'll talk on the plane."

* * * *

Rosa's meatball soup might as well have been made of dishwater. Piper didn't taste a thing as she forced down lunch. She did make an attempt to add to the conversation around the table, but had no idea if she'd made any sense. A mix of relief and anxiety left her slightly nauseous as they said good-bye to Wyatt's sister and niece, Rosa and Tonya, too, and climbed into the SUV she'd assumed was a rental when they'd first arrived.

As with the vehicle, she'd made a number of incorrect assumptions since meeting Wyatt Hunter. Like his plane, and his sister and niece, and believing for even one millisecond she could stroll into his world in *any* capacity and walk out again unscathed. From what she could tell, there were five people in the world who knew the truth about Mandy, and Piper wished with all her heart *she* wasn't one of them.

How the bloody hell had she ended up tangled with the one sexy jock with ties to the highest political game on the planet? At the level of power Wyatt's father moved in, secrets had gotten people killed. She'd already had her nose broken. Forget surviving with her heart intact. Good Lord. She'd be lucky to survive, period.

But if she saw through the ruse, might not others? This wasn't a secret she would be comfortable keeping to herself. She'd have to say something. At least to Wyatt.

Not that she was in any position to judge. Piper didn't have to stretch to see the desperate reasoning behind the decision to hide Mandy from the world, and couldn't honestly say for sure she would have done anything different if she'd found herself in Megan's shoes. The fact was, knowing firsthand the kind of hell that could rain down on a person caught in the crosshairs of the press, Piper would have been just as desperate.

Wyatt didn't say a word in the car on the way to the airport, and Piper was glad to postpone what was sure to be a contentious discussion—if his heated kiss were any indication. Lord, what a mess.

The moment they stepped onto the plane, he directed her to the couch and showed her how to work the seat belt. Once she was buckled in, she opened her mouth, but he held up his hand. Depressing the cue on a wall panel, he gave Curtis, his invisible pilot, the go ahead, then turned, slid onto the couch beside her, and covered her mouth with his.

The tactic was unexpected and incredibly devious. Seriously, how was she supposed to think with every other system but those controlling her girl parts shutting down? Somewhere in the distance, engines revved. The plane turned to begin taxiing to the runway, and her head spun—or maybe the spinning was due to the sweep of Wyatt's tongue, tangling with hers.

G-forces pressed her into the couch as they took off, then eventually eased as the plane leveled out. Throughout the climb to forty thousand feet, a nagging question tugged at the back of her mind. She tried to capture it, but each time awareness floated close to the surface, the brush of Wyatt's palm or sweep of his fingertips on her over-sensitized nerve endings short-circuited her thought process.

A moan was the best she could manage, until a sudden pocket of turbulence and Curtis's voice coming through the speakers dragged her back from the sensual spell Wyatt had cast.

"Sorry about that, Wyatt. We've got some weather ahead. I'm rerouting to try to avoid it."

With a soft growl deep in his throat, Wyatt straightened away from her and cued the button on the wall once again. "Roger that, Curtis."

He dropped his arm and locked his gaze on hers. Her body staged an instant mutiny at the passion darkening his eyes. Nipples puckered, clit throbbing, her body screamed at her to act now and talk later, but there was too much at stake to give in to her baser instincts. When he leaned toward her again, she dodged his kiss.

Using both hands, she shoved up from the wanton sprawl she'd slipped into. "You said we would talk."

"I'd rather we let our bodies do the talking."

So much for avoiding his talented mouth. With a twist of his upper body, he found her neck with his lips and nibbled his way up the sensitive tendon toward her ear.

In danger of sinking back under his seduction, she pushed at his chest. "Wyatt. Don't do this to me. I'm not sure I have the willpower to resist you."

His chuckle rumbled beneath her hands as he slid his lips over her jaw to her cheek. "Your lack of willpower is just one of the many things I like about you."

Her helpless laugh ended on a groan, and she dropped her forehead to his shoulder. "Please, Wyatt."

His chest expanded on a deep breath before he lifted his head. She straightened to look him in the eye, and he cupped her cheek in his palm.

"Okay, duchess. We'll talk, but I'm warning you right here and now, I'm not going to let you walk away simply because you're scared." He dropped a kiss to her nose, then released her and stood.

She hiked her chin to a defensive angle. "This has nothing to do with me being scared."

"That's bullshit and we both know it." Pacing to a block of cabinets several feet away, he opened an upper door and retrieved a bottle and two glasses.

She stared at his back as he poured a splash of what she assumed was alcohol into each. "Even if that's true, you can't tell me I don't have a reason. Good Lord, Wyatt. Your father is running for president of the United States. Even we Brits admit the job is the most powerful position in the world."

He returned to hold out a glass.

She frowned and snatched it from his hand. "You had to have driven past that mob camped out at the end of your father's drive this morning. How long do you think we'll be able to keep our *fling* a secret with every Nosey Parker in the world keen to discover every detail of your father's life?"

Like the secret, disabled granddaughter he apparently knows nothing about. Bugger it all.

Tossing back the dark liquid, she sputtered and coughed as a wave of fire burned its way down her esophagus. With tears springing in her eyes, she glared up at him. "Bloody hell. That was whiskey!"

The arch of his brow didn't hide the humor in his eyes. "As a Scotswoman, I would expect you to enjoy a fine malt now and again." He raised his glass to his lips, then hissed between his teeth after swallowing the shot whole. "Smooth."

"It so happens I detest the stuff, and smooth me arse." She choked on another cough and slapped a hand to her chest. "It's bloody rot. Petrol would be smoother."

His bark of laughter accompanied a sharp grin. "I've got to tell you, duchess, I love it when you talk dirty."

The fire in her throat was too immediate to be embarrassed. She slapped her glass into the hand he held out. "I assume you have water around here somewhere."

He continued to chuckle as he returned to the cabinet where he'd found the whiskey. Setting aside the glasses, he pressed a panel on a lower cabinet and pulled a water bottle from a refrigerated cabinet. He straightened and returned. After handing her the cool bottle, he slid into the chair across from the couch.

"As for the... What did you call the mob at the gate? *Nosey Parkers*?" He crossed one knee over the other in a seemingly easy slump, but she didn't miss the returning tension in the tightening of his lips. "You're right. My father upped his game this morning, but I was born a Hunter, remember? I'm also one of a small handful of league quarterbacks. Do you think I haven't learned a thing or two about dodging the press?"

The subtle bitterness in his tone sliced through her very reasonable anxiety, and her shoulders slumped. How could she not empathize with his frustration over the price of his fame when she'd been an unwilling victim of the same not so long ago? Still, their association was only temporary. She wasn't willing to open an old wound by explaining her past brush with a famous athlete. Thankfully, she had another, much more compelling excuse for avoiding a personal entanglement between them.

"I imagine you have." She dragged in a ragged breath. "But the interest you've faced in the past will be nothing compared to what's coming. Secrets are tricky things, Wyatt. Keeping them isn't always possible."

The tension in his face shed with a teasing twist of his lips. "You have secrets, huh?"

She sighed and stepped off the ledge at the point of no return. "We all do, I think. Even the famous children of presidential candidates—or their *granddaughters*."

His humor evaporated as he stilled. He slid his foot to the floor and his Adam's apple jumped in his throat with his harsh swallow. "Ah, fuck."

Her insides quivered with the compulsion to rise from the couch and wrap him in her arms. Instead, she curled her fingers into her palms and nodded. "Precisely."

He ran a hand down his face and, slumping back in the chair, he studied her for a long moment. "So, what are you trying to tell me? That you're an undercover journalist for some London rag and I can expect to open tomorrow morning's addition and find an exposé on my niece and sister?

She jolted as if he'd slapped her, then tossed up her chin. "Of course not. I would never betray either you or them in such a way. I was simply making a point."

"What point would that be?" He held her gaze. "That anyone who sees Meg and Mandy together can't miss the resemblance or the love?" He sat forward and propped his elbows on his spread knees. "I love Mandy, too, and I'll do whatever it takes to protect her from the public eye, but this plan of Meg's was doomed from the beginning. Despite the steps she's taken to avoid being seen with her daughter in public, I've warned her over and over the day would come when someone would make the connection and word would get out."

"Word won't come from me, Wyatt," Piper was quick to promise.

The wrinkle in his brow smoothed out with a soft smile. "I appreciate that, but the truth will come out eventually. That's just a fact of life. In the meantime, Meg's deception has nothing to do with you and me."

"Wyatt." Piper sighed and dropped her chin to her chest.

"Are you attracted to me?"

"Excuse me?" Her head popped up, and her gaze crashed into his.

"You heard me. I asked if you find me attractive."

Hello! You're a bloody sex god.

She couldn't prevent an un-baroness-like snort. "As if you have to ask."

"I am asking because I want you to say it. If I just don't do it for you, then say it." The intensity in his gaze, as if her answer held the key to the future, held her captive.

"I..."

"Otherwise, I'm asking you not to turn away from something both of us want. Something that just might wind up being more than five weeks of incredible sex."

Her heartbeat tripped into overdrive and left her breathless. *Oh good God. What did he mean by* that?

"Here's the thing, duchess. I've never had a woman stick in my head the way you do."

Piper frowned, unsure if that was a compliment or a complaint.

He chuckled and shook his head. "Don't get me wrong. I want you until I'm so hard I can't breathe, but it's more than that." He straightened and jammed the fingers of one hand through his shaggy hair. A befuddled sort of acceptance replaced the humor in his eyes. "Even when you aren't around, you're in my head. I find myself wondering what you'd have to say about something I saw, or whether you'd have laughed at a joke I just heard. I watch the clock, knowing I'm going to see you soon, and I think, what can I say to get you to do that sexy little eye thing you do whenever you're caught off guard."

She blinked and his smile came slowly. He waggled a finger at her face. "There. That right there. Shit, duchess." He dropped his voice to a seductive croon. "That triple blink you do is hot as hell, and I don't have a fucking clue why. But I'm willing to spend the time to find out."

Piper dragged in a ragged breath as surprise and yearning tangled in her belly and sent fissions of heat racing through her system. She considered slapping her hands over her puckering nipples, but that would just call attention to the fact he had her right where he wanted her.

He slid onto the couch beside her and entwined her fingers with his. "I give you my word I'll keep our relationship private. If that means wearing a fake nose, or changing cars three times and climbing the fire escape to your hotel room, I'll do it. Just give me a chance to discover why you're the first thing I think of when I wake up in the morning, and the last face I want to see before I go to sleep at night."

Her head spun even as her heart beat so hard it slammed against the inner wall of her chest.

Ya see. He's the devil I told ye he was.

She bit her lip and clung to the last vestige of sanity. He'd probably used that line on a dozen women.

A dozen, me arse. More like thousands.

"Say it, Piper." Tight with purpose, his face held no trace of his usual humor.

She stared into his intent gray-green eyes and, for the life of her, she couldn't remember why she was fighting him. It was no use. If he was the devil, then she was going to hell. She stuck out her chin and leapt into the fire. "You know you do it for me." His eyes darkened as he leaned in to kiss her, but she stopped him with a hand to his chest. "How private is this cabin?" He quirked a brow and she nearly growled with impatience. "What I mean is, how discreet is your pilot?"

One corner of his mouth kicked up in a boyish grin. "Very. Curtis has been a trusted friend since we were juvenile delinquents in junior high, but if you were thinking we could make use of this couch, you're out of luck."

"Why?" She glanced around, then back, and her eyes went wide. She'd been sprawled half beneath him for the first twenty minutes of the flight. "Oh, bloody hell. Please tell me there are no cameras."

His smile was wicked and he lowered his mouth to hers. "No, but now that you've mentioned it…" He grunted as she poked him in the belly, then straightened with a laugh. "We'll be landing in a little over two hours. We're going to need a lot more time than that if I'm going to touch you the way I want." He cupped her chin and brushed his thumb over her cheekbone. "You've inspired a few fantasies that require complete privacy without the chance of interruption."

Staring into his eyes full of heat and anticipation, she was in danger of melting down. Now that she'd committed to embracing the madness, the unexpected delay was frustrating, but he had a valid point. She looped her arms around his neck and offered him a cheeky smile.

"Fine, then, but if your friend, Curtis, knows a shortcut to Manhattan, I suggest he use it."

Chapter 15

Even if Curtis had managed to find a shortcut, it wouldn't have made a difference. After a textbook touchdown at LaGuardia, his voice came through the speakers to inform Wyatt a news crew was apparently waiting to greet him. Once again, Piper was left to wonder if the fates or Karma or some other universal force was determined to keep her and Wyatt apart.

Promising to climb her fire escape the first chance he got, Wyatt instructed Curtis to give him fifteen minutes, then see that she arrived safely at her hotel. With a sound kiss and a wincing apology, Wyatt left her in the plane to face the Nosey Parkers inside the terminal.

She spent the rest of the week humming with anticipation but, come game time on Sunday, she was still waiting. It was just her bloody luck there *was* no fire escape leading to her hotel room and, on top of that disappointment, their respective schedules never seemed to mesh. The trouble was, five weeks might have *sounded* like plenty of time to produce the photographs needed for both the Marauders and Wyatt's projects, but her models were all highly professional athletes on the same killer timetable as Wyatt. When he was working, so were they, and vice versa.

Still, she'd made excellent use of her time. With Tuck's dedicated memory card nearly full of usable photographs, she'd moved ahead of schedule with several of the other players on her list.

Climbing from the car at the security entrance of the Marauders' complex, she grinned at the memory of Wednesday afternoon spent with Gabe Tillman in his grandmother's Brooklyn kitchen. The photos of the Marauders' scary veteran center wrapped in a flowered apron as he rolled cookie dough onto sheets would no doubt raise a few eyebrows with the defenders he faced on a weekly basis. And from Thursday evening, the love in Mario Davis's eyes whenever his gaze touched on Carla, his lovely fiancée, was bound to earn him some razzing from his teammates.

After an interminably long week, the waiting would end tomorrow with an evening of carnal delights—or so Wyatt had claimed when they'd spoken by phone this morning. With the team's normal day off falling on Monday, she'd scheduled a group photo shoot for the morning to include all twelve calendar models. She hoped to get a good start on the calendar project by shooting the cover as well as several of the men individually. Wyatt insisted they be done by noon. Apparently, he'd made plans for their afternoon and evening, and that totally worked for her.

As he had last week, Kip kept her company throughout much of the game. Four hours later, free of broken bones or even the slightest bruise, she cheered along with the home team crowd as the Marauders added another win to their season with a 32-7 victory over Seattle.

Returning to her lonely hotel room, she spent most of the night tossing and turning. When she did manage to drift off, Wyatt was there in her dreams. Again. Just as he had been all week. Unfortunately, Wyatt Hunter in dream form was as big a turn on and tease as the real-life version had proven to be so far. Each time she quivered on the edge of climax, he grinned and disappeared. Consequently, she showed up at the Long Island City studio V Fitzpatrick had procured for Monday morning's photo shoot exhausted and more than a little irritable.

"I think we'll sell a lot more copies if we all take off our shirts." Dead center in the back row of men, Jamal Knight flexed his arms in an Atlas pose.

"In that case, my bare chest should be in the front row," Tuck announced with a grin.

"Yeah, taking off my shirt ain't happening," Gabe grumbled, and several of the bigger guys nodded in agreement.

Three men to his right, Mario bent at the waist to sneer down the line at Gabe. "Maybe we should all wear *aprons*."

Gabe broke from his position to stalk toward him. "Asshole. Miss Darrow promised she wouldn't use that shot, and I told you that in confidence."

Laughing, Mario scrambled two rows back on the bleachers Piper had set up and used several of his teammates as a shield. "I'm confident you looked sexy as shit in your grandma's *kiss-the-cook* bib."

Snickers and outright laughter echoed off the converted warehouse walls.

Perched twenty feet overhead on a rented mast lift, Piper watched in horror as her carefully staged groupings fell apart. Wyatt met her pointed glare with a crooked half smile and a shrug as, like boys on a precarious jungle gym, the remainder of the men took sides in Gabe and Mario's impromptu game of chase on the temporary bleachers.

A gasp escaped Piper as Gabe's foot slipped and he went down. He landed on his ass, straddling the bottom bench. Envisioning half the Marauders' starting line on the injured reserve list with broken ankles or worse, Piper cupped her hands around her mouth and screamed.

Quiet descended over the studio as twelve men stared up at her with varying degrees of surprise. Wyatt's shoulders shook with his silent laughter, his teeth flashing in a grin.

She sighed and shook her head. "Gentlemen, we're wasting time. I'll never get the shots I'm after if you don't cooperate." She squinted at Wyatt. "And I *don't* want to be here all day."

Apparently, he received her message loud and clear. His grin winked out and his brows dropped into a scowl. He cleared his throat. "The lady's right. Smarten up and let's get this thing done."

Wedged between the first and second rows of the bleachers, Gabe shoved to his knees, then his feet. His fist shot out and connected with Jamal's belly where he stood on the top row. Four feet off the ground with his arms pin-wheeling, the Marauders' top running back teetered backward. Piper's breath caught in her throat until the two players on each side of him snagged him by the arms and averted disaster.

Jamal regained his footing, but apparently wasn't capable of overlooking his teammate's meaty left hook. "You hit like a fuckin' girl."

"From the looks of it, his grandma taught him how to bake cookies *and* throw a punch," Mario contributed to the trash-talking fest, and the shoving match resumed.

Tuck started to laugh, then ducked to avoid a swinging fist. Wyatt hopped from the bleachers and stayed out of the way.

Bloody hell. It's like herding cats. Shoving two fingers into her mouth, Piper let out a piercing whistle.

Twelve pairs of eyes stared up at her.

"Gabe!" She glared at the Marauders' mammoth center. "No more punching. It's not helping."

"Sorry, Ms. Darrow." He sent her a sheepish wince that tugged at her heart.

She leaned on the railing and curled her lips into an affectionate smile. "By the way, I thought you were *incredibly* sexy in your grandmother's bib." She shifted her best baroness glower onto Mario and then Jamal. "And anyone who has an issue with that can take it up with me."

Snickers sounded from the others, but neither Mario nor Jamal said another word.

Nodding smugly, she straightened from the rail. "Now, you all have exactly thirty seconds to find the positions I had you in. If I have to come down there to reset any of you, I will not be a happy photographer. Believe me, you do not want that."

Her gaze caught Wyatt as he slapped a hand to his heart and affected a sigh. She rolled her eyes and stepped behind her tripod once more.

A half hour later, she had the cover shot she'd been looking for. With the exception of Wyatt, the Fab Five guys took off. She'd be working with each of them in the coming weeks and would shoot the calendar photograph for their individual month then. She spent several hours with the remainder of the guys. By the time noon rolled around, the other seven months were in the can far ahead of schedule.

The moment she snapped her last shot, Wyatt all but shoved the team's all-pro corner back out onto the curb. A second later, the man spoke through the closed door, pointing out he wasn't going anywhere without his helmet and the keys to his Harley. Piper pressed her hand over her mouth to muffle her giggles as Wyatt ripped the door open, shoved the guy's helmet and keys into his hands, and slammed the door in his face.

He turned to face her and threw up his hands in a what-are-you-going-to-do shrug, and she lost the battle with her laughter. Squinting in warning, Wyatt stalked to her, gripped her by the arms, and kissed her long and deep. He wore a self-satisfied smirk as he set her back, then had to steady her when she wavered.

"That's what I thought. Move it along, duchess. We're burning daylight."

Turning her around, he gave her a gentle nudge toward her equipment bag. A residual giggle bubbled up and out of her mouth. Giddy at the proof Wyatt was as impatient to finally experience their *when* as she, she offered no resistance. In less than ten minutes, they had everything packed up and stored in the back of the SUV waiting just outside the studio door.

As he drove them through the streets of the industrial neighborhood, Piper stared out the passenger window. Between the buildings, she caught an occasional stunning glimpse of the Manhattan skyline beyond the East River. Tempted to ask him to stop so she could retrieve her camera from the boot area where it had been stowed, she turned to study his profile.

"If this is a shortcut to your place, it's a dreadful one." She tossed a thumb toward the opposite bank of the river. "The city is way over there."

He grinned and pressed a button on the console. "We're almost there."

"Where?" Confusion wrinkled her brow.

"Here."

Slowing the vehicle, he made a sharp right turn. A loading dock door rolled open in front of them, and he nosed the SUV inside the building.

Surrounded by brick on three sides, the fit was tight, but Wyatt didn't blink an eye as the metal door slid closed behind them.

Piper squeaked as the walls around them began to drop.

"Freaky, huh?" He chuckled. "I had a similar reaction the first time I was here. It's an optical illusion. We're being lifted to the second floor."

"We're in a lift?" She shot him a sidelong glance as the brick around them disappeared and the second floor landing came into view. "Of course. We're inside a vehicle...inside a lift."

His teeth flashed strong and white in his smile. "It's a customized freight elevator. We're perfectly safe."

The floor beneath them jerked to a stop as they reached their destination and Piper grabbed hold of the arm rest. "If you say so."

His chuckle turned into a deep-throated laugh. "Come on, I'll show you around."

He opened the driver's door and stepped out. She exited the vehicle into a garage of sorts, large enough to hold half a dozen SUVs, and joined him at the boot where he collected their bags.

"What is this place?"

He tapped a button on the hatch and stepped clear as it began to close. With a hand to the small of her back, he led her toward the brick wall to their left. "It's home."

"Another home?" She shook her head and he smiled.

"The place in Oklahoma City is a convenience for when family calls. But mainly, it's Meg and Mandy's home."

She nodded, understanding, then arched a brow. "And the condo in the city across the river?"

"Provides me with a place to entertain when necessary and somewhere to crash when I need to. It also keeps the *Nosey Parkers* off the scent of this place." He winked and she smiled.

Toward the front of the building, a repurposed barn door hung from an industrial rail. Recessed into the brick beside the door was a discreet keypad. Wyatt punched in a set of numbers and a humming noise behind them drew Piper's attention. She turned and blinked as the metal grating beneath the SUV lifted several inches, spun the vehicle one-hundred-eighty degrees, and lowered until flush with the surrounding floor.

She faced Wyatt. "That's quite handy."

He grinned and pressed in another set of numbers. The barn door slid to the left, revealing an enormous, open-concept loft.

Piper gasped. "Oh. How lovely."

He held out a hand, indicating she enter before him, and she stepped inside. Wide wood-plank floors gleamed in the natural light courtesy of at least a dozen floor-to-ceiling windows. To the right, the original brick had been left alone on the building's long back span facing the river and city beyond. Otherwise, a soft cream paint covered the rest of the walls and softened the industrial feel of the exposed beam and pipe ceiling and black metal staircase leading to a second level.

One giant room, there were no interior walls to define the different spaces. Strategically placed furniture achieved that end. In the spacious, modern kitchen, top-of-the-line stainless appliances were tucked between glass-fronted cabinets and black granite countertops. An eight-foot-long gas cook-top island separated the kitchen from a large but casual living space with several comfortable looking lounge chairs and the largest TV Piper had ever seen. Beyond a huge sectional couch was a game area of sorts. A lovely, hand-carved pool table held a position of honor. Half a dozen vintage pinball machines and three dart boards lined the wall facing the street.

At the far end of the room, a charming reading nook was tucked beneath the stairs. Skirting the oversized sofa and ottoman, Piper wandered over and studied the built-in shelves loaded with books. Not surprisingly, amongst the mysteries, political thrillers, and classical literary titles were quite a few children's books. Selecting a thin volume from the shelf, she grinned at the cat in his red and white striped hat.

A glass of wine appeared in her line of vision. She accepted Wyatt's offering, and turned to face him. "You have a rather eclectic taste in literature."

He smiled. "I do not like them, Sam-I-Am, I do not like green eggs and ham." With a waggle of his brows, he tapped the rim of his glass to hers. "Mandy knows every line of that one. It's her favorite."

Utterly charmed, Piper grinned. "She's rather sweet, and you're very good with her."

"She makes it easy." Helpless pleasure tugged at his lips. "She loves with the entirety of her huge heart, not holding back a thing, and doesn't have a judgmental bone in her body. That kind of acceptance is rare in this world." A sudden wrinkle appeared between his brows as if he'd just remembered the wall of secrecy he'd helped to erect around his niece had recently suffered its first crack, thanks to Piper. "And when the world finds out about her, they'll show her the exact opposite. She'll be judged and found lacking, and there isn't a damn thing I can do to stop it."

Frustration stretched the tanned skin over his cheekbones and he swallowed his wine in a single gulp.

Clutching fingers of guilt wrapped around Piper's throat and threatened to steal her breath. She should have kept her mouth shut. After all, telling him what she suspected wouldn't make a bit of difference in what happened in the future.

"Wyatt." She rested a hand on his forearm and squeezed.

"Shit. I'm sorry." His chest expanded on a cleansing breath. "I didn't bring you here to discuss my fucked-up family and its secrets. I've got something much more pleasant in mind."

So did she, but that didn't change the facts. "I've obviously opened a painful can of worms and hurt you in the process. That wasn't my intention." Surprise lit his eyes, but she rushed on before he could speak. "I'm a photographer who was given up close and personal access to you and your family."

He nodded, but didn't say a word. After plucking the wineglass from her fingers, he deposited it and his empty glass onto one of the bookshelves, then slipped an arm around her waist and pulled her against his chest.

With her hands tucked between their bodies, she pushed forward in her attempt to ease his mind. "Looking at the world through a lens alters the view, Wyatt. Sharpens it. I tend to see things others won't necessarily."

"That makes sense." He traced her spine with his fingertips, then continued on to her bottom and cupped her cheek in his palm. Clearly, he'd lost interest in the subject, but she was trying to make a point.

She cleared her throat. "What I'm trying to say is, it wasn't until I'd seen all of you together in your natural element that I recognized something wasn't as it seemed. The average person looking at Mandy isn't likely to make the connection to you, and therefore, to Megan."

He dipped his head, spreading heated kisses across her cheekbone to her ear, then hummed appreciatively at her helpless shudder. "All I see is a beautiful woman with a gentle heart and a glass-is-half-full attitude."

The combined warmth of his compliment and his big body pressed to hers interrupted her train of thought and she sighed. "Wyatt?"

"Mm hmm."

He nipped at her lobe, and she frowned. "Never mind. I can't remember what I was going to say."

His dark rumble of laughter vibrated from his chest to hers and her lips curved in an answering smile. As usual, he didn't even have to try and she was seduced. And two could play that game.

Freeing one of her hands from between them, she slid her palm down his chest to his stomach, bypassing his waist to cup the hard length of his erection through the soft denim of his jeans. His quick intake of breath both thrilled and encouraged. She hummed deep in her throat.

"Is there a bedroom anywhere close?"

He swallowed, and his Adam's apple jumped with an audible click. "Right upstairs."

She fluttered her lashes. "Were you planning to show it to me?"

Her world spun crazily and she yelped as he swept her from her feet. With an arm beneath her legs and the other bracing her back, he headed for the stairs. "Duchess, I thought you'd never ask."

Chapter 16

Wyatt climbed the steps to his bedroom, aware he was breaking his number one rule. He didn't bring women here. Ever. He'd spoken the unvarnished truth when he'd told Piper this was his home, but the converted warehouse was more than that. Purchased in Rosa's name with the express purpose of avoiding a paper trail leading to him, it was his refuge, a sanctuary from the glare of the spotlight, the only true escape he had from the pressures of who he was and the life he'd chosen.

Fewer than a dozen people knew the place existed and less than that had visited. The fact that he'd brought Piper here was a move he'd have to consider later, but at the moment, it felt simply…right.

Pressing a knee to the mattress, he lowered her to her back, but didn't join her yet. Sliding onto his hip, he braced his hand on the other side of her slim waist. She didn't say a word, but her green-eyed gaze held a silent question as he took a moment to savor the sight of her.

No sassy phrase was printed over her chest today. Instead, a soft oversized sweater of pale green molded to the swell of her breasts. Combined with the plain black ball cap, faded jeans, and sneakers, the look didn't quite mesh with the debutant vibe she'd projected that first night at the fundraiser. Then again, neither had any of the printed sweatshirts he'd seen her wear since she'd been back in town. Not that he was complaining. She could wear a paper bag and he'd be turned on.

The urge to tug today's cap from her head and bury his fingers in her curls had been driving him crazy all morning. Pinching the bill between finger and thumb, he peeled the hat free. Released from captivity, her curls tumbled around her, bold and bright against his pillow as the afternoon sunlight turned the auburn locks to a silky mane of fire.

Holding her emerald gaze, gone dark with anticipation, he picked up a bouncy curl and tested the texture. Cool to the touch, the thick strands slid over his fingers. "Beautiful. I've dreamed of having you in my bed, of touching you and kissing every inch of your skin until you come apart in my arms."

Her chest rose and fell in erratic breaths. "I've dreamed of you, too."

Delighted at the admission, he grinned and lowered to his elbow so that he leaned over her with several tempting body parts within reach. "You have, huh? That's good to know." He twined a curl around his finger. "What did I do to you in these dreams?"

Her irises dilated until they were a thin rim of green surrounding black. "You made love to me." A crease appeared between her brows. "Sort of."

"Sort of?"

She arched an accusing brow. "I was quite disturbed to learn the dream Wyatt is something of a bounder. Every time he brought me close to climax, he disappeared."

Well, hell. It appeared his little duchess enjoyed a bit of chatter in her foreplay. He was happy to play along. "The bastard." He chuckled at her quick grin. "You should have given the real me a call. The way I remember it, I was right there with you in my kitchen when you came...apart."

A soft moan and she covered her eyes with one hand. "I'm still rather embarrassed by that."

"You shouldn't be. Watching you come was beautiful, and you enjoyed it."

"I couldn't help myself. It was," she peeked through her fingers, "quite lovely."

It was his turn to moan, but fuck. Hearing her admit she'd enjoyed an orgasm he'd given her in that proper British accent was the hottest thing he'd ever heard in bed.

With what little blood remaining in his head rushing south, he dropped his gaze to the luscious mounds of her breasts beneath pale green jersey knit. Once or twice this morning, he'd wondered at the lack of straps that should have been visible beneath the loose neckline. Tugging the soft material to the side, he swallowed at the sight of the naked expanse of shoulder he exposed.

"No straps." He lifted his gaze to hers as his pulse sped up. "What happened to your bra, duchess?"

Her lips formed a silent *oh* and she slid her hand over her belly to pause on her left breast. His pulse kicked into overdrive as she drew the tip of her index finger over the nipple peaking the soft material, then on to the other, before she dropped her hand to her belly.

"Oh, dear. Apparently, I forgot the garment in my race to get to the studio."

He bit back a laugh at her prim response, even as the blood arrived at his painfully engorged cock. Fucking A. Who was the tease now?

"I should probably investigate. Just to be sure."

Her exaggerated sigh lifted her chest and stretched the sweater even tighter against the hardened buds of her nipples. "That sounds like a splendid idea."

Damn, she was beautiful. Covering her mouth with his, he devoured her in a hard and fast kiss before backing away to tug her sweater down by the neckline. The spit in his mouth dried up as the creamy skin of her breast was revealed in slow degrees. By the time her tightly beaded nipple popped free, he was close to panting.

If he wasn't inside her in three minutes, he was going it embarrass *himself*, but he couldn't resist tasting her first. Dipping his head, he took the puckered bud between his teeth and, closing his lips around her, he sucked.

A groan escaped as her body arched beneath his chest. He straightened and stared at the glistening peak of her nipple, then slid the hem of the sweater up and over her head exposing all of her to his hungry view. Tossing the garment aside, he treated himself to the silky feel and taste of her once again. With hands, tongue, and teeth, he stroked and laved her soft skin. She squirmed beneath him, her fingers snatching at the hem of his T-shirt and tugging.

Shifting away from her, he reached behind his back. He fisted his shirt between his shoulder blades and yanked it over his head. Both of her hands had come to rest over his pecs before he'd fully turned back to her. With a gentle shove, she tumbled him to his back and rose to her knees. She traced her fingertips over the crouching tiger tattoo on his right shoulder and upper arm, then rested both her hands on his abs.

"You're beautiful, Wyatt, and now it's my turn to touch."

His heartbeat pounded out a tango in his chest, and he covered her hands with his, delaying her exploration. "Duchess, as much as I want your hands on me, I think we should hold off on that for this first time." Wrapping his fingers around one of her wrists, he moved her hand past his stomach and brushed her palm over his crotch. "You've already got me primed and ready to blow."

"Oh my." Her chest quivered with her quickened breathing as she went to work on the button fly of his jeans. "Then we'll simply have to hurry this time."

Several flicks of her nimble fingers dispersed the buttons, and she tugged the denim down his hips. When she curled her fingertips into the waistband of his briefs, he groaned.

"I mean it, duchess. I'm damned close."

Her eyes flashed with intent as she peeked up at him. "I can see that, but it *is* my turn."

She shimmied his briefs down his thighs and his erection sprang free. Humming deep in her throat, she shoved his underwear and jeans to his ankles. Toeing off his loafers, he kicked free of his clothes.

"I'll make you a deal." Naked to the waist, she bent over him. "I won't touch you...with my hands."

Fuck. Me. Dead.

His head slammed to the pillow, and he hissed through his teeth as her cool curls brushed over his thighs at the same time her hot mouth all but swallowed his cock.

Once. Twice. A third time, she measured him with her lips, teeth, and tongue. Helpless against the wet heat surrounding him, his hips jerked convulsively. Her hum of encouragement vibrated through his shaft and the drag of her lips on his sensitized skin as she pulled back was nearly his undoing.

"Piper." Her name was little more than a plea as the tingling forerunners of climax tightened his balls.

She swirled the tip of her tongue across his slit and her green eyes, hazy with passion, met his. "Did I mention I might have forgotten my knickers as well?"

His surprised bark of laughter cut off abruptly as she licked the tip, took him deep, and sucked. The orgasm hit him so fast, so powerfully, he couldn't prevent it. Stabbing his fingers into her hair, he attempted to tug her free at the last second, but she resisted his efforts. A guttural moan rattled his chest, and his cock twitched through multiple excruciatingly pleasurable jettings as he surrendered to her will.

Several moments later, with his chest cavity swelling and contracting like an overworked bellows and his heartbeat still somewhere close to stroke range, Wyatt lifted his head. He blinked at Piper as she crawled up his body, her eyes glazed and hot and a smug curl on her lips.

He dropped his head back to the pillow and shut his eyes. "I'm going to need a minute, duchess."

"I know." She settled beside him, tucking close with her head against his shoulder and her hand over his heart. "What is it you Yanks say? I rocked your world?"

His snort of laughter ended on a coughing wheeze.

She lifted her head and he opened his eyes to find her staring down at him. A grin stretched her full lips. "You can thank me later." She batted her lashes. "When you can breathe again."

Her squeal echoed off the high ceiling as he bolted up and rolled her to her back. "We Yanks have another saying." Resting on one elbow, he cupped her right breast. Tweaking the tightly budded nipple with his thumb, he didn't miss her subtle gasp.

"What would that be?"

"Payback's a bitch." With a grin, he lowered his fingers to the waist of her jeans. "Did you really forget to wear your knickers?"

She batted her lashes. "I don't know where my head was this morning." He flicked open the snap and peeled the zipper down, and she shivered. "Of course, my absentmindedness might have had something to do with a certain bold and tidy gentleman promising me an evening full of *carnal delights*."

He didn't give her a chance to prepare, simply slid his hand into the opening of her jeans. Sure as shit, the little darling had gone commando. She was wet and hot, and his cock twitched with renewed life as he plunged a finger inside her. Adding a second, he withdrew and plunged again, then repeated the stroke several more times. Her hips swiveled, undulated. She ground against his palm. He rotated his hand, massaging her clit, and captured her keening cry with his mouth.

With her body still quivering, he rose to his knees. He removed her heels, then stripped her jeans from her hips and legs. Tossing the denim and her shoes over the side of the bed, he spread her thighs and knelt between them. Her swollen folds glistened with the result of her passion. He bit back a tortured moan, and stroked himself as she watched.

"Wyatt." She reached for him. "I want you inside me."

Her brutal honesty was almost as sexy as the need shimmering in her eyes. "Soon, duchess. I've got one or two other *carnal delights* I need to explore first."

Walking backward on his knees, he lowered to his stomach and cupped her ass in his hands. She whimpered as he lifted her, and jolted at the first flicking lick of his tongue against the hard nub of her clit. Sweet and musky, her essence made his mouth water, his nostrils flare, and his cock throb as he alternately sucked and licked.

Incredibly responsive, she mewled deep in her throat. It wasn't long before she was bucking against his mouth as she reached her climax. Starting over, he built her back up until she cooed with desire, staying after her until she shattered a second time while screaming his name.

Only then did he let her rest, and then, only long enough to retrieve one of the condoms he'd tossed into the bed-stand drawer before traveling the half mile to the studio this morning. Sprawled boneless and naked, she followed his movements with heavy-lidded eyes as he rolled the condom over himself.

Propped over her on his left elbow, he used his right hand to position the tip of his cock at the entrance to her channel. A flex of his hips, and she stretched around him. Retreating slightly, he pressed forward, pushing beyond the tip before retreating again. A third foray into paradise, and he was buried to the hilt. His groan merged with hers.

Ripples of pleasure skipped up and down his spine as he paused to enjoy the exquisite squeeze of her incredibly tight walls. Beads of sweat broke out on his forehead, and he had to move. Slowly at first, he swiveled his hips in a lazy roll. Seduced by the spark of returning heat in her eyes, he picked up his pace. She matched his ever-increasing frenzy, rising and falling in time with him. Hands clinging to his shoulders and a slim calf wrapped around the back of his thighs, she arched from the mattress to meet him and took his heavy thrusts as if they were her due.

She threw back her head, mouth open in a silent scream, and the sudden milking of her internal muscles was his undoing. His balls contracted, and he buried himself deep, shuddering beneath the violence of his orgasm.

Lost in a sultry fog, he wasn't sure how long he lay atop her. As she shifted beneath him, he pushed up on his elbows. "Sorry, I must be heavy."

"You make a lovely blanket." Her jaw snapped on a wide yawn, and he smiled.

"You okay?"

"Fabulous." Looking as if she didn't have the strength to lift it, she brought her hand to his face and cupped his cheek. "You're a talented and generous lover, Wyatt."

Turning his head, he held her gaze while pressing a kiss to her palm. "I was inspired."

The pink tinge of a blush bloomed over her cheekbones, and he shook his head. She'd just matched him lust for lust. The fact she could still blush surprised him as much as it charmed. Dropping his forehead to hers, he chuckled.

"I'm in danger of losing my heart here, duchess." The whispered words were out of his mouth before they'd even registered.

She froze beneath him, her eyes wide. He swallowed a vicious curse. Pressing a kiss to her nose, he disentangled their bodies and rose from the bed.

I'm in danger of losing my heart? Fuck. Where the hell had that come from?

Like the coward he'd suddenly become, he avoided her gaze as he swept his briefs from the floor. Instead of entering the attached bath to dispose of the condom, he hurried toward the stairs. He needed a few minutes to scrape the holy fuck off his tongue before any post coital conversation could begin.

"I'm going to get us something to eat. I'll be back in a couple."

Chapter 17

Piper sat up and tugged the rumpled comforter from beneath her hip. Wrapping it around her naked breasts, she blinked at the speed with which Wyatt disappeared down the stairs. *Bloody hell. What just happened?*

She'd been kidding with her comment about him making a good blanket. Up until that point, she'd been hotter than a banked fire and, considering he'd experienced at least two orgasms of his own, she'd assumed he had been, too.

But she wasn't hot now.

Chilled to the bone by his sudden coolness, followed by his rapid retreat to the first floor, she chewed her bottom lip. Though he'd whispered the words, she'd heard them clearly. He'd said he was in danger of losing his heart. Then…what?

Ha! 'Tis a basket of rubbish he was feeding ye. The only danger to that devil's heart would'a been if he fell down the steps while scramblin' to get away once he'd gotten his leg over with ye.

She stared at the empty space where he'd disappeared, and her pulse catapulted into rapid fire. Surely, that wasn't it. He'd said he thought about her. Wanted the time to discover why.

Ye know why. Tis what men do. Like yer cheatin' fiancé, Wyatt Hunter has had his way with ye and now he's ready to move on. And ye played right into his hands. Her inner nag snorted. *Forgettin' yer knickers? Blimey, had the first Baroness of Delaney known what her line would come to, she'da become a nun.*

Piper slapped a hand over her eyes and groaned, but now wasn't the time for *I told you so's*. She dropped her hand to her lap and eyed the windows running the length of the front wall. Perhaps she could tie the bed sheets together and shimmy down the building to the street below.

Right. With yer luck, you'd come up short and spend the afternoon dangling above the sidewalk before ye fell and broke both legs.

With a grimace, she shoved aside the comforter and climbed from the mattress. She very well may be a disappointment to her ancestors, but the current Baroness of Delaney didn't escape through third story windows and she didn't run. Especially when she'd done nothing wrong.

She scooped her jeans and jumper from the floor where Wyatt had dropped them and welcomed the growing kernel of anger in her belly.

For heaven's sake, they were consenting adults and it wasn't as if this was his first sexual encounter. By all accounts, he was an expert in the field and, in view of the way her body still hummed, the reports were spot on.

A low growl escaped her throat. Considering his expertise, if he was uncomfortable with women once he'd shagged them, then he shouldn't bring them to his flat. Good God. He owned his own plane. Surely he could afford to spring for a neutral location, like a hotel room, where he'd be free to be on his way once the deed was done…instead of pacing around downstairs, wondering how the devil to get her to leave without tossing her out.

She jammed a leg into the wrinkled denim, then the other, and yanked the jeans over her naked bottom and hips. Bugger it. It wasn't as if she'd forced any kind of demands on him. Well, other than the money, but that was business. Bloody hell, she'd expressly insisted on a no-strings arrangement with no long-term commitments.

She scowled at her pretty green jumper and wished like hell she had a brassiere stashed away somewhere. Knickers, too. Shoving her arms into the sleeves, she dragged the sweater over her head as heat suffused her cheeks. Her nag had a point. She'd been incredibly easy for him. Wyatt probably considered her a trollop not worthy of another thought now that he'd had it off with her.

The wanker.

Stomping into her heels, she headed for the stairs. If he'd decided they were done personally, fine. She could live with that, but he didn't have to be a…prick about it. She nodded smugly at the Yank insult and decided it fit Wyatt perfectly. After all, a shake of the hand or a pat on the head might have been a cool ending to what had just passed between them, but either would have been far less insulting than bolting from the bed and running like hell while she was still vibrating from his touch.

She hesitated only slightly as she spotted him upon reaching the bottom step. Bare chested and footed with his hair sexily mussed from her fingers, he stood at the kitchen island in only a disreputably faded pair of jeans. The makings of a sandwich were spread out around him. The knife in his hand stilled over the tomato he'd been slicing, and he looked up. His forced smile made him look like he'd been sipping the juice from the pickle jar near his elbow.

Definitely a prick.

She stalked past him, stopping to collect her camera bag from the couch where he'd left it. Hefting the strap onto her shoulder, she faced him with a bugger-off tilt of her chin. "I didn't see a pedestrian door when we arrived. Is there a secret passage somewhere to let me out, or shall I ride down with the SUV?"

He cocked his head. "What are you talking about? Where are you going?"

"Back to my hotel." Adjusting the bag's strap, she shrugged. "Never mind, I'm an intelligent woman. I'll figure it out on my own."

"Duchess, wait..."

She ignored him, and turned toward the exit. Behind her, metal clattered, and he cursed beneath his breath. She hurried her steps. Chin high, she somehow managed to hold on to her pride, a difficult thing with the residual stickiness between her thighs reminding her just how big a fool she'd been.

He caught her before she reached the barn door. Tucking an arm around her from behind, he dragged her to a stop. His chest swelled against her back as if he were dealing with something he'd rather not. "Hold on a minute, duchess."

She stiffened her backbone. She'd become accustomed to the nickname. In fact, she'd found it rather charming, but now... If they were to be nothing more than business associates—and their professional relationship had bloody well better still be in effect because there was no way she was returning his money—then he could damn well address her by her given name.

"I'd rather you not call me that. Especially since our association from here on will be of a professional nature. I insist you call me Piper or Miss Darrow."

His sigh was audible as he lowered his head to press his cheek against hers. "I'm sorry, Piper."

Surprise caught her off guard, but only for a moment. She twisted her head clear of his cheek. "Yes, well. That makes two of us. Now, if you don't mind..."

He tightened his arm when she attempted to step forward. "Give me a minute to explain."

She leaned her upper body to the side and turned her head to look at him. "Explain what, exactly? I'm not some virginal missy who doesn't know how men think. I get it, Wyatt. We shagged and it was lovely, but now we're done, and you're not sure how to get rid of me."

His brows dipped together in a frown. "What the...? Not even close." He released her, but only to straighten and turn her to face him. Gripping her upper arms, he looked her dead in the eye. "Jesus, duchess. What kind of men have you been with that *that's* your opinion of how we think?"

She arched a brow, but wasn't going anywhere near that minefield of questioning. "I asked you not to call me that." She gave in to a derisive snort. "And please, you couldn't get off me fast enough when the deed was done." The flash of guilt in his eyes was painful to witness but, instead of increasing her anger, a sadness she hadn't expected filled her heart. She blew a windy sigh. "Look. We agreed at the beginning there would be no strings or obligations. I suggest we cut our losses and move on."

His fingers briefly clenched around her arms. "What if I don't want to move on? What if I want to move forward?"

She blinked, but if she was shocked by his question, it seemed he was as well. An agitated wrinkle creased his forehead, and he released her arms. She stared at him as he jammed a hand through his hair, disturbing the mussed locks even further. She waited for him to correct himself and, when he didn't, she shook her head.

"You don't mean that." He couldn't. Not in the way she wanted him to, anyway. Men like Wyatt didn't have relationships; they had flings. He was a player. A playboy. A professional athlete who had his pick of women and had proven through the years that variety played a key role in who he spent his time with.

Been there, done that. Didn't buy the T-shirt because it was bloody ugly and hateful.

Then again, perhaps she should have. Maybe then, her heart wouldn't be tripping in her chest at the thought he might have actually *meant* his whispered comment—before he'd rolled off her and fled.

He dropped his arms to his sides and blew a half-pained snort. "I've never meant anything more in my life and it scares the fuck out of me."

Her head went fuzzy, and she must have gone pale because his face tightened with alarm. She didn't argue as he slid an arm around her waist and guided her back to the couch. He very gently lowered her to the cushions and squatted before her, then took her hands.

"Yeah, I know. I had a similar reaction. Which is why I took off so quickly. I needed a few minutes. Truth is, I didn't expect to discover I have feelings for you, much less speak them out loud."

She swallowed hard, but he seemed to have moved past his panic.

He squeezed her fingers. "Can I get you something? Water? A glass of wine?"

"Thank you, no."

"Whiskey?" He smiled softly at the narrowing of her eyes. The bulk of the concern drained from his face. "That's better."

She dropped her gaze to their hands, but hadn't realized she'd been clinging to his fingers. The smart move would be to tug free, but she couldn't bring herself to break the connection. "We had a deal, Wyatt."

"Deals are renegotiated all the time."

True, but... "Hey."

She lifted her gaze to his.

"I'm not suggesting we jet off to Vegas tonight. All I'm asking is you keep an open mind. See where things lead."

The dizziness returned as her heartbeat pounded in her ears. She shook her head to clear it. "See where things lead? Wyatt, your father is running for president of the United States."

That reality killed the humor in his eyes, and he winced. "Yeah, there is that." Releasing her hands, he slid onto the couch beside her. He didn't ask, simply scooped her into his lap and wrapped his arms around her. "I think you should know, you're being investigated by my father's campaign."

"What?" She struggled against his hold. "Let me up, please. I've got to go."

"No, you don't."

"Yes, I do. I really do."

"You're panicking and there's no need." He held her gently but firmly, and she gave up the fight. Rubbing a soothing hand up and down her spine, he pressed a kiss to her temple. "It's not as big deal as it sounds. They investigate anyone with a connection to the family."

"Not a big deal? Bloody hell. I'm being investigated by the probable next president of the United States." She squeezed her eyelids shut on a whimper. "I've fallen down the rabbit hole."

His palm stilled on her lower back. "You haven't killed anyone, right? Don't head up an international mob syndicate? Aren't hiding out here in the States because you're wanted by Interpol?"

She coughed dismissively and met his gaze. "Don't be ridiculous."

He grinned and resumed his soothing strokes. "I admit, I don't understand the ball cap and sweatshirt routine, but figured you have your reasons for wanting to keep a low profile."

Bugger it. Obviously, he'd recognized her attempt to disguise herself as exactly that. She blew a frustrated huff. "Wyatt, I..."

"There's just one problem, though."

Whatever explanation she'd been about to give—and she had no idea what that was—stalled in her throat. She blinked. "What kind of problem?"

He slid his hand past her waist to cup his palm along the left cheek of her bum. "You may want to exchange the jeans for a pair of baggy sweats. A woman who wears denim the way you do is impossible to overlook."

Relief sagged her shoulders. "I'm serious, Wyatt."

"So am I. You have one of the finest asses I've ever seen." He squeezed her cheek in emphasis, then brushed his lips over her temple. "Talk to me, duchess."

Fear mixed with an underlying desire to do as he asked, and fear won. "What would be the point? In case you've forgotten, we live on different continents."

"In case *you've* forgotten, I have my own plane."

His grin was so boyishly self-satisfied, she couldn't help smiling, but it faded quickly.

He sighed, but didn't give up. Brushing a fingertip down her cheek to her jaw line, he crooked his knuckle beneath her chin and lifted her face. His eyes darkened with intensity. "I'm interested in you, Piper. Several days ago on my plane, you admitted you were interested, too. Less than an hour ago, you opened yourself up to me in the most elemental way a woman can, and I've never seen anything more beautiful."

He dipped his head and brushed her lips with his before straightening. "My father *is* running for president. I can't change that any more than I can change the fact that you make my heart pound and my dick hard. Dad's staff doesn't give a shit about you, but I do. Forewarned is forearmed. If I'm going to defend you against whatever they find, I need to know what's coming."

She dropped her gaze, but he wasn't having any of that.

"Hey." He jiggled her slightly until she looked up again. "Dad's paranoia aside, I want to know more about you. About your favorite foods and television shows. What makes you happy and those things that have made you sad in the past. Like the asshole who taught you to have such low expectations when it comes to men."

Her fear was no match for the glow of hope sparking in her chest. If she was being honest with herself, she'd been more than interested in him from the very beginning. He hadn't gone so far as to touch on the L word but, then, she didn't love him, either. She wasn't so stupid to have allowed herself to go down that road again, but she did like him. A lot. As V claimed, it was impossible not to.

Like no man she'd ever met, he had an uncanny ability to keep her off guard, and the way he could draw a laugh from her even when she tried to hold back made him a temptation nearly impossible to resist. The trip between like and love would be a very short one but, the question remained, could they possibly overcome the daunting barriers circumstances had created in their individual lives?

Her stomach twisted into knots. The scars left after her failed engagement had long since healed, but the thought of baring them was still bloody uncomfortable. However, if she and Wyatt were to have a chance at moving forward as he'd suggested, they needed to start somewhere. And if she was reading the situation wrong? If sharing the details of her life blew up in her face?

Well, she'd simply deal with it. She was the eighth Baroness of Delaney, after all. She'd deal with it, right after she hired a hitman to kill Wyatt Hunter dead.

Mentally rolling her eyes, she sucked in a ragged breath and jumped in. "I was once engaged to Cody Beckett."

Chapter 18

Cody Beckett? The soccer dick? That explained a lot. Especially Piper's initial aversion to Wyatt as an athlete. With Beckett as her yardstick, it was a wonder Wyatt had gotten within ten feet of her.

He grunted. "My condolences."

Her tension was broadcast in the thin line of her lips, if not in the uneasiness shadowing her eyes. "The breakup was my decision, although Cody would argue with my version of events."

She slid from Wyatt's lap and he let her. She was talking, which was what he'd asked, but she wasn't happy about it. If moving around made her feel better, he was good with that. But just in case... He rose to his feet and placed himself between her and the exit.

Propping his hip against the side of the couch, he crossed one bare foot over the other as she dug into the outside pocket of her camera bag. "You misunderstand, duchess. I wasn't commiserating with you on the breakup, but on the fact you spent any amount of time with the asshole."

The truth was, he couldn't imagine his duchess giving Beckett the time of day, never mind agreeing to marry him. Wyatt had only met the captain of the London Guardsmen once, at a party in Cannes last spring. A petite blonde, whose name Wyatt couldn't remember, had dragged him to France for the film festival. Drunk as shit, Beckett had publicly felt up a young waitress, then chastised her for delivering his double martini with only two olives instead of three.

Bent over her bag, Piper paused and cocked her head to look at him. "You know Cody?"

"Not really. I met him once. My first impression was that he's an elitist dick with narcissistic tendencies. You're way too good for him."

And there was the triple blink.

She straightened with her phone in her hand. "Thank you. That's one of the nicest things anyone has ever said to me."

Wyatt winked, relieved by the return of her smile. "We aim to please, ma'am."

"Yes, well, don't get too cocky. You asked me to talk to you, and I've only just begun." Thumbing her phone, she typed something in and stepped in front of him. She kept her gaze on the screen as if waiting for a page to load, then held the phone out to him.

Curious, he took the device and spun it so he could see what she found so interesting. He read the headline and looked up. "The Gold-Digging Baroness?"

"That's me." She crossed her arms and bumped her chin toward the phone. "By the way, I'm not a duchess. I'm a baroness."

He glanced from her to the phone and back. The bold text fronting the article read, *With her scheme to bilk Beckett of his millions exposed, the Gold-Digging Baroness has holed up on her cash-strapped country estate.*

Scrolling down, he stopped at the photo of a redhead glancing into the lens over her shoulder while ducking into a garden doorway. In her hand, she carried a—he held the phone closer—shit, was that a chainsaw? The photo was grainy, but there was no mistaking Piper's face or the sweetly curved behind molded lovingly by faded denim.

He slowly lifted his head. "You're fucking kidding me?"

"I wish," she grumbled, then angled her chin at a proud angle. "It's a pleasure to meet you, Wyatt. My name is Piper Darrow. I'm the eighth baroness of the Delaney. Or, as Google refers to me, *The Gold-Digging Baroness.*"

She lowered her arms to her sides. "For the record, my country estate is indeed cash-strapped. Frighteningly so. A situation I was unaware of until my father's death three years ago. However, contrary to what that article and others like it claim, I never expected Cody to bail me out. In fact, I have never asked him for a single shilling."

She dropped her gaze to the phone in Wyatt's hand. "*The Gold-Digging Baroness* moniker was a creation of Cody's monumental ego and, of course, the press and his fans believed every one of his lies as if they were gospel." She looked up with a wry laugh. "Why wouldn't they, when no sane woman would walk away from Cody Beckett to run a B&B in the wilds of northern England?"

She hiked her chin even higher. "And, for the record, I'm perfectly sane. Delaney Manor is not only my home, it's a legacy handed down to me through four hundred years of Delaney women. Selling it, as Cody insisted I do to pay off my creditors, was no less out of the question then than it is now. As the Baroness of Delaney, the estate is my responsibility. One I don't take lightly, especially considering there are others who depend on the estate for their livelihoods."

Her chest heaved with an indignant sigh. "I was vilified by Cody's vicious toadies in the press as they snuck around the grounds and popped from the bushes, but I will not apologize to anyone for doing what had to be done to preserve my legacy. Nor will I apologize for opening my home to strangers or earning a living by accepting odd job offers like the ones from you and the Marauders."

She stood before him with her eyes full of wary expectation as if waiting for him to accuse her of bilking *him* out the funds they'd agreed upon. Of their own accord, his hands curled into fists. His duchess—shit, she was a real-life baroness—was no more a gold-digger than he was a politician.

The tension in her stiff stance scraped at him, and his heart accelerated straight past interested into uncharted territory. He wasn't willing to name the change, not until he'd had the opportunity to examine the shift from every angle but, though he expected panic to follow, it never came. Instead, a rightness he'd never experienced settled over him.

In the meantime, the starkness in her eyes made him want to hunt down Cody Beckett and break him in two. Wyatt promised himself that day would come but, for now, what he wanted more than anything was to bring back her smile.

He cocked his head. "A baroness, huh?"

"That's correct."

He dragged his palm over his chin and jaw and studied her in silence for a moment. "So. Am I supposed to curtsey or something?"

She hiccupped, half laugh, half relieved sob. His stomach muscles clenched painfully as she stepped into him to press her forehead against his chest. Sliding her arms around his waist, she held on as if he were a lifeline, and his eyelids briefly slid closed.

"I'll take that as a no." He wrapped her in a loose hold. "I'm not up on the whole royal thing. Which is higher? Baroness or duchess?"

"Duchess." She spoke against the bare skin of his chest, making it hard to concentrate. "But my title isn't of a royal line. In simple terms, my grandmother, eight times over, was granted the title by writ to be passed to the next female in the Delaney line. I'm the eighth."

He didn't know what the hell a writ was, but he got the point. Piper wasn't in line to take up residence at Buckingham Palace. Thank God. As it was, Walter Crowley was going to shit himself when Jennings handed in his report. Wyatt made a mental note to call Meg the first chance he got.

He contracted his arms in a gentle squeeze. "Are you hungry? I'm starved."

Piper leaned back to stare at him, disbelief widening her eyes. "Am I *hungry?*" She shook her head. "Wyatt, that article you read is only one of dozens. Your father and his campaign will not be happy with you once they learn you're spending time with a woman whose name and face were plastered all over the tabloids for months."

He snorted dismissively. "My father and his campaign are never happy with me."

"Maybe not, but I'm..."

"With me." She bit her bottom lip and satisfaction surged through his veins. He didn't know where, exactly, this thing between them was headed, but the fact that he'd left her speechless said she wasn't averse to exploring the possibilities. He dropped a kiss on her nose and released her to round the island, returning to the sandwich he'd been making. "We can keep our relationship quiet for the time being if that'll make you more comfortable, but I'm not turning my back on what could be between us because of some imagined problem my father or his political machine might have."

She heaved a sigh and followed him to slide onto one of the stools fronting the island. "I don't want to be a point of contention between you and your father."

He lathered slices of bread with a grainy mustard, and twisted his lips in a smirk. "Yeah, I wouldn't worry about that. Points of contention pretty much rule our relationship and always have." He layered Gouda over thick slices of ham. "Anyway, considering you're a bona fide baroness, he'll no doubt consider you an improvement over quite a few of the women I've dated through the years." She arched a brow and he shrugged. "Either way, it doesn't matter. If not you, he'll find something else to bitch about. He always does."

"I'm sorry, Wyatt. I was very close to my Da. I can't imagine what it's like to always be at odds with a parent."

He glanced up and wasn't surprised by the empathy in her eyes. She had a soft heart and it showed. And that fucking accent... Damn, who knew the word Da could be so sexy? He grunted deep in his throat and turned to retrieve a couple of plates from a cabinet. "The relationship between my father and me has always been more like that of CEO and employee than father and son."

"That's sad, but you have Meg and Mandy, and Rosa, too. If you don't mind my asking, what happened to your mother?"

After slicing the sandwich down the middle, he arranged the halves on the plates. "She was killed by a drunk driver when I was six. Meg had just turned one."

Piper slid a hand over her heart, but didn't offer random platitudes like most would. He appreciated the restraint, but had to wonder if her silence on such a painful subject was a natural byproduct of her proper, English upbringing or something more personal. He'd put money on the latter.

He slid one of the plates in front of her along with a napkin. He'd left a bottle of wine breathing on the end of the island. He picked it up and lifted a brow in question. She nodded.

"What about you?" He handed her a glass. "You say you were close to your father, but didn't mention your mom."

"She died within an hour of my birth."

"Shit." He hesitated, then poured himself a glass and set the bottle aside. "Sorry. What happened?"

"I was several weeks premature and had some trouble breathing." Her shoulders went stiff, and she dropped her gaze to her glass. She scraped her thumbnail down the stem. "The midwife attending the birth was busy taking care of me and didn't notice my mother was struggling as well. The doctors called it a postpartum hemorrhage. She'd bled to death before anyone knew there was an issue."

"Jesus. That must have been tough." The haunting sadness in her eyes was tempered with acceptance. The combination wrenched his heart, and he was tempted to skirt the island and hold her until the remembered grief faded. Before he could move, she nodded.

"It was for Da, for a long time. I missed her, too, in my own way, but she's never been more than an abstract image in my mind. She was the star of each of the stories Da shared with me over the years and the heroine of all my childhood fairytales, but he was the one who made sure I knew I was loved."

Wyatt leaned his hands on the edge of the island, absorbing the nuance of emotion crossing her face. Yearning, simple pleasure, wonder, all took a back seat to a profound sadness she couldn't disguise as she spoke of the man who'd raised her. "He sounds like a good man."

"He was the best." Genuine affection dampened the strain of sadness as she smiled.

"What about extended family?" He rounded the island to take the stool to her right. "Do you have anyone else around you now that he's gone?"

She set aside her wine and picked up her sandwich. "I do have one cousin who I've never been close to, but Tilly Perkins has been the housekeeper at Delaney Manor since before I was born. Her daughter, Moira, is the sister I never had. She co-manages the B&B with me and her mother feeds the guests." She bit in to her sandwich and hummed in appreciation. "Oh my. I didn't realize how famished I was," she said around a mouthful of ham and cheese.

He chuckled and ripped off a large bite of his own. They'd worked up an appetite earlier. If he had anything to say about it, they'd need to refuel a number of times before the night was done. For the moment, however, she was talking, just as he'd asked. He was content to listen.

She reached for her wine. "Then, of course, there is Angus."

He waited as she sipped, then set aside her glass and bit off another bite. When she said nothing more, he frowned. "Who's Angus?"

"Angus Graham." She swallowed, then wiped her mouth with her napkin. "He's Alick's brother."

"Yeah, that tells me a lot." Wyatt didn't quite grumble the words, but it was close. And the fact he was bothered by her rattling off the names of faceless men said more about that shift he'd experienced a few moments ago than he wanted to acknowledge.

She cocked her head, her eyes twinkling with teasing laughter. "Alick is my favorite model. I included a photograph of him in the Marauders' fundraiser last week. Apparently, there was quite a bidding war over him. But then, I can understand why. There is just something about a man in a kilt, especially when it's the bold blue and green pattern of the Graham tartan. So manly and sexy at the same time."

She hummed appreciatively, deep in her throat. "A wealthy, female stock broker paid a fortune to take Alick home with her." She sighed and nipped at her sandwich.

An image of the scarf Piper had worn the night of the team fundraiser flashed in Wyatt's mind. Plaid silk in blue and green. The same pattern as the kilt worn by the old-time fisherman in the largest of her photos. The little minx was playing him. He narrowed his eyes and she burst out laughing.

"Angus is Alick's twin. They turn seventy-nine a week from Tuesday."

Wyatt shook his head, though he was utterly charmed by the dimples creasing her self-satisfied smile. "Smartass."

"Just returning the favor after that comment about your father preferring a baroness over your *other* women."

Okay, *that* he could live with. He propped his elbows on the counter. "Jealous, duchess?"

She snorted. "That's baroness, thank you very much."

"You'll always be a duchess in my eyes." He waggled his brow and straightened. "Do the sexy old kilted twins live at your manor, too?"

"Just Angus." She pushed her mostly finished sandwich aside and picked up her wine. "Alick lives in Inveraray, not far over the Scottish border.

TO WIN HER SMILE

The first Baroness of Delaney came from there. The sea has always been Alick's first love, but Angus prefers the solidness of the ground beneath his feet—when he's not climbing a ladder." She shook her head, but her grin relayed her affection for the old man. "He's been a jack of all trades at Delaney Manor since my mother was a little girl. She was their cousin, twice removed."

"Inveraray." Wyatt settled comfortably on his stool and sipped his wine. "You mentioned spending your summers there as a girl."

"I did?" She squinted. "When."

"That first day, in Tuck's kitchen."

"Oh." She smiled, but then her brow wrinkled slightly. "Da split our summers between there and Italy where I met CC. He sold the villa in Cinque Terre about five years ago and the cottage in Inveraray a year later. I thought he'd sold the homes because we barely found the time to visit them anymore, but it turned out he was liquidating properties to pay for some much needed repairs and an extensive renovation at Delaney Manor. I wish he'd told me what was happening at the time."

"Maybe he didn't want to worry you."

She nodded. "Probably, but I've been left with plenty of worries, despite his keeping me in the dark. Not that I'm complaining, mind you. Delaney Manor is my home and I love it, but it's a lot of work. At five hundred acres, the estate grounds are mostly wooded and don't require a lot of maintenance. Other than the occasional removal of a fallen tree or such, which Moira or I handle *if* we manage to get to the chainsaw before Angus does."

Which explained the photo in the online article. "A baroness skilled in the use of power tools." Wyatt whistled through his teeth. "I'm getting a hard-on."

She snorted a laugh, but he noted she shot a quick glance at his crotch. He grinned and she rolled her eyes.

"As I was saying, the wooded areas aren't a problem, but the lawns and gardens are still quite extensive and keeping up with them can be a bit time consuming. Then there is the manor itself. It's over four hundred years old. Even with the updates Da had done, it seems there is always wrench work to do. When I've finished here in a few weeks, I'll be in the position to hire a new handyman, and I'll have a battle on my hands when Angus finds out."

Wyatt cleared his throat. "If you need…"

She shut him down with a shake of her head. "Stop. You're helping already, more than you know. In fact, the completion of your calendar project will put us back in the black for good, so don't say another word."

He held up his hands in surrender. He didn't know a damn thing about the real estate market in northern England, but five hundred acres of virgin woodland had to be worth a bundle. Walking away from Cody Beckett hadn't been much of a hardship as far as Wyatt was concerned, and he was damned glad she had, but she'd also been willing to roll up her sleeves and go to work rather than cashing in.

Jesus, a chainsaw. She obviously loved the estate and the people who helped her run it. Delaney Manor and its staff was something he planned to check out.

He shook his head, spun on his stool, and held her gaze.

"Do we have a deal, duchess? We let this thing between us play out and see where it leads?"

She studied his face, her eyes full of sober consideration. "Maybe. If we keep things between us private. For the time being, anyway." He dipped his chin in a nod. "*And* you agree to follow the guidelines set out in our original agreement. I won't have anyone suggesting the Gold-Digging Baroness is at it again. I pay my own way or it's a no-go."

He resisted the urge to grind his teeth. Like anyone who truly knew her would believe something like that of her. If he was ever in the same room with Cody Beckett again, he was going to rearrange the fucker's face. Sliding from his stool, Wyatt scooped her from hers into his arms.

"Done." Covering her mouth with his, he sealed the deal with a kiss, straightened, then plucked her wineglass from the island.

She grinned and wrapped an arm around his neck.

"Grab the wine, if you don't mind."

Reaching out with her free hand, she snagged the bottle, and settled into his chest. He spun toward the stairs and she dropped her head onto his shoulder. The flick of her tongue behind his ear nearly buckled his knees before he'd made it halfway to the second floor. He had to pause to regain his balance.

"Have mercy, duchess, or we're both going down."

"Oh, I'd planned to and I'm glad to know you will be as well." She laughed as a guttural growl climbed up and out of his throat.

He took the remaining stairs two at a time.

Chapter 19

"I thought we agreed to keep our relationship quiet from the public for the time being." Piper frowned as Wyatt parked the SUV in front of the Malones' Long Island farmhouse.

He slid a hand behind her neck and drew her forward to receive his kiss. "The Malones and the others aren't the public. They're friends." Straightening, he removed the key from the ignition and opened his door. "And they already know we've been spending time together."

Of that, Piper was certain, and she had no one to blame but herself. Well, except Wyatt, of course. It was his fault she was walking around grinning like a ninny. Those eighteen hours they'd spent locked away in his loft condo had set the pattern for the past two weeks. She'd maintained her hotel suite, returning there each afternoon to shower and change at the end of her work day, but her nights had passed wrapped in Wyatt's arms in his bed in Long Island City.

She couldn't remember ever being as happy and, apparently, it showed. CC had taken one look at Piper's face when she'd arrived at the Tuckers' home the next morning and announced, "I told you so." V had had much the same reaction when Wyatt had popped his head through her office door, interrupting their first Friday Fab Five meeting to wink at Piper. The Marauders' PR consultant hadn't said a word. Hadn't needed to. The smug satisfaction in her smile spoke volumes.

Piper hadn't bothered attempting to defend herself against either woman. She had no idea if this fling between her and Wyatt would last, but she'd agreed to give it some time. And she couldn't regret the decision. He was a fabulous lover. Generous, attentive, and fun loving, he could make her believe she was the only woman he'd ever looked at in that hotly sensuous way.

That was a whopper if she'd ever told herself one and, in the dark recesses of her mind, the saying *If something is too good to be true, it probably is* haunted her. Wyatt Hunter was definitely too good to be true. There was also the specter of some enterprising reporter catching them together, not to mention the interest from his father's campaign but, God help her. She couldn't bring herself to care.

She'd never met a man who could make her laugh the way Wyatt did. A trait she found incredibly sexy and impossible to resist. Whether the heat between them proved to be a quick flash or a banked fire, she was having a bloody blast and planned to enjoy every moment while it lasted.

She exited the vehicle and hefted the strap of her camera bag onto her shoulder, then rounded the hood to take the hand Wyatt held out. As they climbed the steps to the porch, he tucked her close to his side. Lifting their linked fingers, he pressed a kiss to her knuckles. She couldn't prevent her shiver, then dug her elbow into his side at his self-satisfied chuckle.

"There you are." Gracie Malone swung the door wide. She smiled at Piper, then smirked at Wyatt. "Tuck bet the guys you wouldn't show."

Piper blinked and turned to Wyatt, who snorted.

"Tuck's an ass."

"That is the general consensus." Gracie grinned and waved them inside. Piper's confusion must have shown, because Gracie grimaced and linked arms with her to explain. "At one time or another, we Gridiron Girls have done some matchmaking for each of the guys inside. Tuck is convinced we've got Wyatt in our crosshairs."

Matchmaking? Oh, bugger it. Her and Wyatt's relationship was complicated enough without their friends sticking their noses into the mix, no matter how well-meaning their intentions. Piper tensed and chewed her bottom lip.

"Jesus," Wyatt grumbled beneath his breath.

Gracie patted his chest as she passed by him. "Lighten up, Hunter. We're fresh out of available leg shackles this evening. Tonight is dinner with friends, nothing more." Tugging Piper down the hallway toward the back of the house, Gracie didn't seem to care that Wyatt could hear every word she said. "Besides, from what V and CC say, you're doing just fine on your own."

Piper didn't have a chance to respond as the hallway opened into a large family kitchen. Wyatt caught up to them at the doorway. In front of a room full of his friends, he lifted Gracie's hand from Piper's arm and replaced it with his own. He moved his gaze around the kitchen. Beginning with Gracie, he paused on all five of the Gridiron Girls.

"V and CC are right. Piper and I are doing just fine. So, ladies, although I've heard you have a damned fine track record, butt out. We don't need your help."

Male snickers competed with several feminine snorts. Caught between horror at the not so subtle power play, and delight at his blatant possessiveness, Piper curved her lips in her best *yes-I'm-a-baroness-and-above-all-this* smile.

V met Wyatt's gaze with an approving grin, then turned to Piper. "You haven't technically met my husband, Sam."

Gracie handed Piper a glass of wine as Wyatt made introductions. She knew all the women, of course, and had met Tim Tucker, Kris's husband, when they'd passed through London last year. New to her were Sam Fitzpatrick, Jake Malone, and Max Grayson—Jessi Tucker's cage-fighting champion husband.

Talk about a power group. Wyatt's friends and their wives represented more talent and success than one would expect to find in half a dozen Fortune 500 outfits.

As the wine flowed, and friendly laughter filled the air, Piper glanced around in wonder. There must be something in the Manhattan water that grew larger than life men who were too handsome for their own good. She snapped several photographs and was tempted to send a few along to Moira, but thought better of it. Her friend was likely to burst a few blood vessels.

Two hours later, with dinner behind them, Piper wondered if her thoughts hadn't somehow reached across the pond. The sound of muted bagpipes caught her ear, and she glanced toward the hallway where she'd left her camera bag.

Wyatt leaned close to speak in her ear. "I think Scotland is calling."

She smiled and met his gaze. "It's Moira, actually, but you're close. The manor is less than twenty minutes from the border."

"Do you need to take it?"

She bit her lip. She spoke to Moira every morning, including today. If she was calling again, she must have a reason. "I probably should." Rising, she excused herself and retrieved her phone, moving farther into the hallway before answering. "What's wrong?"

"How do you know something is wrong? Maybe I'm just calling for an update on Operation Sex God."

Piper grinned. "I told you, details of that operation are on a need-to-know basis."

"But I *need* to know," her friend insisted in a whiny tone.

Piper laughed and shook her head. "Sorry, dearest. What's going on?"

A hesitation, then a soft sigh came through the phone. "It may be nothing."

"You wouldn't have called if you weren't concerned. What is it? Is Angus okay?"

"He's fine. Okay, he's not fine, exactly. In fact, he's rather upset."

"Moira." Concerned and frustrated at her friend's evasiveness, Piper switched the phone to her other ear. She happened to turn toward the dining room doorway and found Wyatt watching her from his seat at the table. Warmth spread from her belly to other, more sensitive parts of her body.

She forced herself to look away. "What happened?"

Another sigh. "Actually, I was hoping you could tell me. We had a visitor this afternoon while I was off to Glasgow. Apparently, Abigail arrived with her estate agent and demanded Angus give them both a tour of the property."

Piper shivered as her blood chilled. "Bugger."

"That's exactly how Angus reacted to her demand. He told her to bugger off. You can imagine how that went over."

With a grimace, Piper turned her head and her gaze found Wyatt's. He lifted a brow in question. She attempted a smile but, if his sudden scowl was any indication, she failed. He shoved back his chair to stand and she turned away.

"What did Abigail say?"

"She called him a snooty Scot." Moira's snort spoke volumes. "If anyone would know snooty, it's her. But then she went into the office and confronted Mum. She demanded to speak to you and, when Mum told her you couldn't be reached, she insisted her estate man be allowed access to the house and grounds. Mum didn't tell her to bugger off, but she may as well have. She suggested Abigail and her *friend* vacate the premises before the authorities were called. Your cousin threw a fit and said, come the first of the year, we'll all be looking for a new home."

Fury tightened Piper's chest. She may owe her cousin a great deal of money, but the manor was her home and had no bearing on Da's stipulation.

"What's going on, Piper? What did she mean?"

Her eyelids slid closed. She'd hoped to pay her cousin off without the residents of the manor ever having been aware of the deadline. With Abigail pushing her way onto the property and making demands, keeping them in the dark was no longer an option. Thanks to the Marauders and Wyatt's projects, meeting the deadline wouldn't be a problem, but explaining why she'd kept the detail to herself was something Piper would prefer to do in person. How she was going to pull that off when she was close to six thousand kilometers away, she hadn't a clue.

With a sigh, she answered Moira in the only way she could at the moment. "Nothing. How did Abigail leave things?"

"She said she'd be back on Wednesday."

Bollocks. Two days. Piper rubbed at the headache blooming between her brows.

"Trouble at home?" Wyatt's deep voice spoke near her ear.

She jumped and suppressed a shiver as he ran his hand down her spine to her waist.

"Is that the sex god?" The breathy demand whispered through the phone Piper held to her ear.

Telling Moira to hush would only encourage her. Dipping the phone from her mouth, Piper shrugged. "A tiny bit of trouble. Nothing I can't handle."

With the other half of your payment and a restraining order.

"It's him, isn't it?" Moira didn't bother to whisper this time. "It is utterly unfair for the man to look like that and come with a smoky bedroom voice as well. Bugger. Now I'm not going to be able to sleep tonight."

Piper covered her laugh by turning into a clearing of her throat. "Please tell Angus not to fret, Moira. I'll have an answer for you tomorrow."

Wyatt cocked his head and held Piper's gaze. "With this week's bye on the team schedule, I've got four days free and a private plane. If we leave now, we could be at Heathrow in eight hours."

Moira's squeal nearly pierced Piper's eardrum. Slapping her hand over the ear piece would have been a waste of time. From the grin on his face, Wyatt had heard.

Piper shook her head. When the bloody hell had she lost complete control of her life? "I appreciate the offer, but that's not necessary."

"Are you daft?" Moira complained loudly. "Bring him to visit. In his plane!"

"But I insist." Wyatt plucked the phone from her hand and held it to his ear. "I assume this is Moira."

The lilting murmur of her friend's voice reached Piper's ears, but she couldn't make out the words, which was more than a little disturbing, considering the source. Wyatt held Piper's gaze. The way he twisted his lips said he was fighting not to laugh. She bit her bottom lip. Perhaps it was a blessing she couldn't hear what Moira was saying.

"That's the plan, if Piper agrees." He dipped his chin. "What do you say, duchess? I'd love to see your manor."

Damn him. He knew exactly what he was doing, appealing to her with that rakishly charming smile. The fact he was asking instead of plowing forward with his own agenda only made denying him more difficult. Especially since taking him up on his offer would allow her to speak to her friends in person. Still, a transatlantic flight to visit her home wasn't part of their original deal.

"Fine, but I'm paying for my airfare." He smirked, but she stood her ground. "Those are my terms."

He shook his head while speaking into the phone. "We'll be there in the morning, Moira." A slight pause. "No, we'll pick up a car and drive ourselves." He laughed. "Oh, I'm definitely looking forward to meeting you as well."

Thumbing the screen, he handed Piper the phone. Dimples bracketed his anticipatory grin as he plucked her camera bag from the hall table and turned her toward the front door with a hand to her lower back. "Thanks for dinner, Gracie," he called out, "but we've got to go."

"Where?" Several of the women, including V, called back.

Wyatt swung the door open and spoke over his shoulder. "Road trip, and that's all you need to know."

Chapter 20

Wyatt cast a sidelong glance at Piper. Head turned toward the passing scenery, she sat stiffly in the passenger seat of the Land Rover that had been waiting for them upon their arrival in Glasgow. He frowned. When he'd asked after the problem on their way to LaGuardia last evening, she'd claimed it was nothing more than a slight hiccup in the running of the B&B. The tension riding her shoulders since she'd spoken to Moira said otherwise.

After two weeks of holding Piper as she slept, he knew her body well. Something more than a hiccup had kept her from relaxing completely in the plane's comfortable bed. Though she'd slid into his arms without complaint, she hadn't been able to settle and had dozed restlessly throughout the overnight flight.

He dropped his gaze to her hands, twisted together in her lap. The knuckles had gone white from being clenched so tightly. He bit down on a frustrated sigh. Her lack of trust in him rankled. She'd clearly opened herself up to him physically but, emotionally, she was still holding back. Call him greedy, but he wanted it all. He wanted her laughter *and* her tears. Wanted to be her everything, not just a warm body she slept with for a time.

He'd told her he was in danger of losing his heart, but he'd been wrong. He hadn't lost it. He knew exactly where it lay. In fourteen short days, his sexy redheaded duchess had managed something no other woman had. With her soft heart and scrupulous sense of responsibility, she'd somehow plucked that beating organ from his chest and held it in her hands.

Fuck yeah, he wanted it all. He wanted to wake up to her smile every morning for the rest of his life. He wanted Piper, all of her. And if he was going to win her, it was time to up his game.

"Talk to me, duchess. You're wound up like a spring, so don't try to tell me there's nothing bothering you."

Her gaze cut to his, and the smile she offered him was strained. "It's nothing I can't handle."

He shook his head and turned his eyes back on the roadway. "I don't doubt you could handle just about anything, but I'm here. I want to help."

"I told you, you're already helping enough."

He bit down on a scowling smirk. *By hiring her to create the calendar* was what she'd said the last time he'd tried to offer his help. "Then the problem is financial in nature?"

It must be. Thanks to his father's investigation, the minute details of her financial situation were the only question mark left, and it was only a matter of time before Jennings finagled a way into opening those records. Just as Wyatt had predicted, Walter Crowley had figuratively shit himself at learning Piper held a legit title in Europe. The savvy political advisor would eventually find a way to spin that tidbit to the campaign's advantage. In the meantime, he hadn't made much of a fuss over the Gold-Digging Baroness crap. Apparently, Walter was not a Cody Beckett fan. Who knew?

Her laugh was little more than a cough. "You're not going to let this go, are you?"

He shot her a quick glance and quirked a wry brow.

Irritation flashed in her eyes. "Very well. The problem isn't financial. Well, not really." Her sigh blew through the vehicle, and she shook her head. "My father's will included an old stipulation granting a large sum of money to his only sister, Claire. She passed a decade ago. Consequently, with his death, the bequest fell to Claire's heir, my cousin, Abigail."

He turned his head at the flat tone of her voice. "The cousin you said you've never been close to?"

She snorted. "Never been close is an understatement. She's a rather nasty woman. A snotty elitist who has absolutely no concern for the feelings of anyone she considers her inferior. Which is just about everyone." Her shoulders jerked in a shrug. "Anyway, either by fate or design, I'm not sure which, Da included a three-year grace period to disburse the funds owed her. If he hadn't, I would have been forced to sell the estate long ago. The money is due to Abigail no later than December thirty-first of this year."

"How much?" He met her gaze in a sidelong glance.

Her lips flattened with distaste. "Five-hundred-thousand pounds."

"Fuck. Me."

She actually smiled. "I know, right?" She dropped her head to the rest and turned to look out the windshield. "I've managed to put some funds aside in the last three years and, thanks to you and the Marauders, I'll have more than enough to pay Abigail off once the projects are complete."

His fingers tightened on the steering wheel. Such an easy fix and yet, she would never ask. "I'll have the balance transferred to your account as soon as we arrive at the manor."

She snapped her head around to squint at him. "No, you will not."

"Jesus, Piper. It's your money."

"Until I've completed the job, no, it isn't."

Damn stubborn woman. What difference did a week or two make? He frowned and she reached over the console to squeeze his forearm.

"I appreciate the sentiment, but the money isn't the problem." She returned her hand to her lap. "Because I didn't want to worry the others needlessly, Moira, Tilly, and Angus aren't aware of the deadline. Not telling them was a mistake on my part. Apparently, Abigail has become impatient. She showed up at the manor yesterday and made some threats based on a situation they aren't aware of. I'm here to put their minds at ease and set the record straight."

She said nothing more, and he was content to allow the silence to reign, for the moment. They were on her turf now, and would be for the next forty-eight hours. She'd handle the manor affairs as she saw fit, but that didn't mean he couldn't watch and listen. She may not like it, but if there was a way he could help, he would. In the meantime, he hoped witnessing her in her natural environment would provide the key to smashing through her self-erected barriers once and for all.

Twenty minutes later, she directed him off the highway and onto a country road. Several miles had passed before she shifted forward in her seat. She pointed at an opening in the stone fence running along the roadway to their left.

"This is it." Her breathy announcement was a mix of nerves and pride.

Wyatt slowed the Land Rover and turned through the open metal gate. On one of the thick pillars was an aged iron plaque, engraved simply *Delaney Manor - 1618*. The walls of Piper's beloved home could be seen through the foliage at the end of the long drive. At least thirty mature maple trees lined the gravel driveway like sentinels on watch. The earthy scent of fall drifted to his nostrils as they passed the acres of leaf strewn lawn between them and their destination. A white wooden fence followed the line of the drive off to the left. On the right, beyond a small stone wall, a pond glimmered in the early morning sunlight.

"There are no guests in residence at the moment, and none scheduled until the weekend. We are quite sensitive to the concept of privacy here at Delaney Manor. You'll be able to wander the estate freely without the worry of being recognized." She spoke without glancing his way and he shook his head.

He wasn't the one concerned with recognition, but he understood. She still saw their relationship as temporary. He meant to change her mind on that. In time, she would need to come to grips with his celebrity and his family name but, for now, he'd play duck and hide if it made her happy.

He shot her a grin. "You sound like a tour guide."

Her smile came easily for the first time in what seemed like days. "Sorry. Habit. A good portion of my responsibilities here at the manor are that of a tour guide. One with a title."

She turned to glance forward as they rounded a bend and the house came into view. Wyatt blew an appreciative whistle. Christ. The place belonged on a postcard.

A fountain sat at the center of a large parking area the width of the house. Rounding the fountain, he eased the vehicle to a stop. Elaborately carved pillars and a detailed archway framed the double wooden doors at ground level. Above the impressive entry, an intricate façade rose to the roof line above the third story.

The house was enormous. Seven tall chimneys rose from several steeply pitched rooflines. At least two dozen windows faced the three story structure, in a pale yellow stone faded with age. To the left, clinging vine covered an archway leading to a courtyard and a second wing not much smaller than the main section of the home.

"Bloody hell. Angus, are you kidding me!" Piper was out the door and hurrying beyond a wide opening in a row of high hedges before Wyatt had even shifted into park.

He left the bags in the back to follow her. The murmur of her voice grew louder as he walked around the graveled drive to an unattached, four-bay garage. The doors were open and several of the slots held vehicles. An elderly man Wyatt assumed to be Angus clung to the rungs of a tall ladder, rubbing the glass of a second floor window with a handful of newspaper.

Piper frowned up at him with her fisted hands on her hips. "What happened to the boy from town that Moira hired?"

The old guy didn't bother looking at her. He stretched out far enough even Wyatt winced.

"Young Frasier Cameron, you mean? He's a good lad. Works hard. But 'Tis a school day, don'tcha know." Angus scrubbed a spot on the glass before straightening. The ladder shifted beneath his weight.

She whimpered. "And this couldn't wait until he was done for the day?" She pressed a hand to her chest. "Please, Angus, come down before you slip and break your neck."

He twisted his head to glare at her from above. "I'm doin' me, job, lass. A job I've been after since long before you were a twinkle in yer Da's eye. I won't be slippin'." He shifted his gaze to Wyatt. "Who is this, then? The American footballer Moira's been croonin' over?"

Piper slapped a hand over her eyes before glancing back at Wyatt. Her eyes held a plea and her hand flopped to her side. He stepped forward as she returned her gaze to Angus on the ladder.

"Yes, this is Wyatt Hunter. And if you'll come down from there, I can introduce you proper."

Angus turned his scowl on Wyatt. "Women." He jerked his head in Piper's direction. "I changed this one's nappies, yet now that she's grown, she thinks I'm too feeble to do the job she pays me to do."

"That's not true," she grumbled.

"Ha!" The old man started down the rungs.

Her shoulders dropped in relief. "I would just prefer you keep your feet on the ground while doing the job I'm paying you to do."

"Is that so?" Angus reached the ground and turned to her with a squint. "Then you'll be tellin' me where you've hidden me chainsaw, lass. There be a branch danglin' over the nature path beyond the pond. We can't have it fallin' and conkin' a guest on the head, now, can we?"

She chewed her bottom lip.

Angus shot his eyes heavenward. "It's a bloody branch, lass. I'm not plannin' to trim the whole of the woods. A swipe or two, and the job is done."

She surprised Wyatt by laughing and stepping into Angus's arms. "I've missed you, cousin." After pressing a kiss to his cheek, she pulled her head back to grin at his huff of dismissal.

"Ach, now. You'll not be gettin' by me with a kiss and a grin. There's work to be done around the place, and someone has to do it." He shifted his gaze to Wyatt. "You're a strappin' young lad. You can help."

"Angus, Wyatt is a guest." Piper stepped clear of the old man's arms.

"I'm happy to help." Wyatt rubbed his hands together and winked at her. "I haven't had the chance to fire up a chainsaw in years."

Her jaw dropped open, but a grin transformed Angus's face. "There's a lad."

Wyatt smiled. "If you'll give me a few minutes, sir. I'd like to see to it our bags are settled inside first."

Angus nodded and turned back to the ladder.

Piper grabbed her cousin's arm. "If you promise to leave the ladder work for Frasier, I'll cough up the location of your power tools."

He grinned, obviously pleased with himself for winning her capitulation. "Sure, and I could do that."

She dropped her hand to her side with a sigh. "Check in the boot of the Woodie."

He jerked his gaze to a pre-war era wood-paneled station wagon parked inside the garage, then back. The grin slid from his face, replaced with impressed disbelief.

"Ach, 'Tis a clever lass ye are, hidin' me tools beneath me verra nose."

She laughed and batted her lashes. "I'll send this strapping lad out to you in a few minutes once I've introduced him to the ladies."

Busy retrieving the chainsaw from the trunk of the car, Angus waved them on without looking their way. Wyatt shook his head and chuckled as she linked her arm with his and led him toward the front of the house.

"I like him."

She grinned and tossed a glance over her shoulder. "So do I." She squeezed his arm. "It was very sweet of you to offer to help him."

"Sweet, hell. I was serious about getting my hands on his chainsaw."

"Ha. Ha." She rolled her eyes and he laughed.

"It's a guy thing. You wouldn't understand."

Her smile softened before she looked away. "Regardless, I'm in your debt. Over the past six months, he's suffered a few dizzy spells. He makes a stink about us hiding the more dangerous tools, but he understands why. He'll be pacing the path waiting for you so he can go out and do manly maintenance again."

Wyatt paused at the back of the Land Rover and turned her in his arms. "My pleasure, duchess." He pulled her close and took his time kissing her. The unevenness of her breathing pleased the shit out of him when he finally let her up for air. "I like having you in my debt. You can pay me back later tonight."

Her eyes, already a bit hazy, glittered with anticipation. "You've got yourself a deal."

She waited while he gathered their small carryon bags, then led him inside the house, pausing in the grand foyer. It was obvious, even to his untrained eye, whatever her father had spent on the renovations had been well worth the price tag. If the outside belonged on a postcard, the inside should've been featured in one of those fancy homes magazines.

Glossy wooden floors met classic wainscoting, intricate crown molding, and exposed dark wood beams. Furnished in a mix of old and new, each room they passed throughout the quiet house was more inviting than the next. He had yet to meet Moira or Tilly, but Piper loved them both. No doubt they would turn out to be as welcoming as Angus, and he could see why she'd made a success of her B&B. The combination of his beautiful duchess, her charming staff, and the superior lodgings would tempt anyone staying at her manor to book a return visit before leaving.

Passing beneath one of several archways, they left the long central hallway behind to enter the kitchen. Along with the ceilings, at least sixteen feet high and featuring exposed wooden rafters, the same warm stone from outside had been utilized to soften the look of the modern industrial appliances. Oversized windows let in plenty of natural light and the scent of baking bread made Wyatt's mouth water.

A sixty-something woman with salt and pepper curls clipped short wiped her hands on the apron wrapped around her plump waist, then opened the door of one of three ovens to check the contents. At the long granite island at the center of the room, a petite strawberry blonde leaned over a ledger, chewing on a pencil. She looked up, spotted Piper and him…and screamed.

Chapter 21

"I swear, luv, I don't know how you held out against him as long as you did."

Piper peeked around the refrigerator door to roll her eyes at Moira. "Come away from the window. They'll be back soon and he'll catch you watching."

"As if he's not used to women watching him." A delicate snort flared Moira's nostrils as she pivoted and returned to the island. "Besides, it's not like I can make a bigger fool of myself than I already have." She slid onto one of the stools and dropped her forehead to the granite surface with a groan.

Piper grinned, understanding completely. How often had her legs gone weak just from the sight of him? "I wouldn't worry about it, dearest. I'm sure you're not the first woman to scream when he walked into the room."

Moira rolled her head to the side to leer. "You can be such a bitch."

Piper laughed and selected a water bottle from the bottom shelf. The embarrassed look on Wyatt's face had been adorably sweet as Moira had followed up her scream by bolting from her stool to stare at him with her mouth gaping like a landed fish. Quite a feat, that. Piper couldn't recall the last time Moira had been rendered speechless. Probably because it had never happened.

But, sweeter yet, had been Wyatt's reaction to Tilly. Or perhaps the correct term would be bittersweet. For all practical purposes, the manor's housekeeper had raised Piper. While more than a little old school and forever conscious of appearances, Tilly wasn't blind. The moment the introductions were complete, she'd volunteered to show Wyatt to his room on the second floor and admonished Piper to take her bag to her own room...on the *third*.

Piper's chest heaved on a heartfelt sigh. She'd still been humming with anticipation over the debt she'd promised to repay that evening. Yet, neither by word nor action, had Wyatt challenged Tilly's rule by objecting to the sleeping arrangements. He had, however, met Piper's gaze as he'd followed the older woman from the kitchen, and the wry laughter in his eyes had nudged her heart ever so much closer to the edge of a cliff she was hoping to avoid.

"I really should hate you."

Piper blinked and mentally shook herself. Happy to ignore the manic thumping of her heart, she shut the refrigerator and turned to face her friend. "Whatever for?"

Moira straightened on the stool. "For bringing him here and ruining me."

Piper broke the seal on her water with a droll smirk. "You insisted, remember? And just how did I ruin you?"

Moira glanced out the window to where Wyatt had disappeared down the path into the woods with Angus nearly an hour ago, then back. "By dangling the perfect man in front of me when he's clearly not available. I'll never find a guy who matches up, no matter how hard I try."

Piper laughed and climbed onto the stool beside her.

Grinning, Moira took hold of her hand. "I'm thrilled for you, luv. You deserve the best and it looks as if you've found him."

Piper smiled but, even to her, it felt forced. She squeezed Moira's fingers. "Don't jump ahead of yourself. There is no guarantee this thing between us will last past the next couple of weeks."

"You said he asked for the time to see where things lead." Confusion creased Moira's brow.

"Yes, and things could lead straight into a brick wall."

And that brick wall wasn't something Piper wished to consider, not while she was having such a lovely time enjoying the moment. So far, she'd avoided that cliff, but she was definitely teetering on the edge. Like a moth to the flame, she couldn't resist Wyatt, and hadn't tried very hard. The day would come, however, when he'd be gone.

The truth was, while she was a baroness, Wyatt was American royalty. Their lives were worlds apart. With each consecutive day, the reality of their existences simmered closer to the surface. Sooner or later, they would each have to go back to their own. She belonged here in the wilds of northern England, and the shining spotlight of championship sports and high power politics were his home.

"Piper, you're looking at this all wrong."

She sighed and bent her head to rub her cheek against Moira's. "I love you, dearest, but I didn't fly all this way to talk about Wyatt and me." She turned her head as Tilly reappeared and attempted to clear the nerves from her throat. "I need to speak to you both about Abigail."

Tilly huffed and rounded the island to check the loaves of bread baking in the oven. "Claire Eaton was a lovely woman. Both she and your da would be horrified at the wretched brat that girl has become."

"I can't believe she had the gall to show up here with her estate agent." Moira's lips flattened in a scowl. "What the he…heck," she shot a wincing glance at her mother's back, "could she be thinking, presuming to have any say over the manor? The nerve of the woman."

"She has the gall and the nerve because she believes I won't have the funds in time."

Tilly straightened and slowly turned to face Piper. "In time for what, exactly?"

Glancing between Tilly and Moira's confused stares, Piper blew a guilty sigh. "I misled you all when I told you Da's will required the disbursement of the funds due Abigail *only* when they became available. The truth is, I have until the end of December, and my cousin knows it."

Hurt slowly filled Moira's blue eyes. Tilly didn't say a word but, then, she didn't need to. Her silence was more condemning than if she'd lashed out with angry accusations. The back of Piper's nose stung and her eyes began to mist as she pleaded for understanding.

"I'm sorry for not telling you the truth from the beginning, but I didn't want you to worry."

Tilly huffed and turned back to the oven. Snatching a pair of mitts from the hook beside the stove, she donned them to retrieve the bread. She placed the hot tray on the stovetop and shook her head. "The manor and its business may be your concern, young lady, but we're a family. Families share their worries and it lessens the load. I taught you better."

"Mum, don't." Moira slid a hand over Piper's and squeezed. "Can't you see she feels bad enough already?"

"Here now, what's this?"

Piper whipped her head around. Angus stood in the doorway with Wyatt behind him. She met his watchful gaze, then quickly spun away to swipe at the tears hovering on her lower lashes.

"What have ye done to make me lass cry?" Angus demanded of Tilly.

Tilly propped her fists on her ample hips and returned his glare. "I've done nothing, but your *lass* can't say the same."

Angus's eyes darkened and he slowly turned his head Wyatt's way. Horrified at the obvious direction of her cousin's thoughts, Piper slid from her stool. "Don't look at Wyatt, Angus. This is me." She shook her head. "It's all me."

Angus was no happier than Tilly to learn Piper had kept the deadline from them, but her promise to send Abigail and her estate agent packing tomorrow went a long way toward smoothing his ruffled feathers. He did, however, insist he be allowed to accompany her to Glasgow when she settled the debt with her cousin—the moment she returned to the manor after finishing in New York.

Wyatt remained silent throughout the discussion but, holding her hand in his as they explored the grounds after a dinner of sandwiches made of Tilly's fresh bread, he repeated his offer to transfer the balance of what he owed her immediately.

"That's not necessary."

"Maybe not, but the offer is still on the table."

"And I appreciate it." Sniffing the air, she changed the subject. "Is that sawdust I smell?"

He grinned. "I had to promise your cousin I'd let him take the Land Rover for a spin before he let me anywhere near his damn chainsaw. He's planning to take the SUV out in the morning to search for more *troublesome* limbs to bring down."

She laughed as she led him down the path toward her favorite spot on the estate.

"This place is beautiful, duchess. It's easy to see why you love it so much." Wyatt tucked her arm through his. "I'm curious. For a woman so protective of her privacy, it must have been difficult to open your home to strangers."

She looked away and her shoulders heaved with a sigh. "Actually, it isn't as bad as I'd feared it would be. At times, it's a lot of work, but that's to be expected." She smiled. "Tilly is in her element. She loves to cook and absolutely adores chatting with guests from all over the world, and Moira is surprisingly good at managing it all." A laugh gurgled in her throat. "Angus stays clear of the guests for the most part but, thankfully, those visitors who *have* crossed paths with him seem to have been charmed by his gruffness and straightforward speaking."

"It's probably the accent." Laughter sparkled in Wyatt's eyes as he attempted a Scottish burr. "An insult dropped on yer head is a lot easier ta swallow when it comes at ye in a lyrical tone." He cocked his head, looking quite proud of himself.

She batted her lashes. "I think you may be right about the accent, but you should probably keep your day job."

He squinted at her in mock affront. "Ach, yer a cruel lass, ye are."

She bared her teeth in a grin, but then cleared her throat. Bloody hell. He sounded suspiciously like her inner nag.

They walked together in companionable silence for a time, eventually leaving the open pathway behind for the wooded foot path circling a good portion of the estate's land. An occasional break in the thick forest offered a partial view back toward the shrinking manor house and formal gardens.

At one such clearing, he bumped his chin toward a dwelling far off in the distance. "What's that?"

"The estate's buildings include three free-standing cottages. They are spread out at one kilometer each, leading toward the coast. That one is the farthest from the main house. Some of our guests prefer a bit of solitude to the family style atmosphere of the manor's accommodations."

He glanced down at her, then back toward the cottage and other buildings dotting the land. "Shit, how many people does the estate sleep?"

"All together, the cabins will accommodate twenty-two and the bedrooms in the main house will hold another twenty-eight."

"Fifty?" He shook his head. "How the hell do you manage an enterprise of that size with such a small staff?"

"The simple answer is, we can't, so we don't bother to try. With careful scheduling and time management, and some help from the local villagers, we handle an average of twelve guests per weekend. Any more and we're stretched thin, plus we've found a consistent twelve guest schedule optimizes our income potential."

She grinned at a chipmunk, chattering at them from behind a thick tree root. "With very few exceptions, we're empty on Tuesdays and Wednesdays. Guests who wish to stay through mid-week are encouraged to book one of the cottages. Having the main house to ourselves two days a week allows us to catch up with inventories or cleaning, or to simply enjoy a lazy day without the concern of bumping into a stranger in the den or kitchen."

They rounded a bend and she tugged him toward a smaller trail leading off the main one into the thicket. "Come on."

"Where to?"

She dropped his arm as the well-traveled pathway narrowed rapidly and forced them to proceed single file. She spoke without looking back. "I'm going to show you the best view on the estate."

He chuckled and she briefly glanced over her shoulder. "What?"

Pointedly dropping his gaze to her bottom, he sucked air through his teeth. "I'm already looking at the best view."

Her laughter echoed through the trees as she led them through wild shrubs and beneath low-hung branches on a track she'd traversed a thousand times before. Here and there, the tall trees on each side of the trail gave way enough to allow dappled sunlight to dance like fairy points of light on the forest floor. Several kilometers later, the bramble and brush opened up onto a rocky outcropping and she drew a breath of sea air.

Below and to their left was the Atlantic. As far as the eye could see, sunlight played chase with the occasional chop of a wave. Up and down the stretch of rocky shoreline, sea fowl rode the current of the wind before dropping into the water to pick up dinner. Far off to their right, the pitched roofs of the manor house could be made out beyond the wild expanse of virgin forest.

"Wow." Wyatt wrapped his arms around her from behind, easing her back to his chest and pressing his cheek to hers.

She lay her arms over his at her waist and looked out over the familiar vista. "I told you."

He contracted his arms, pulling her into closer contact with his body, and she couldn't miss the interest pressing against her bum.

"It's not as fine a view as your ass in those jeans, but it's damn close."

She snickered and he paid her back by sliding his palm up to cover her left breast. The fire his touch always inspired flared in her belly. "This is my special place. My very favorite place in the world." He kneaded her gently, and she hummed her pleasure. "Da used to bring me here as a little girl and we would listen to the cliffs."

Wyatt rubbed his cheek against hers. "Listen to them?"

She smiled at the memory. "When the wind blows just right, it sounds as if the cliffs are singing. When I grew older, I came here to think and dream."

"What did you dream?" He dragged the pad of his thumb over the tight peak of her nipple.

"Oh," she said with a sigh. "The usual. That I could step off the cliffs and fly along with the gulls. Or that I would one day travel the world snapping my photographs." He closed his teeth over her earlobe. "Or that a handsome jock would appear one day, right on this spot," she exaggerated her natural shudder, "and make me shiver."

He chuckled and dropped kisses along her shoulder. "Tilly put me in a bedroom on the second floor."

She sucked air. "Yes, I know."

Freeing his other arm from beneath hers, he skimmed his hand down to cup her through her jeans. "Your bedroom is on the third."

"Unfortunately, yes." A shift of his hips proved his interest had grown as he touched her, and she wiggled her bottom just enough to make him sweat.

He hissed air through his teeth. "I'm feeling a little dizzy, duchess."

With the heel of his palm pressing against her heat and his talented fingers plucking at the hardened tip of her breast through her blouse, it

Mackenzie Crowne

was becoming increasingly difficult to concentrate. What had he said? Oh, right. Dizzy. She'd never been a fan of sex on a twigs and leaves bed but, in an emergency, she could be flexible.

She sighed and arched her neck to give his mouth better access. "I'm a little off-balance myself." And this encounter was rapidly becoming an emergency. If they hurried, the Rose Cottage couldn't be more than a ten-minute walk.

"It's Tuesday." He latched on to the tendon in her neck and she quivered beneath his open-mouthed kisses.

"Tuesday?" she groaned.

His pained laugh vibrated through her as he dropped his forehead to her shoulder. "You said there were no guests. I think we should check out the closest unoccupied cottage. We really should lie down until the dizziness passes."

Spinning around, she jammed her fingers into his hair and kissed him soundly. She grinned as she pulled back. "Why, you lovely man. You read my mind."

Chapter 22

Piper ejected Tuck's SD card from the slot in her laptop and inserted Wyatt's. He and Angus were off somewhere chasing manly pursuits with the chainsaw. Hopefully, they'd find something to keep them busy long enough to miss Abigail's visit this morning. Piper wouldn't mind skipping it herself. Time spent with her cousin normally ended in a bout of high blood pressure followed by a migraine.

To keep both from overtaking her as she waited, Piper had spent the last hour organizing the shots she'd be turning over to V at Friday afternoon's meeting. With little over a week to go in both contracts, the work was pretty much done. She was more than satisfied with the results of her labor, and expected Caroline Wainwright and the Marauders to be so as well.

There were still two shots to get for Wyatt's calendar. She'd finished the photos for every month but January and February, and was scheduled to shoot Jamal Knight's Mr. January later in the week. She'd saved Wyatt's February Super Bowl extravaganza session for last, and planned to take her time next week to produce the perfect image.

Her hotel suite was booked through a week from Monday but, after that, she just wasn't sure. They hadn't discussed the details of how things would work between them going forward, but access to each other would be greatly diminished once she'd returned to the manor full-time. Sure, she'd be flying in for his games, at least for the next two months, but weekend stopovers in random cities wasn't the same as curling up together every night.

He'd said he wanted to see where things led. If the anxious longing squeezing her heart at the thought of saying good-bye to him every Sunday evening was an indication, she'd already tumbled from that cliff she'd been trying to avoid.

She shoved aside the nausea the knowledge produced and eyed the clock on the mantel. Abigail was due to arrive in a half hour. Once she'd set her cousin straight, Piper didn't want anything interrupting the hours she and Wyatt had left here at the manor. Refocusing on her laptop screen, she was soon immersed.

Back and forth she went. Keep this shot, delete that. As incredibly photogenic as Wyatt was, V would have plenty of choices for her Fab Five project.

Some time later, Piper stilled her fingers over the keyboard. Her throat tightened as she stared at the photograph she'd snapped of Wyatt with his sister and niece. With a quiet sigh, she studied the shot she'd taken in Wyatt's den the afternoon of Richard Hunter's presidential announcement.

Everything, from the lighting to the composition, and especially the models, called to her as an artist *and* a woman. For obvious reasons, the shot could never be made public, but she couldn't bring herself to delete it, either. Perhaps she'd gift Megan with a print. One she could display somewhere in her private quarters.

With an internal nod, Piper saved the shot to her hard drive.

"I was quite disappointed you weren't out front to meet us when we arrived, Cousin. It's been ever so long since we've had the chance to spend any quality time together."

Piper jumped at Abigail's deceptively soft purr which, of course, was completely at odds with the dislike shining in her china blue eyes. Piper lifted a brow at the ridiculous implication that either of them had ever willingly sought the other's company. The fraudulent inference was no doubt for the benefit of the man behind her cousin.

Piper closed her laptop on the den's small desk and stood. Leave it to Abigail to find an estate manager who more closely resembled Jude Law than the slick car salesman one normally associated with real estate hacks. Mr. Tall, Dark, and Handsome carried the requisite briefcase, but the tailored and obviously expensive suit would have placed him at home in any of the world's most powerful boardrooms. He remained in the den's open archway, his expression blank as his gaze drifted from Piper to Abigail and back.

Piper ignored him to turn to her cousin. "Please. You can hardly stand to be in the same room with me and, believe me, the sentiment is mutual."

With the sham that they shared anything but animosity exposed, Abigail gave up the act. "How true." She wandered farther into the room and trailed her fingertips along the edge of the distressed wooden mantel. "For three years, I've put up with your excuses and have yet to see a pound of my mother's inheritance." Selecting the smallest of the decoratively displayed white enamel pitchers, she studied the delicate pottery. Her nose wrinkled in distaste, and she replaced the antique on the mantel. Dusting her hands, she faced Piper. "Obviously, you don't have the cash, but you do have this drafty old house."

The estate manager cleared his throat before Piper could suggest Abigail bugger off.

"I apologize for intruding on your time, Baroness Delaney. My name is Broderick Faulkner."

Bloody hell. Piper snapped her head around. Proper etiquette demanded she acknowledge the man with a polite smile, but she couldn't manage to dredge one up. Her temporary paralysis had as much to do with name recognition as it did the odd sensation she was staring into the eyes of a predatory jungle cat.

Literally. His watchful, unblinking eyes were a beautiful, feline gold.

Broderick Faulkner. The man was no common estate agent. Even if Piper hadn't received his phone call shortly after Da's death, she would recognize his name. Anyone who had dealings in the north of England would. And now that she'd met him, it was easy to see why the wealthy land-developer had gained a reputation for succeeding where his competition had failed. Clearly, tenacity played a role, but any opponent he faced would be at a distinct disadvantage while trapped by the glow of his catlike eyes.

She mentally shook her head at the rare flight of fancy and dipped her chin in greeting. "Mr. Faulkner, I'm afraid you've arrived here under a false assumption. As I mentioned in our previous communication, Delaney Manor is not now, nor was it ever, for sale."

"Broderick, please." He flicked an accusing gaze at Abigail. No emotion showed on his handsome face as he looked back. "And if that's the case, then I definitely owe you an apology. I was led to believe you and your cousin were on the same page when it came to the sale of the estate."

Piper met her cousin's unhappy sneer. "Abigail and I have rarely been on the same page about anything."

"Then you have my money?" Abigail demanded, dropping any pretense of civility.

"I will." Piper smiled widely and, bugger, did it feel good to watch the color drain from her cousin's face.

Fury replaced the usual sour countenance Abigail reserved for anyone she couldn't manipulate into giving her what she wanted. "You had better. If I don't have the funds in my hand at one second past midnight on December thirty-first, my lawyers will tear you to shreds. When I'm through with you, your precious estate will wind up on the auction block and sell for a fraction of what you seem to believe it's worth."

Broderick lifted a brow as if surprised by the vehemence spewing from Abigail's mouth. Piper almost felt sorry for the guy. He wasn't the first to be fooled by her cousin's piquant blonde looks and soft voice.

The smile he offered Piper didn't come close to reaching his eyes. "I'm sorry to have wasted your time, and mine. If you'll excuse me…"

Surprisingly, Abigail had the grace to look a bit nervous as she turned to Broderick. With good reason. The tick in his clenched jaw clearly pronounced his displeasure.

"If you wouldn't mind, Broderick, I really must powder my nose before we go. I'm sure Baroness Delaney will see you to the foyer."

Anything that would expedite Abigail's departure worked for Piper. She nodded and held out her hand.

Broderick pinned Abigail with a stern stare. "Be in the limo in five minutes or find your own way back to Glasgow."

Piper bit down on a snicker as Abigail hurried toward the bathroom off the kitchen, which happened to be the opposite direction from the angry man framed by the pale stones of the den's archway. He stepped backward, then waited for Piper to pass by him as she entered the hallway. He matched her stride toward the front of the house and the foyer. Once there, he faced her and the frustration in his eyes was a point in his favor.

"I apologize again. Although I can't deny my interest in the estate still stands, especially the southern section of the shoreline I mentioned when we last spoke, I'm not a man who enjoys wasting his time." His lips flattened as he glanced down the empty hallway. "Any more than I appreciate being played for another's benefit."

Piper nodded and mentally wished Abigail a lovely ride back to the city. What she could possibly have hoped to gain by facilitating the sale of Delaney Manor, Piper wasn't sure but, in the process, Abigail had tugged on a tiger's tale. One whose cage she now had to share for the long one hundred-twelve kilometers between the manor and Glasgow.

The golden glow in Broderick's eyes softened as he reached into the inner pocket of his suit jacket. "I understand completely why you aren't anxious to part with Delaney Manor. The estate is beautiful. I'd have a difficult time letting go if it were mine." He retrieved a business card and held it out. "The financial concerns between you and your cousin are none of my business but, if the funds you're counting on should fall through, I hope you'll give me a call. I can guarantee the project I have in mind for the land will be completed with care and an understanding for the distinctiveness of the area."

With the shake of her head, she took his card. Holding it up, she smiled. "Thank you, but please. Don't hold your breath." She blinked as the stern lines of his handsome face fell away with his easy laughter.

"Ach. Have we missed ye tossin' yer bratty cousin out the door, lass?"

Piper was still smiling as she turned to find Angus standing behind her with Wyatt at his side. He surprised her by stepping forward and draping his arm over her shoulders.

"Wyatt Hunter?" The land developer lifted a brow, his gaze bouncing between Wyatt and her.

"Yes, and you are?"

Although she was secretly thrilled at the clear possessiveness in Wyatt's action and tone, Abigail was still in the house. Piper bit back a wince and made the introductions. The two men spent the next few minutes speaking football with Broderick admitting he had an aunt in Queens who was apparently Wyatt's biggest fan. All the while, she chewed her bottom lip and watched the hallway for sign of her cousin.

To Piper's knowledge, Abigail didn't know a thing about American sports but, bloody hell. Richard Hunter was a worldwide figure, and her cousin wasn't stupid. Even if she didn't recognize Wyatt physically, she was bound to put two and two together should she hear any part of the conversation between the two. As luck would have it, she emerged through the den archway just as Wyatt gave Broderick the name of a contact at the sports complex.

"Tell Aunt Beatrice to call that number. Doug will make arrangements for her to watch the game from a Marauders' skybox set aside for friends of the players."

Piper bit back a groan as Abigail headed straight for the celebrity in the manor's foyer.

"Why, heavens, how awful I missed the introductions." Angus's scowl didn't faze her a bit. She batted her lashes and held Wyatt's gaze. "It's an honor to meet you, Mr. Hunter. I'm Abigail. Piper's cousin."

Angus had never suffered from a case of tact. He snorted loudly, his gaze running up and down Abigail's steel-gray silk dress. "More like a piranha in a fancy frock."

God forgive her, Piper had to bite the inside of her lip to keep from laughing as Wyatt looked down his nose at her cousin, then turned back to Broderick as if Abigail hadn't said a word.

"Beatrice is welcome to bring a guest, of course."

Angus enjoyed a healthy snicker at the flags of obvious outrage coloring Abigail's cheekbones. As she stomped out the door without waiting for Broderick, Angus asked of no one in particular, "Was it somethin' I said?"

* * * *

Five days later, Piper punched in the code and let herself inside the private lift to Wyatt's loft condo. She tightened her fingers around the handle of the bag she carried and grinned. Before leaving the manor last Wednesday evening, she'd stood at her dresser, studying the contents of her underwear drawer as she recalled Wyatt's reaction to her missing knickers. In the end, she hadn't selected a single piece because, really. Why mess with a good thing? But she hadn't been able to resist the sexy black bra and panty set she'd spotted in a window downtown, and couldn't wait to experience Wyatt's reaction when she modeled the matching garter belt and hose.

Tonight was a celebration, after all. Jamal had proven an easy subject to work with. His Mr. January photo was safe and secure on the SD card in her bag. Her part in the project was nearly complete and, according to Caroline who'd seen the photos Piper had already submitted, the calendar was going to be a huge success.

Wyatt's Mr. February shot still remained, of course, but Piper had a few ideas on how to present him, and couldn't wait until tomorrow afternoon to get started.

With yesterday's bye, the Marauders' players didn't have today off as they did most Mondays. She didn't have a lot of time to prepare before Wyatt was due home from the complex, but with the sensual anticipation running through her veins, that wouldn't be a problem. The echo of her laughter trailed her as the doors of the private elevator whooshed open beneath the metal staircase and she stepped into the loft.

Her laughter cut off on a stilted scream, and she stumbled to a stop. Heart in her throat, she cast her mind about for a weapon to defend herself against the huge bald man leaning against the kitchen island. Nothing came to mind. Certainly nothing strong enough to take down a man who looked like he could bench press half the Marauders' offensive line without breaking a sweat.

"Have a seat, *Baroness*," someone other than Mr. Tree Trunk Arms demanded.

She yelped and jerked her head toward the living area. She didn't recognize the speaker, an older man in a wrinkled suit and a bow tie.

Baroness? What the…?

Relief crashed into her and loosened the muscles in her legs as she spotted Wyatt sitting on the couch. Her shoulders sagged beneath her shuddering sigh. "Bloody hell, Wyatt. Your friends frightened the crap out of me."

The instant heat of her blush wasn't surprising, but Wyatt wasn't amused by her slip of the tongue as she'd expected. With his legs spread wide and his elbows braced on his knees, he jerked his chin toward the older man who had spoken.

"Piper, this is Walter Crowley. My father's campaign manager."

She blinked at the sound of her name on Wyatt's lips. He'd spoken it so rarely, his use of it was jarring, but he'd made it clear he and his father weren't close. She supposed the use of her nickname in this situation wouldn't be appropriate.

"How do you do, Mr. Crowley?"

He said nothing in reply. No greeting. He simply watched her with intent gray eyes.

"And Devon Jennings. He also works for the campaign."

She returned her gaze to Wyatt, disturbed by the flat tone of his voice, but he wasn't looking at her. She shifted her focus to the bald guy. Jennings didn't bother acknowledging her, either, and the hairs on her arms stood on end. She slowly dragged her gaze from the bald man's predatory stare.

"What's going on, Wyatt?"

"We have a few questions, Ms. Darrow." Mr. Crowley indicated the chair across from the couch. "Have a seat."

On shaking knees, she lowered to the edge of the cushion and set the bag of underwear on the floor beside her feet.

"Wyatt?" For a moment, he held her gaze and she silently pleaded with him to tell her what was wrong. She could think of only three people he cared enough about to put that stark look in his eyes and, as he lowered his head to stare at a spot between his shoes, the bottom dropped out of her stomach. "Oh, dear God. Not Mandy?"

Wyatt jolted as if he'd been lashed by a live wire. Before she could push to her feet to go to him, Mr. Crowley stepped in front of her. He held out a photograph.

"The digital signature on the bottom left corner is yours, is it not?"

Piper didn't bother looking for the scrolling initials she knew would be there. The image itself proclaimed the photograph as hers. She snatched the 8x10 glossy from the man's fingers as her throat threatened to close. "Where did you get this?"

"I'm asking the questions. You're answering."

She shook her head and stared at the photo of Mandy as her Unkie White read to her. "It's mine."

A harsh breath heaved in her chest as she dragged her gaze back to Wyatt's face, then wished she hadn't. His eyes were no longer stark. They were full of heat, but not the sensual burn she'd come to know and crave. His eyes were hot with condemnation as he dropped his gaze to the photo, then lurched to his feet and crossed to the bar.

As he slammed ice into a tumbler, she turned back to Walter Crowley. "I don't understand. How did you obtain a copy of this?"

"Richard Hunter's campaign was contacted by The *London Bugle News* an hour ago. As a courtesy, they provided him with the photograph they'll be running in the morning along with an article concerning his biological granddaughter."

She couldn't breathe and, when she turned to Wyatt, she wasn't sure she ever would again. His face held no emotion. Not the usual joy and pleasure for life that made him the man he was, or even fury that the prediction he'd spoken only days ago would soon come to pass.

"Why?" He leaned both palms on the bar top, and his angry gaze bore into hers. "Damn it, I offered to transfer the funds you needed. Twice." He shoved straight, not waiting for an answer. Self-disgust twisted his features as he turned his back on her as if he hated himself for even asking.

Even without the numbness spreading out from her heart to her limbs, she was too shocked to stand. He thought *she* was responsible for the photograph finding its way into the filthy hands of the *Bugle*'s slimy owner?

"Wyatt. I didn't do this." She shook her head and fought back the tears that demanded release. "I wouldn't."

He ignored her plea as Walter Crowley slid the photograph from her lifeless fingers. The campaign manager slapped the glossy sheet against his thigh and his cold gray eyes sliced into her like knives. "I understand you owe a large sum of money through an inheritance obligation."

The words, spoken in accusation, slammed into her like stones. A silent cry lodged in her throat and stole what was left of her breath. Her aching heart soundly rejected the notion as a cruel joke, but there was only one place Walter Crowley could have gotten that information.

Her horrified gaze jerked to Wyatt. She stared at the rigid lines of his back, mentally willing him to turn around and tell her this was all a mistake. But that wasn't going to happen. She'd find no refuge with Wyatt, not when he believed her capable of such a heinous act.

Good Lord, didn't he know her? The man had spent every spare moment of the last few weeks laughing with her or whispering darkly sensual secrets in her ear. The nights had passed with her wrapped in his arms, held so closely she'd forgotten where she ended and he began.

But she remembered now.

Blinded by Wyatt's irresistible smiles, his sweet gestures, and his pretty words about moving forward, she'd forgotten that first and foremost, Wyatt Hunter was a player. A champion, just like Cody Beckett. For men like them, competition was life and winning was the only option. Everything he'd said or done had been nothing more than a means to an end. With blind focus and cold calculation, he'd easily claimed what he'd been after, getting her into his bed, while her foolish heart had been slipping ever closer toward that precarious cliff she'd rightly feared.

A band of pain compressed her chest. How bloody stupid of her to have fallen in love with a man incapable of the emotion.

A toxic mix of shock, humiliation, and hurt roiled in her belly. She swallowed against the noxious brew burning its way past her esophagus. The air in the condo was set at a comfortable seventy-two degrees, as usual, but chills raced over her skin as she faced Walter Crowley once more.

He tucked the photo into a file on the counter. "I hope the one hundred thousand pounds the *Bugle* paid you was worth it." The snap of his briefcase latches closing made her jump. "But you should know, making enemies with the Hunter family is not a healthy way to live."

She stiffened. It would be easy enough to prove she hadn't received a shilling from London's top gossip rag, but she didn't bother suggesting the campaign manager check the facts. What would be the point? Wyatt's behavior proved he didn't think much of her integrity, a deal killer for any future they may have had. In the meantime, if she wasn't mistaken, she'd just been threatened by the right-hand man of the possible next president.

Fear overtook her despondency and insisted she get out of there as fast as humanly possible. "Are you threatening me?"

"I would never threaten anyone, *Baroness*. Especially not in front of witnesses." He smiled for the first time since she'd walked into the condo. It wasn't an improvement.

"Walter."

Piper jerked at the sound of Wyatt's softly spoken admonishment.

The campaign manager shrugged. "You will be allowed no further contact with anyone in the Hunter family, Baroness, nor will you have access to anything involving the campaign. I suggest you get on a plane and return to England with all due haste, and count yourself lucky myself or Mr. Jennings haven't been left to mete out justice."

He said nothing further, and she blindly collected the bag at her feet. It took every ounce of energy Piper could call upon to stand. She couldn't feel her legs and prayed they held her as she crossed to the elevator. Stepping inside, she turned and pressed the button for the ground level exit. Though pride insisted she not look his way, her mutinous gaze found Wyatt's tensed profile, and the blessed numbness encasing her heart was no match for the jagged fissure of despair tearing it in two.

Outside, she staggered to the corner and tossed the bag of underwear in a public trash can before hailing a cab. Arriving at the manor the next morning, exhausted and grimy, she was rocked by the knowledge she hadn't actually known what a broken heart was until now.

Chapter 23

Piper stared at the open page on her laptop screen and dragged in practiced, even breaths. For three years, she'd been working toward the day her bank balance would top the figure needed to buy her life back. Yesterday, she'd reached that seemingly impossible goal, but only for a brief time.

Moira had nearly had a coronary upon learning Piper had rejected Wyatt's transfer for the balance they'd agreed upon, but she couldn't, in good conscience, accept payment for a job she hadn't completed. And the thought of taking money from a man who believed the worst of her left her skin crawling with shame.

In truth, she'd been surprised to find the transaction pending in her account, and not just because of the way things had ended between them. Considering the wild frenzy of press over the last four days covering the story of Richard Hunter's secret granddaughter, she was amazed Wyatt had time to think of anything else.

Backing out of the page, she shut down the machine. She rolled the cord and stored both it and the laptop in the outer pocket of her largest camera bag. A glance around her bedroom brought a sigh as she pushed to her feet. Hefting the strap onto her shoulder, she snatched her jacket and a small suitcase from the chair as she left the room.

Stealth and quite a bit of luck delivered her to the back walkway without the anticipated run-in with Moira or Tilly. As much as she loved them both, she was too heartsick to maintain a stiff upper lip under their constant fussing any longer. And, after today, she was going to need some time and privacy to mourn on her own.

Angus wore a disapproving scowl as Piper slipped into the garage. She shook her head and loaded her things into her SUV. "Don't look at me like that, Angus. I know what I'm doing."

He snorted. "I'm not so sure about that. Runnin' instead of givin' himself the chance to come around smacks of cowardice, and a coward is somethin' ye've never been."

She blinked back the tears that remained right there at the surface. "Come around to what? To the realization he doesn't think enough of me to know I never would have done what I've been accused of doing?"

His bushy brows met over the bridge of his nose like an angry caterpillar. "I've known ye since you were no more than a sprite, lass. Think ye, I can't tell ye've lost yer heart to the big Yank? Never once, when ye were looking at that bounder Beckett, did yer eyes come alive the way they did whenever they landed on yer American footballer." Her eyelids slid shut, but Angus wasn't finished. "From what ye told me, the wee girl is his heart. Can ye blame him for goin' a bit bonkers in the circumstances?"

With a sigh, she shook her head. "No, I can't, but neither should I have to plead with the man I love to get him to listen or to believe in me."

He dragged a callused palm over his jaw. "Aye, yer right on that account."

She stepped forward and wrapped her arms around his waist. He accepted her squeeze with one of his own. "I'm doing what needs to be done, just as I always have." She pulled free and slid into the SUV's driver seat. "Tell Moira and Tilly I'll be in touch when I know where I'll be."

He nodded and squinted as she started the engine. "Ye be careful out there, and give me best to yer bitch of a cousin."

She smiled and, tapping her fingertips to her lips, she blew him a kiss before guiding the vehicle down the drive. There wasn't a soul to be seen as she turned onto the road in the direction of Glasgow. Less than five minutes into her drive, she eyed the narrow lane veering off toward the coast. Biting her lip, she continued straight ahead and told herself the memory of standing on her cliffs with Wyatt had nothing to do with her reluctance to return there, even to say good-bye. The plain truth was, a nostalgic side trip to bid farewell to her special place would only make the task ahead of her more difficult.

She arrived in Glasgow an hour prior to her first appointment. With the famous Buchanan Quarter just around the corner, she killed some time window shopping, but still arrived at Broderick Faulkner's swanky offices thirty minutes before expected. Whether he was simply efficient, or afraid she'd change her mind if left to wait, Broderick cleared his office of the half dozen employees he'd been meeting with to devote his time to Piper and their business.

Her hand shook as she scrawled her signature over the papers that would shrink Delaney Manor's land mass by close to a third but, all in all, she'd made the best deal she could under the circumstances. The previous Baronesses might haunt her for turning over a large chunk of the estate for Broderick's exclusive golf resort, but she'd had little choice. With less than three months to the deadline, she was forty thousand pounds short with no viable prospects for closing the gap. To save the whole, she'd been forced to sacrifice a piece.

The fact that Broderick's piece included her beloved cliffs was just another bruise on her already battered heart.

The successful land-developer had pulled some strings with his banking friends. Before the ink was dry on the contract, Piper's bank balance had swelled more than ten times over. She'd never have another financial worry in her life, and Tilly, Moira, and Angus would be free to run the B&B as they saw fit without worries over the bottom line. There was one other small silver lining in this whole twisted nightmare. Abigail would never see the healthy commission Faulkner had promised her in return for her so-called assistance in convincing Piper to accept his deal.

Twenty minutes later, satisfaction tempered the crushing sadness in Piper's heart as she stood in Abigail's living room.

Her cousin looked up from the half million-pound cashier's check, eyes wide with disbelief. "Where did you get the funds?"

"Actually, I have you to thank for the source." A surge of satisfaction rushed through Piper's veins. "Broderick Faulkner said to say thank you, by the way. He'd basically given up on the idea of convincing me to sell. Thanks to your little power play last week, he and I concluded the deal on our own and he saved that hefty commission you had demanded."

Abigail's jaw dropped open, but she quickly covered her surprise with a scornful laugh. "Oh, how the mighty do fall. So much for your precious legacy."

Piper started to turn, but her cousin wasn't finished.

"But I suppose you had little choice." She sniggered. "It's not as if your wealthy boyfriend was about to cough up the cash you owed me. Especially with him dealing with the craziness over your *lovely* photo of his retarded niece."

Piper would have been sickened by her cousin's vicious and blatantly bigoted comment if she weren't struggling to breathe. "How did *you* know I took the photograph?"

Up came Abigail's chin. "Don't be dense, Cousin. The signature on the bottom of the photo was obviously yours."

Piper curled her fingers into fists as her suspicions were confirmed. She nodded, when what she wanted to do was slap the sneering smile from her cousin's face.

"You're right. The signature was mine, but the photo the *Bugle* ran was blown up, cutting it out. Only someone who had access to the original would know the signature had been there."

The sneer slid from Abigail's face, replaced with her laughter. "Well, aren't you the clever little sleuth. You really shouldn't leave your laptop lying around where just anyone might come along and learn your secrets."

The breath clogged in Piper's throat as she remembered leaving her laptop in the den to escort Broderick to the foyer. Abigail hadn't the time to snoop through the many files it contained, but she wouldn't have had to. From what Piper recalled, the photo had been right there on the screen when she'd closed the laptop. A cell phone was all her cousin would have needed to capture the telling image.

Bloody hell. Thanks to Abigail's lack of respect for anyone's privacy, combined with her vicious nature, Piper's world had been ripped apart. Her heart had been broken, and she'd given up a part of her soul when she'd signed over the cliffs. Even worse was the horror and heartache Wyatt and Megan were no doubt going through. He was right. There were bigots in the world like Abigail who would look at Mandy and find her wanting for no other reason than their high opinion of themselves.

"I don't understand you, Abigail." Piper glanced around the open floor plan of the flat located in one of the most expensive neighborhoods in Glasgow. "You've been given everything. Looks, brains, wealth, but it's like you're not happy unless you're making someone else miserable with your schemes."

"What would you know about it, *Baroness*? You walk around with your nose in the air, believing you're better than everyone else." Flags of angry color stood out on her cheekbones, growing brighter with every word. A deep breath seemed to drag her back from the edge of hysteria but, when she smiled, there was no humor involved. "But you don't seem to be able to hold on to a man, do you? A simple whisper in the right ear and Wyatt Hunter dropped you faster than one of his footballs."

A chill ratcheted down Piper's spine at the hatred in her cousin's voice. "If you were angry with me, why involve an innocent little girl who's never hurt a soul? Why not announce to the world the Gold-Digging Baroness had snagged herself another athlete?"

"You think I wouldn't have if I'd had the time to scroll through your laptop to find a photo of you and your cold American jock? There's no money in hearsay, Cousin. The rags only pay for proof."

Disgusted by her cousin's bald greed and heartsick over the fallout, Piper shook her head. "Enjoy your inheritance, *Cousin*. You may, however, want to set aside a few thousand pounds to hire yourself a bodyguard. It's only a matter of time before Richard Hunter's political machine learns the name of the *Bugle*'s source."

The color leached from Abigail's face, and the first genuine smile in days tugged at Piper's lips. "Oh, and Angus sends his regards."

* * * *

Wyatt called the snap and rolled back from the line to survey the field. It had been said of him, by both fan and detractor alike, that his greatest asset as a QB was his situational awareness. Like a gift from nature, that awareness could be sharpened with determination and focus, but it wasn't something a player could be taught. One either had it or he didn't.

For Wyatt, the gift manifested itself as a subtle recalculation of time. Things simply seemed to slow whenever the ball was snapped, allowing him the opportunity to discern the patterns playing out in front of him and choose the most advantageous option available. So far today, the slowing had increased to a sluggish crawl. A couple of times, he'd been tempted to stroll through the slow motion slideshow going on around him and walk into the end zone. After six days of nothing more than an hour or two of fitful sleep per night, the ability to maintain his concentration on such a level was as welcome as it was surprising.

Thirty yards downfield, Tuck lifted his hand, signaling Wyatt on the breakdown by Buffalo's rookie safety. The world snapped back into real time as Wyatt released the ball in a spiraling bullet. He pumped his fist as six more points appeared on the board, and accepted the celebratory congratulations of his teammates and the coaching staff as he trotted from the field.

He shed his helmet and dropped to the bench as the kicking team took the field. Today was living proof the superstitious crap he'd followed for years was nothing more than fucking bullshit. There had been no pre-game visits to his lucky charm's office or last-minute phone calls to her cell. Or, as had been the case more recently, no scouring the sideline for a deceitful redhead with a fine ass.

He and the boys had taken the field and blown out Buffalo all on their own.

"Where's Piper? I haven't seen her all day."

The hair on his arms stood on end. Shit. Had he conjured her name with his thoughts? He shot Kip an annoyed glance. "She's done."

Surprise lifted the young man's brows. "What do you mean, she's *done*?"

"I mean, she won't be back. Your bodyguard skills are no longer needed." Wyatt shifted his gaze back to the field. "You're blocking my view, kid."

Kip danced to his right. "This week or ever?"

"Ever." Wyatt ignored the dull throb of his heart.

"But she's this year's lucky charm."

Wyatt grunted. "Not anymore."

"Why not?"

"Christ, Kip. Will you get the fuck out of my way?" Wyatt leaned to his left to follow the action on the field, but the move was purely for show. Out of the corner of his eye, he witnessed the flash of embarrassed hurt on Kip's face before he wandered down the line in search of safer ground.

Lashing out with his foot, Wyatt kicked the edge of the empty bench beside him. It crashed over, causing several milling members of the offense to scramble clear of harm. Sam Fitzpatrick looked up from his tablet to send Wyatt a questioning glance, but said nothing. Tuck wasn't as circumspect. He slid onto the bench at Wyatt's side.

"Damn, Wyatt. Did you forget to apply your hemorrhoid cream?"

"Not funny, Tuck." Wyatt kept his eyes on the field.

"Have you called her?"

"Jesus." Wyatt squeezed the bridge of his nose. V had asked the same question yesterday and now Tuck. Which was exactly the reason a man shouldn't bring a woman to meet his friends. Inevitably, they got involved and, when the relationship exploded after the woman turned out to be a lying bitch with a financial agenda, they felt entitled to a say in the matter.

"CC's worried. She hasn't been able to reach her."

Wyatt snorted. "You can tell CC not to stress it. Piper's a big girl. Trust me, she knows *exactly* what she's doing and how to take care of herself."

Tuck dropped his elbows to his knees and nodded briskly as Buffalo's quarterback went down beneath a vicious sack. He smiled at the defensive line's chest bumping celebration. "CC says there is no way Piper sold you out. I don't know the lady all that well, but I'm having a hard time believing it, too."

Wyatt slowly turned his head. He met Tuck's gaze, and swore beneath his breath. "Neither you, nor your wife, are privy to the details or dynamics of what went down between me and the…lady. Because I consider you a friend, I won't tell you to stay the fuck out of my business, but I will ask that you do us both a favor and steer clear of the subject of Piper Darrow."

Tuck nodded and rose to his feet. The usual humor in his eyes was nowhere to be seen. "No problem, my friend, but for this. You've got more natural talent for sizing up a person's character and getting it right than just about anyone I know. Yet, like the rest of us, you didn't pick up a single negative vibe from her. Not until that rag in London somehow got involved. The same rag that dragged her through the mud three years ago, in case you hadn't noticed."

He cocked his head, and the intensity in his eyes deepened. "Can you really see the proper Baroness of Delaney playing footsie with the same people who staked out her estate and made her life miserable?"

Unease tightened Wyatt's shoulders. Considering CC's friendship with Piper, of course Tuck would know her history. A history she could have fabricated to cover her true agenda. Christ, what other explanation could there be? She'd fucking stood in front of him with understanding in her eyes and promised the knowledge of Mandy's true parentage would not come from her, but she'd also admitted the photograph was hers. If she hadn't given it to the fuckers at the *Bugle*, how had they gotten their hands on it?

His scowl must have broadcast his train of thought, because Tuck shook his head.

"If Piper really is a gold-digging bitch who fucked you on the off chance of discovering your father's secrets so she could sell them to the highest bidder, she missed her calling. She belongs in Hollywood."

Several hours later, the questions Tuck had triggered multiplied exponentially thanks to a two-day old e-mail from Wyatt's accountant. Slumped on the couch in his loft, he stared blindly at the highlight reel playing on the big screen.

Even if everything else Piper had ever told him was complete bullshit, her debt to Abigail was legit. With his own eyes, he'd witnessed Angus Graham's furious reaction to learning about the looming deadline, and Jennings had inadvertently verified her honesty on the subject by producing her financials this past Friday morning.

If the balances listed were correct, and Jennings wouldn't have presented Wyatt with a copy if he wasn't absolutely sure of the validity of his illegal snooping, Piper was still forty thousand pounds short of telling her cousin to go fuck off.

Christ. She'd had her reputation dragged through the mud and set aside her photography, a career she clearly enjoyed, to save Delaney Manor. He'd seen first-hand what the estate meant to her. More than a roof over the heads of those she loved, the buildings and grounds skimming the rocky coast near the Scottish border were her heart, her legacy, just as she'd claimed.

So, why the hell would she deny his transfer of the remaining funds?

He kept coming back to the same question. Why would a woman willing to sell out a special needs kid reject payment for a job she'd actually done when she clearly needed the money?

Sitting forward, he snatched his cell from the coffee table and punched in a number. Before the first ring had ended, the call was answered simply, "Yes."

"This contact at the *Bugle*. Did he specifically name Baroness Delaney as the source of the photo?"

A hesitation, then, "Since the photo was digitally stamped with her signature, he didn't need to." Another pause. "Why? Do you have information we don't?"

Wyatt ignored the uncertainty compressing his chest like a steel band. For nearly a week, that moment when she'd realized he didn't believe her and her wounded eyes had turned away from him had haunted him like a specter. If he was letting wishful thinking fog his judgment where she was concerned, he would only extend the painful longing he'd refused to recognize. But if he'd let his fear for Mandy blind him to the truth of Piper's innocence...

His chest expanded on a ragged breath. "No information. Just doubt. Whatever it costs. Get me a name."

Chapter 24

"At least tell me where ye are, lass."

Piper rested her elbows on the small bistro table and propped her chin in her hand. Her lazy gaze followed a woman in a floppy hat below her balcony. The wide brim kept the sun from the woman's face and head, and was wrapped in a bright red ribbon that dangled down her back. The bold tail swished to and fro as she strolled along Bourbon Street.

Though nowhere near as busy as it had been last evening, the pedestrian walkway was far from empty as the visitors to *the city care forgot* enjoyed the chilly, mid-December morning. Rounding a corner, the woman and her hat disappeared.

Piper sighed. "What difference would telling you where I am make when I'll be moving on in an hour?"

"I'm simply wantin' to relieve Tilly's mind. She's been in a state since ye left the manor…without sayin' good-bye, I might add."

Piper welcomed the soft glow of pleasure warming her chest. She hadn't had much to smile about in the two and a half months since she'd walked out of Wyatt's loft condo, and the return of her humor felt good. "For years you've been complaining about Tilly's bossy state of mind. Now you want to relieve it?"

"Ach, 'tis disrespectful and stubborn ye are."

She imagined his eyes narrowing the way they did whenever he voiced a complaint. "You know I love you, Cousin."

A dismissive huff. "Charmin' me won't do the trick, lass. I'm worried about ye, too."

Guilt stabbed at her, and she softened her voice. "I know you are, but there's no need. I'm fine. Really, I am, and if I come to feel that's no longer the case, you'll be the first person I ring. I promise. But I need some time, Angus."

She eyed the historic architecture of Bourbon Street reflected through her water glass and rose to collect her camera from inside the hotel room.

"Ye've had nothin' but time. Nearly three months. If ye were home where ye belong, the people who love ye wouldn't be concerned with whether or not yer carin' for yerself proper."

She returned to the balcony with camera in hand. "I *am* caring for myself, but I'm not ready to come home. Not yet. A woman deserves to lick her wounds in private, and I'm just now learning to breathe again. I'm not coming back until there is no longer a reason for all of you to hover." She dipped her knees and studied the play of light on her water glass from different angles. "Give Tilly my love, and tell Moira I'll call her in a few days."

"Lass..."

Piper thumbed the screen, disconnecting the call, then let her eyelids slide closed. Couldn't her friends see she was handling the situation the best way she knew how? Working again gave her focus while the constant travel kept her busy. Busy enough in those first few weeks that she didn't dwell on the ache piercing her heart every time she recalled the look of condemnation on Wyatt's face. And busy enough to give her a viable outlet later as the ache slowly slid into anger.

Snapping her eyes open, she shoved aside the memory and drew the camera to her eye. She clicked several dozen photos before she got the shot she wanted. Studying the camera's screen, she returned inside and slid the balcony door shut against the chilly breeze.

This was what she needed. To be productive again. As much as she loved the manor, Moira was right when she'd commented that there were other things Piper would rather do with her life than play the proper baroness for their guests.

Like her heart, Piper's creativity had been locked away for three long years. Her heart had taken a beating at being released, but her artist's eye gloried in the ability to wander free once again.

She'd had no plan after signing her deal with Broderick and settling things with Abigail, other than to go where the wind blew. Surprisingly, the chilling breeze had blown her straight back to Manhattan. Temporarily, anyway. Although the impulse was probably childish and had definitely been rash, the instinct had been a good one. She'd needed closure, but she'd also needed to attend the Marauders' game that first Sunday and every Sunday thereafter.

Her photograph might have been the vehicle, but *money* was the driving force behind Abigail's heartless actions. Money had ripped apart the world

Piper had only just begun to believe in and caused the man she'd fallen in love with to turn his back on her. It was a matter of principle she earn every bloody shilling Wyatt had paid her, even if he was never aware of the fact. While there was nothing she could do about the calendar project, she *could* fulfill the promise to see the season through.

As it turned out, someone *else* quickly became aware of her efforts.

It seemed Karma enjoyed an occasional bit of mischief. Choosing a seat as far from the field as possible hadn't produced the results Piper had hoped. But really, what were the odds several high rows of the middle balcony section of the stadium would be set aside for family and friends of the team's volunteers? Or that Kip would stop by to visit with his father, sitting four rows below Piper, before the game?

Concerned the young man would blab to Wyatt about her presence when that was the last thing she wanted, she'd asked Kip to meet her after the game. Over a slice of decadent cheesecake while awaiting his train back to Boston in Penn Station, she'd explained her convoluted reasoning for being at the game. She'd expected him to run straight to Wyatt and spill the beans. Instead, Kip had understood. He'd surprised her by insisting she make use of his season seat for the next game since his father wasn't able to attend and it would be empty.

The pattern repeated itself the following week. Two hours before kickoff, she found Kip waiting at the Will Call window to see her to her seat. With seven days before the next game, she'd flown back to Europe and spent the week wandering aimlessly with nothing but her camera for company. Two days in Amsterdam, the next in Paris. A stopover in Barcelona, then it was back to the States and Houston for the Marauders' next gridiron battle.

The next two and a half months had passed in a haze of football and constant travel. In the process, she was close to fulfilling her lucky charm promise and had produced what she hoped to form into a sort of photographic journey across the world. And she knew exactly who she wanted to help her promote it.

She dialed CC's number before she could change her mind.

"Piper!" Her friend answered on the second ring. "Oh my God. Where have you been? Are you okay? Wyatt's been..."

"I love you, dearest, but before you say another word, I want your promise you won't bring up his name."

"But..."

"I mean it, CC. I've finally gotten to a place where I'm not constantly fantasizing about hiring a hitman to...take him out. I'd like to keep it that way."

CC surprised her by laughing, but then sighed. "Okay, whatever you want. How are you? *Where* are you? I've tried to call and so has Wy—er... Hmm. How are you?"

So had Wyatt is what CC had been about to say. Piper didn't need to be reminded. His first call had come the day after she'd sold the cliffs. She hadn't answered, of course. As far as she was concerned, anything he had to say could be relayed through her attorney. She'd done nothing wrong. It might have taken her a while to get over the hurt, but she had eventually and what had been left behind was anger. Anger that he would think such a thing of her in the first place. That he'd refused to listen when she'd tried to explain.

But what really made her mad was that he'd believed the word of the rag newspaper who'd printed the photograph over hers. She'd considered hiring that hitman for real after listening to Wyatt's message saying he'd spoken to a contact at the *Bugle* and was sorrier than he could express. He'd screwed up, he'd said, should have trusted her, and could they talk.

She'd changed her phone number that very day.

Gritting her teeth, she dragged in several calming breaths and shoved Wyatt, the bloody wanker, to the back of her mind.

"I'm doing quite well, actually. I've been working again. Really working, and it feels fabulous."

"I'm so happy for you, Piper," CC said softly.

Piper had to clear her throat. "Which is the reason for my call." She explained her idea for a traveling display featuring her photographs and asked if a show of its type was something CC would welcome in her gallery.

"Are you kidding? I'd love it. What's more, I know quite a few gallery owners who might be interested in such a project."

Excitement danced up Piper's spine. "I was hoping you'd say that."

"How soon can we meet so I can take a look at the work?"

The dancing tingle in Piper's spine screeched to a halt like someone had switched off the music. It wasn't that she didn't trust her friend, but CC loved her husband, and Tuck was one of Wyatt's best friends. Piper would rather avoid any accidental-on-purpose chance meetings if she could.

"I'm afraid meeting physically will be impossible as I'll be on another continent for the next little while. However, I can e-mail the files directly to you so you can check them out." She bit her tongue at the flat-out lie, and shot a silent prayer for forgiveness toward heaven. Christmas and the New Year had come and gone, but for those who followed football, the true holiday season was about to begin. She'd be in Manhattan for the divisional round game next weekend and, hopefully, the conference championship the week after that.

"That's fine, of course, but..." CC's disappointment was evident in her tone, and it wasn't in her to hedge. She normally spoke her mind. The fact that she would hesitate now was enough to put Piper on edge.

"What is it you aren't saying, CC?"

"You told me not to bring up his name."

Piper slid her eyelids shut. This was the reason she'd been reluctant to speak to CC all these past months. They'd known each other since they were little girls, when CC had arrived in Italy timid and skittish after she'd been kidnapped and her father had used the notoriety of the abduction to jumpstart his lagging rock 'n' roll career.

Despite her youth, Piper had recognized the fragility of the friend she'd met on the beach. She liked to believe she'd played a small role in CC's recovery but, the truth was, the skinny girl with haunted eyes was one of the strongest people Piper had ever met. CC had managed to claw her way back from the horror she'd survived with little help from others. That kind of strength was rare in this world, and Piper had never been able to deny her anything.

"What's on your mind, dearest?"

"You," CC said softly. "And Wyatt. You know I love you, but this situation has hurt you both."

Piper somehow contained the gasp that wanted to come and clamped down on the angry tears stinging the back of her nose and throat. "Situation? CC, what he accused me of was filthy and unforgiveable."

"Yes, it was, and he was wrong. Terribly so. He made a mistake, Piper, and he knows it." Another hesitation, then, "I've never seen him like this."

Despite the renewed pain squeezing her heart, Piper was curious. "Like what?"

"Like he no longer cares. I've known him for a long time. Football is everything to him. The team is two games away from doing something no other has. Tuck can barely contain himself, yet Wyatt can't seem to work up the enthusiasm he's always shared with his teammates."

Piper frowned. He certainly hadn't looked like he didn't care to her. Whatever CC was seeing, it hadn't shown up on the field. Focused as usual and supremely talented, he and his teammate friends had spent the season taking apart respectable offensive and defensive lines as if they weren't in the same league.

"I miss his smile, Piper, and I miss you." CC's sigh was long. "I'm afraid I won't see either again unless the two of you work things out."

Breathing was difficult. Piper shook her head, then pressed her fist to the bridge of her nose. "Give it time, dearest. You'll see me again, and Wyatt will find his smile once he's done what he's set out to do."

Chapter 25

"I'm sorry, but the lass doesna want to be found. Every time I ask her where she is, she says she's fine and refuses to say more." A sigh, then, "Ach. The past three years have been a trial for the lass, what with the world dumpin' a load of trouble on to her wee shoulders by takin' her da and threatenin' to steal her manor. She carried the load like the lady she was born to be and deserves some time to herself to mourn all she's lost. She'll come home when she's ready."

Wyatt scraped a palm over his face. After nearly three months, he was losing his mind. "Thanks, Angus. As usual, I appreciate you letting me know she's okay."

He disconnected the call and dropped his head to the back of the couch. The guilt of knowing he'd contributed to the load she'd carried tangled with frustration to tie his guts into knots. But whatever emotion her absence from his life had delivered at any given time, none came close to the pain of missing her—except maybe the agony of knowing what she'd given up because of him.

He blinked at the ceiling and breathed through the band of anguish that compressed his chest every time he thought of that fucking deal she'd made with Broderick Faulkner. According to Angus, the manor house and most of the land remained in her possession, but Christ. She'd given up her beloved cliffs. Damn it, but for one photograph, she'd completed the job Wyatt had hired her to do. Yet, rather than accept another dime from him, she'd sacrificed the place where she and her father had shared their dreams.

The fact that she had was a hard pill to swallow and made it clear how badly he'd fucked up.

After years of condemning his father for his paranoid judgment of everyone around him, Wyatt had reacted little better. In a fit of rage and fear, he'd ignored everything his heart knew about the kind of woman Piper was. He dragged a palm down his face. Jesus, he loved her. He loved Piper

Darrow, but instead of giving her the benefit of the doubt, he'd behaved like a prick, and the best damn thing that had ever come into his life had walked out without a backward glance.

The irony of how well things had worked out for everyone other than Piper wasn't lost on him. After a brief period of panic, Meg had taken advantage of the public nature of the *Bugle's* exposé to force their father to accept the reality of his granddaughter's existence. That Mandy was little more than a campaign prop to his father made Wyatt's stomach turn but, just as he'd predicted, the campaign had spun the story to their advantage. They'd even seen a significant bump in the polls as a result.

As for Wyatt himself, professionally, things couldn't have gone any better. As if fate had stepped in to see history done, he and the Marauders had marched forward, blowing through teams in their pursuit of a third consecutive Super Bowl. The whispers of a possible perfect season had grown with each additional win until they had become an earsplitting roar. With the playoffs underway this week, even his most ardent detractors had been caught up in the frenzy of positive speculation over the team's odds of pulling off the impossible.

But, personally...Without Piper to share it with, his dream season had become nothing more than a weekly rehash of the same hollow achievement. Too late, he'd realized he'd held everything he ever wanted in his hands and had thrown it all away when he'd let her walk out of his life instead of standing by her side. He loved her and had to make things right between them but, to do that, he'd need to find her first. In the past three months, he hadn't come close.

Thanks to Faulkner, she now had millions at her disposal and could go anywhere in the world she wanted. Apparently, that was exactly what she was doing. Like Angus and Moira, CC Tucker swore she had no idea of her friend's location, but from the photographs Piper had contracted CC to show in her downtown studio beginning last week, his duchess had been on the move with stops in Sydney, Tokyo, Athens, New Orleans, San Francisco, and Boston.

The soft buzz of the doorbell drew him from his musings, and he climbed to his feet. Not many knew of the loft's existence, and those who did, knew to call before showing up. He frowned as he stalked to the reading nook to retrieve his tablet. Swiping his fingertip over the blackened screen, he swore beneath his breath at the video of the half dozen people caught by the camera outside the small lobby downstairs.

On the tablet's screen, he watched V poke at the panel beside the door. The buzzing resumed and, with a shake of his head, he cued the intercom. "I'm not home."

"Then you should definitely let us in." Tuck looked straight at the camera lens and smirked. "I think you're being robbed. Some asshole just answered your doorbell."

Sam Fitzpatrick shook his head and smiled. CC elbowed her husband as Jake and Gracie Malone laughed.

V rolled her eyes, then managed to knock the breath from Wyatt from two floors below. "If you want to know where Piper is, open the door." She smiled smugly as he swiped at the tablet and the outer lock clicked open.

"Where is she?" he demanded the moment the elevator doors whooshed apart.

"Hold your horses, big guy." A very pregnant Gracie Malone was the first off the elevator car. She glanced around the loft with a wrinkle creasing her brow while shedding her winter coat. "Where's the bathroom? I have to pee."

Wyatt pointed to the far wall without taking his eyes from V.

"Don't say a word until I'm back." Gracie wagged a finger at V before hurrying off.

He glared at her back. After all this time, he finally had a clue to Piper's location and they wanted him to wait?

V squeezed his arm in reassurance as the others filed into the loft behind her and peeled out of their heavy coats. "Breathe, Wyatt. Piper's not going anywhere in the next five minutes."

"Who wants a beer?" Tuck made himself at home behind the bar.

"It's ten o'clock on a Monday morning," CC pointed out.

Tuck met Jake's gaze, then Sam's. "Bloody Mary?"

Jake snickered while Sam grinned, but they both nodded. Tuck turned to Wyatt with a questioning arch of his brow.

Wyatt scowled. "Am I going to need alcohol for this conversation?"

"It's a definite possibility."

Fuck. "Make mine a double."

"What did I miss?" Gracie hurried toward them from the far end of the room.

Tension bunched Wyatt's shoulders as he turned an impatient glare on V. She, however, was busy digging through her purse.

"Tuck is playing bartender," CC answered.

Gracie joined Jake on the couch. "It's not even noon."

CC eyed Tuck and held up her hands as if to say *I rest my case.*

"Bloody Marys don't count." Tuck smirked and handed Sam and Jake their drinks. "They're a breakfast beverage."

Wyatt's patience hit the wall. "For fuck's sake, enough already. Where is she, V?"

V squinted at him while handing Sam a disk she pulled from her bag. As a friend as well as the team's offensive coordinator, Sam had spent many an hour with Wyatt studying game tapes over pizza and beer. He knew his way around the loft's top of the line media center.

"At this exact moment," V said as Sam slid the disc into the Blu Ray, "I can't honestly say where Piper is."

Disappointment nearly knocked the wind out of Wyatt. He scrubbed a hand down his face.

"But I believe I know where she'll be next Sunday."

Wyatt dropped his arm to his side. "How could you possibly know that? Have you spoken to her?"

"No. I told you, the only communication I've had with her has been via e-mail, but I have spoken to Gracie and she's spoken to Kip."

Wyatt shot a quick glance Gracie's way. What the fuck did Kip have to do with anything?

Tuck rounded the bar and handed Wyatt his drink. "The kid has been in touch with Piper all along."

"What?" Wyatt whipped his head around as Tuck took a seat next to his wife. "How? Where?"

Sam cued the DVD. "At the Marauders' sports complex."

CC nodded. "It seems she's been in the stands for every game this season."

Wyatt's gaze bounced from one friend to another, but he found no answer to the question burning in his mind. What the hell was she doing at the Marauders' games? It wasn't as if she was a fan particularly. She'd known nothing about football when they'd first met and had only agreed to be on the field as part of the job. But the job was no longer a consideration, and she'd made it more than clear she wanted nothing to do with him.

He studied what looked like a security tape running on the TV, and sure enough. There was Piper walking along an inner corridor of the stadium with Kip. Wyatt squinted, attempting make out their location.

"Where is that?"

"Upper terrace level, north corner end zone." V turned to Wyatt. "Caroline doesn't advertise the perk but, each season, she makes a block in that section available to the on-field volunteers. Each receives a not-for-resale seat to share with a family member or friend. Kip normally gives his seat to his dad."

On the screen, the kid said something and Piper turned her head. Seeing her smile was like taking a fist to the gut. Wyatt fought an instinctive flinch.

"Kip is on holiday break and spent Sunday night at the farm instead of heading straight back to Boston after the game." Wyatt turned as Gracie spoke. "In years past, he's always made a point to bring his father by the farm before a game at least once a season. That hasn't happened this year, and I asked Kip why. He got all jittery and changed the subject. From his blush, I assumed there had to be a girl involved."

Wyatt shifted his gaze to Jake, who shook his head as if to say, *what are you going to do?*

Gracie angled her chin defensively. "I happened to stop by the complex this morning and dropped in to see Jason Goodwell in marketing. Did you know his department keeps a copy of all footage shot inside the stadium?" She batted her lashes and didn't wait for an answer. "Well, I did. What you're looking at is the security film from outside the volunteers' seating section roughly two hours before kickoff on Sunday. Jason and I also went back and looked at film of the seating section from every home game. Kip's dad is in his seat for the first few games. For the Buffalo game, Piper shows up a couple of rows behind him. From that point on, Piper took over Kip's seat."

They'd beaten Buffalo in a major blowout the Sunday after the photograph had first appeared in the paper. Two days after she'd made her deal with Faulkner. Holy shit. Had she returned to Manhattan after signing the papers and been there for that game as well?

Wyatt was moving before he'd consciously made the decision to go.

"Wait. What are you doing?" V demanded as he grabbed his coat from the closet near the garage exit.

"Road trip." He shoved his arms into his sleeves. "Lock up when you leave, Tuck."

V groaned and immediately headed Wyatt's way. "Your last two road trips ended with bruised shoulder muscles, then a broken heart."

He opened his mouth but, if he'd planned to argue her point, he never got the chance. She waved a dismissive hand in front of his face as she passed. "I'm coming along to keep you out of trouble."

"You're not going anywhere without me." Sam handed his glass to Jake and followed V and Wyatt into the garage to climb into the back seat of Wyatt's SUV. "Where are we going?"

"Boston," Wyatt and V said together.

* * * *

"I'm sorry, Wyatt. She made me promise not to say a word. To anyone."

Kip's hangdog expression said he expected Wyatt to be pissed, but it was amazing what knowing how to find Piper had done for his outlook.

He shook his head and bit back a grin. There was a time Kip's loyalty had belonged unquestionably to Wyatt, but things had shifted the moment his duchess arrived in town. Not that he could blame the kid. Though young, he was still a man, and Piper Darrow's natural charm couldn't help but draw the male of the species in.

"Don't stress it, Kip. Although you would have saved me a hell of a lot of frustration if you'd mentioned you'd seen her, I understand why you didn't." He smiled as the kid's shoulders lowered with relief.

A burst of laughter drew Wyatt's gaze to the closed door. Luck had been with them as they'd arrived at Boston College. Catching Kip between lectures, Wyatt and Sam had caused a near riot as they'd climbed the stairs to the kid's second floor dorm. The ever-increasing voices from the hallway indicated the crowd had grown significantly in the ten minutes they'd been there.

Wyatt ignored the noise and turned back to Kip. "But I've got to know. Are you sure she'll be in the stadium this Sunday? Did she say she would be or are you simply assuming?"

"She'll be there." Kip nodded vehemently. "She said she'd made a promise to be at every game and wasn't about to go back on her word, even if you turned out to be a..." He slid his gaze to V and Sam.

V sighed. "Go ahead and say it, Kip. We all know he deserves whatever insult she threw his way."

Sam scrubbed his palm over his mouth, no doubt to hide his smile. Wyatt shot V a squinted glare, but she was right. He'd gladly accept whatever insults Piper wanted to heap upon him as long as she'd let him apologize once she was done.

He turned back to Kip. "Even if I turned out to be a what?"

The kid's Adam's apple clicked on a harsh swallow. "A bloody arse who wouldn't know the truth if it sacked you."

V turned her bark of laughter into a cough.

Sam didn't bother. His grin stretched from ear to ear. "That nails it. You've *got* to marry this woman. She's perfect for you."

"She is, isn't she?" Wyatt couldn't contain his own chuckle as he worked out the plan brewing in his head. "You said she normally arrives at least two hours before game time?"

"So far, yeah." Kip shrugged. "She mentioned something about some gridiron ladies, and how if she's already in the rafters before they show up, they're less likely to spot her."

V's nostrils flared in an affronted snort, but Wyatt's grin widened.

"Perfect. That'll give me just enough time." He winked at Kip. "I'm going to need your help, kid."

"Whatever you need, you've got it."

Wyatt whipped out his phone and swiped his thumb across the screen. "Just let V know when Piper arrives. I'll do the rest."

V narrowed her eyes. "Who are you calling?"

"Reinforcements."

Chapter 26

Piper slid a sidelong glance toward Kip as they rode the freight elevator to the terrace level of the Marauders' stadium. A slight frown marred his brow and his thumbs moved over the screen of his phone at Mach speed.

As he'd done every home game for the past three months, he'd met her at Will Call but, today, he was unusually distracted. Not that she could blame him. Today was huge. In just under two hours, the Marauders would be kicking off for the conference championship. It was early yet, with only a small portion of the eventual crowd on hand so far, but the excitement in the stadium was already tense and palpable.

She was a bit jittery herself, but her excitement was tempered by the bittersweet knowledge that today was the last game she'd be attending here in the Marauders' complex. If…no, *when* Wyatt and the guys won today, they'd be off to Phoenix for the Super Bowl and the last stop in their history-making season.

She refused to admit the hollow pit in her belly had anything to do with the thought of never again sitting in the stands to watch Wyatt play. After all, once the season was over and she'd fulfilled her promise, she could finally make a clean break from the disastrous Wyatt Hunter chapter in her life. No, the bittersweet tug on her heart was due to the knowledge that this was the last time she'd see Kip. Not to mention the "regulars" as she had begun to think of the friends she'd made among the guests of the team's volunteers who had watched the games with her for eight of the last thirteen Sundays.

Kip's phone dinged and he swiped back a reply.

Piper sighed. "Things must be crazy downstairs today. If there is something you need to get to, I can find my own seat."

His gaze jerked to hers, then slid away. "No, that's okay. I'm where I'm supposed to be." His lips pulled tight in what looked like a wince to Piper, and he shoved his cell phone into the pocket of his khaki slacks. "I mean, I've got plenty of time before I'm due on the field."

The lift arrived at the terrace level and he hurried her from the car. Taking her elbow, he led her to the left in the direction of her seat but, from the way he twisted his head to stare in the opposite direction, something else had his interest.

She stopped at the edge of the tunnel leading to the stands and turned to him. Rising on her toes, she pressed a kiss to his cheek. A blush had already bloomed on his high cheekbones when she lowered to her heels.

"I can't thank you enough for the kindness you've shown me."

He shuffled his feet, clearly uncomfortable. "It was nothing."

"On the contrary. I know how highly you think of Wyatt. Most young men would have held a grudge against a woman who allegedly tried to harm their hero. You didn't, and your support means more to me than I can say."

The blush darkened, but he held her gaze. "You didn't do anything wrong. It just took Wyatt a little while to prove that to himself."

And that was the problem in a nutshell. Wyatt had needed proof while Kip had given her the benefit of the doubt from the beginning. Pointing that out to Wyatt's biggest fan, however, would be a waste of time. She wrapped her arms around his waist and squeezed, then smiled as he squeezed back.

"Do you think you'll ever be able to forgive him?"

And... There went her smile.

She stepped back and sighed. "It's complicated, Kip."

"No, it isn't. Not really. He screwed up, Piper, plain and simple, but he's a guy." He cocked his head and the charm he'd graced her with during those first few Sundays was there in his boyish grin. "We guys do stupid shi...er stuff when a pretty girl is involved."

A soft laugh escaped, and she shook her head. "There's a woman out there somewhere who is going to give that charm you use like a weapon a run for its money."

A dimpled grin was his only reply.

"I'm going to miss you, Kip. You have a standing invitation to come visit me at the manor."

"Really?" Surprised excitement glittered in his eyes.

"Anytime you want."

He barked a sharp laugh. "That'd be wicked cool."

She grinned and patted his arm. "I can take it from here if you'd like to head down to the locker room."

"I'll head down in a few minutes. I want to say hi to the 'regulars' first."

They continued down the tunnel, leaving the shade of the interior hallway behind. The moment they stepped into the bright sunlight, a chorus of voices greeted her from the stands. As she climbed the steps to "volunteers' row," she smiled at Brian McNulty, a friendly pastor of a small congregation in the Bronx. Sitting on either side of him were Andrea Cooper, a resident at New York Presbyterian, and Mark Howell, a retired construction worker from Queens.

All diehard Marauders followers, the super fans had rallied en masse that first Sunday upon discovering Piper's lack of understanding of the game. Picking up where Kip had left off, they'd filled in the gaps in her football education. She paused on the landing and arched a brow.

"Wow. You're all here early." She was normally the first to arrive each week. Seeing them all seated already was weird.

"We didn't want to miss it."

Mark grunted as Andrea's elbow connected with his arm. Piper shot her a questioning glance as she slid into her seat at the end of the row.

The blonde intern's smile held a sharper edge than usual. "We didn't want to miss any of the pre-game stuff. It's not every day your team plays for the right to go to the Super Bowl."

"That's right." Brian nodded enthusiastically—a little *too* enthusiastically.

Piper passed her gaze from one to the next. Other than possibly Kip, who continued to hover beside her seat, she technically didn't know these people all that well. However, over the course of three months, she'd gotten to know their expressions, whether it be sheer joy at a fabulous play or nerves over a third and long situation. At the moment, they all wore questionable smiles. The kind people employed when faced with something embarrassing and weren't sure what to say.

She dropped her gaze to her chest and did a quick check of her blouse to make sure all the buttons were done. Nothing wrong there. Next, she slid her fingers over her hair, but found no discernable issues with the loose braid hanging over one shoulder. Curiosity morphed into unease as she looked up again and found all four grinning like Jack Nicholson in that first Batman movie.

"Bloody hell. Stop that. You're beginning to freak me out." Shading her eyes with her hand, she glared up at Kip. "What? Do I have food in my teeth or something?" She shrugged her small camera bag from her shoulder, intent on retrieving her small compact, but Andrea's gasp stopped her.

"Oh my." The intern pressed a hand to her chest as the sound of bagpipes filled the air.

Piper followed her gaze to the landing twenty rows below them. Her own gasp caught in her throat as Wyatt began to climb the steps in her direction with the rest of the Fab Five at his heels.

It had been almost three months since she'd seen Wyatt up close. From the frantic thudding of her heart, the effect he'd had on her from the beginning hadn't faded.

Or his outfit could be to blame. What there was of it.

Although all five of the men were dressed similarly, it was Wyatt she couldn't look away from. Probably because he was the only one among the men not wearing a shirt. Or maybe not. Whether he was stark naked or fully clothed, when Wyatt Hunter was around, Piper found it difficult to focus on much else.

And the object of her focus right now left her breathless.

A bold blue and gold sash sliced diagonally from his shirtless right shoulder. Clipped to his left hip by a traditional broach, the woolen weave highlighted his roaring tiger tattoo and left the vast majority of his chest and torso bare. She swallowed as her gaze dropped to the kilt riding just below the ridge of muscle delineating his six-pack abs from his lean hips.

The pale snakeskin cowboy boots on his feet weren't exactly traditional, but it was highly improbably anyone looking at him would give a flying fig. Especially if the person doing the looking was a woman.

But it was his eyes that held Piper pinned in her seat. Perhaps it was a trick of the sunlight playing on his shaggy blond hair but, as his grayish-green gaze tangled with hers, his eyes seemed to glow, not unlike the way they had whenever he'd had her alone and beneath him.

She blinked and forced herself to look away…which is when she noticed the stir he was causing.

A growing crowd scrambled up the stairs behind the players. Thankfully, quite a few of the stadium's seats had yet to be filled, but those fans who had already arrived had noticed the developing situation on the terrace level and were watching. Those in close enough sections had abandoned their seats to rush toward the action.

A slightly hysterical laugh burst from her throat. Of course, they'd noticed. Who wouldn't notice four kilted men marching up the stairs led by a half-naked sex god and followed by a trio of bagpipers? Then there was…oh, good Lord. How the devil had Wyatt managed to sway Angus over to his side? And was that…? Holding on to her mother's hand, Mandy poked her head around Tuck's hip to give Piper a gummy smile.

A flood of questions gushed into Piper's mind, then flew out again just as quickly as she spotted two men lugging full-sized cameras on their shoulders. One had the lens pointed straight at her. A cry of dismay stuck in her throat as she looked up at the Jumbotron. Fifty feet wide and thirty feet tall, her pale face stared back at her.

"Breathe, girlfriend," CC whispered from the row behind Piper.

She twisted her head around to stare at her friend. The other four Gridiron Girls stood behind her. "Where the devil did you come from?"

Gracie waved a hand. "We came up through the tunnel in the next section." She jerked her head to the seating section off to Piper's right. "Wyatt didn't want us spoiling his surprise, but there was no way we were going to miss his performance."

Piper groaned deep in her throat. "Please tell me you didn't set this up?"

"This was all Wyatt." CC grinned as she glanced beyond Piper, presumably at her kilted husband. "With a little help from his friends. When he told the guys what he meant to do, they insisted on being his backup."

Gracie shook her head and laughed. "They look like a chorus line of William Wallaces on steroids."

V chuckled, then leaned close to squeeze Piper's shoulder. "Time's up, Piper. Just give him a chance. Please?"

She slammed her eyelids shut just as the bagpipes wheezed to an end.

"I'm sorry, duchess."

Wyatt's deep voice broke the odd silence filling the air around her. She opened her eyes and faced forward. He stood in front of her, his face a mask of intensity. When she said nothing, he squatted in front of her. At eye level, he held her gaze.

"I should have trusted you. I should have trusted what I knew in my heart to be true. That you are one of the most kind-hearted, straightforward, ethically strong women I've ever had the pleasure to meet. If I'd trusted that truth, I would have known straight off you weren't capable of the kind of deceit you'd been accused of."

She didn't make a fuss when he reached for her hand, but neither did she return the squeeze of his fingers. How could she when she was busy controlling the helpless shiver caused by his warm hand holding hers? He rubbed his thumb over the back of her hand and she lost the battle. It wasn't her fault. She hadn't realized how much she'd missed his touch.

Satisfaction gleamed in his eyes and he dipped his head closer. "I know how much you hate the limelight."

She bit back her sardonic snort, and glanced around at close to three hundred people jammed close and hanging on his every word.

His smile leaned toward a grimace as she met his gaze once again. "I promise, after today, I'll do my damnedest to ensure your privacy. But, after the way I acted, I figure I deserve to stand in front of plenty of witnesses as I beg the woman I love for her forgiveness."

"The bigger they are…" Jamal said with a smirk.

Piper ignored the men's laughter and blinked at Wyatt's declaration. Her heart slammed against her ribs. He loved her?

As if she'd posed the question aloud, he grinned. "Yeah, I love you. Which is the reason I'm wearing a skirt." He ignored Angus's affronted snort. "The reason I'm here, in a *kilt*."

She had to swallow before she could speak. He was here, and he loved her. "I noticed that but, the question is why?"

"You told me once a kilt made a guy look manly and sexy. I wanted to impress you."

"You can impress me anytime," a woman offered from somewhere in the crowd and set off a chorus of laughter.

Wyatt chuckled, then spoke without looking away from Piper. "I appreciate the offer, sweetheart, but there is only one woman in the world I'm interested in impressing, and she's sitting right in front of me."

Several feminine sighs could be heard, along with a couple male grunts. Wyatt ignored them all.

"I'm here in front of," he glanced around, "a shitload of strangers, begging you to give me one more chance. Begging you to give *us* one more chance." He lowered his head and his voice, speaking low enough only she and those closest could hear. "I won't screw us up again, duchess. You have my word on that."

Tears stung at the back of her nose as he lifted his head.

"In addition to the fans here today, millions of others will see me making a fool of myself later when they watch the tape. Would I subject myself to that humiliation if I didn't love you?" He shook his head. "If I didn't love you, I'd be downstairs preparing for the most important game of my career."

"Yet," she said softly.

A wrinkle of confusion creased his brow, and she turned her hand over to grasp his.

"As your lucky charm, I can say with utmost certainty, the most important game of your career comes *after* you win today. It comes in two weeks."

He grinned as the crowd around them voiced their agreement with whoops and whistles and *hell yeahs*.

"Duchess, before I head downstairs to exchange my sexy kilt for shoulder pads and a helmet, I need to ask you a question."

He dropped one knee to the floor and slid his hand inside the sash at his waist. An excited murmur of startled gasps rippled through the crowd. One of the Gridiron Girls actually squeaked behind Piper. Wyatt's face wavered through the tears welling in her eyes, and she struggled to draw enough breath.

He held out his hand. A small, pale blue box tied in a white bow rested on his palm. "Piper Darrow, eighth baroness of Delaney, will you put me out of my misery and become my wife?"

"Auntie Pipah!" Mandy announced and Wyatt grinned.

A fat tear plopped onto Piper's cheek. Angus sighed and drew her attention.

His chest lifted on a scoffing snort. "Both Moira and Tilly said to tell ye the lad behaved like a horse's arse, but he seems to have learned his lesson."

Wyatt arched his neck to shoot Angus a pointed stare.

He grinned, winked, then turned back to Piper. "Go on, lass. Put the lad out of his misery already."

A round of *yeahs* and *do it, alreadys* filled the air as Piper met Megan's gaze through the crowd. With a dip of her chin, his sister gave her silent approval. They shared a smile and, plucking the box from Wyatt's palm, Piper rose from her seat. Sliding an arm around his shoulders, she lowered to sit on his knee and looked into his hopeful, beautiful eyes, then repeated the same answer she'd given him that day on the cliffs.

"Why, you lovely man. I thought you'd never ask."

Epilogue

"You're looking quite dapper, Angus."

"Aye, that I am." Resplendent in traditional highland dress of kilt and tartan pinned at the shoulder by his prized, antique clan badge, Angus grinned. "And yer lookin' quite lovely yerself. Ye make a bonnie bride, Cousin."

Piper smiled, her gaze dropping to the envelope he held out. "What is it?"

"'Tis from himself. He said to tell ye, there's been a change of plans."

Piper blinked and accepted the thick packet. She tugged the sheaf of official looking documents from inside and unfolded them. The breath stalled in her throat as she read the included note written in Wyatt's bold hand. Stunned, she lifted her gaze to stare at her cousin.

Approval flashed in his eyes. "Aye. The lad'll do. I'm thinkin' yer Da would agree."

Helpless tears sprung in her eyes, and she shook her head. "How did he do this?"

A snort flared Angus's nostrils. "Love is a strong incentive, lass, and the lad obviously knows yer heart." He turned and snatched the white woolen cape from the hook on her bedroom door. Turning back, he shook out the cloak and held it open for her. "Come on with ye, now. Tilly and Moira have already left with yer friends. The parson is waitin', and the lad'll be wonderin' what's keepin' ye."

With a last glance at the shocking papers, Piper set them on her vanity and picked up the small bouquet of rose blooms. Rising to her feet, she turned so Angus could wrap the cape around her shoulders, left bare by the off-the-shoulder cut of her wedding gown. Dipping her knees, she gathered the lacy material of the dress's sweeping train in one hand and followed her cousin from her bedroom.

They reached the manor's foyer and she cast a quick glance into the lounge where the small service was *supposed* to be taking place. The room was empty. Angus rested his hand on the small of her back and urged her out the front door. A hiccupped laugh broke free as she spotted the enclosed golf cart decorated in blood red roses and greenery.

Angus grinned at her side. "Wyatt had the cart delivered from Glasgow first thing this mornin' along with a half dozen others just like it. His mates caused a stir drivin' the women up the trail after Tuck challenged them to a race."

She jerked her gaze to Angus. "Oh, Lord. Please tell me no one was hurt."

He chuckled. "The lads didn't get the chance to take up Tuck's offer, not with their wives givin' them all the stink eye."

Relieved, Piper laughed, then eyed the tiny vehicle. To cut costs, she'd traded in the manor's roomy SUV for a compact sedan. Tilly hadn't been pleased by the downgrade. She'd claimed a vehicle that small was nothing but a deathtrap. Refusing to drive it, she'd taken to using the manor's ancient "Woodie" instead. Compared to the golf cart, the sedan was practically a stretch-limo.

"Tilly actually got into one of these?"

Angus laughed and wheeled the cart about toward the path leading into the woods. "Aye. She said it was darlin'." He shot her a sidelong grin. "She shooed Moira to the passenger seat and took the wheel herself."

Piper grinned and shook her head as they climbed toward the newly drawn line of the manor's property. At the top of the rise not far from the cliffs, she blinked. Shortly after they had made their deal, Broderick Faulkner had installed a discreet fence along the new border of the golf resort's land. A week ago, his fence line had cut straight across the forest path she'd walked her entire life. This morning, the wooden rails had been adjusted to run parallel with the last hundred meters of the trail leading to her special place.

She pressed a hand to her chest and fought against the tears stinging her nose and eyes. Selling off a portion of the property had not only been necessary, it had been the right thing to do. The sale had allowed her, Moira, Tilly, and Angus to remain on the land they loved, but the loss of her cliffs had left her heart wounded.

Wyatt had somehow managed to find a way to heal that wound by convincing Broderick Faulkner to return the acre of land surrounding Piper's cliffs. She had no idea how Wyatt had done it, but his wedding gift was the sweetest gesture she could ever have imagined and one more reason why she loved the man to distraction.

A breathy sigh escaped her lips. If someone had told her she'd be this happy five months ago—Lord, three *weeks* ago—she would have called them a nutter. A weepy laugh gurgled in her throat. Then again, she shouldn't be surprised. It wasn't every day a woman fell in love with her very own larger-than-life hero.

That wasn't to say there wouldn't be challenges in their future. If the past three weeks were any indication, living in the glare of the spotlight aimed on Wyatt and his family wouldn't be easy. As predicted, the public nature of his kilted proposal had whipped the press into a frenzy. The team's divisional title win, followed by their historic Super Bowl victory, only increased the oppressive press interest dogging Wyatt and Piper at every turn.

Meeting Richard Hunter had been a tense experience, for both her and Wyatt, especially with Walter Crowley looking on. Wyatt insisted contact with his father would be a rare occurrence, and she hoped that was the case. She hated the edgy nerves Wyatt had shown during the half hour they'd spent in his father's presence. From what she could tell, V was right. The relationship between father and son was barely civil.

Megan, on the other hand, had been wonderful. Her future sister-in-law had taken it upon herself to face the press and welcome Piper to the family. She'd also given some invaluable pointers on how to handle the constant attention.

Still, for Piper, having Wyatt back in her life was worth any discomfort she might have to face. She'd missed him so much, and not just the way he could heat her body to the melting point with a simple look. In those months they'd been apart, she'd desperately missed the way he could make her laugh seemingly without trying. Since that Sunday he'd found her in the stands to tell her he loved her, she'd found her smile once again.

"We're almost there, lass."

Piper turned her head at Angus's softly spoken observation and glanced around. He slowed the cart and turned onto a newly widened path leading to the cliffs. Her heartbeat raced as they reached a small clearing. Off to the right sat the carts that had delivered their wedding guests up the trail. To the left, a path disappeared into the trees.

Angus pulled the cart to a stop and exited to round the hood. He held out his hand. She placed her fingers in his and slid to her feet.

He clucked his tongue and studied her face. "Ye look so much like yer mum. It's as if I'm seein' her pretty face again." His smile wavered beneath the tears flooding her eyes, and he cleared his throat. "Both yer lovely mum and yer da would be proud of ye this day. I'm honored to stand in their stead."

Fearing she would choke on the lump crowding her airway, she squeezed his fingers in lieu of speaking. He turned, tucking her hand in the crook of his arm, and led her toward the muted sound of the Atlantic crashing against the rocky coast.

He chuckled as she sniffled and tugged a folded cloth from the sporran at his waist. She accepted the handkerchief and dabbed her nose, then clutched his arm with frantic fingers as the cliff clearing came into view. He brought them to a stop at the edge of the silk runner leading to a linen-covered pillared archway framing the view of the ocean beyond.

Two rows of stark white chairs sat to each side of the temporary aisle. Her gaze paused briefly on CC and the Gridiron Girls and their spouses, then moved on to Megan. Piper returned her warm smile, then arched a brow, surprised to find Broderick Faulkner sitting in the chair on the other side of Mandy. He dipped his head in a greeting nod before turning to face the arch once more.

Piper followed his gaze and promptly forgot all about why the real estate mogul was in attendance. The butterflies returned as her gaze landed on her groom.

With Tuck at his side, Wyatt turned his head. His familiar gray-green eyes gleamed in the sunlight and held her captive. The butterflies rioted violently as his lips curved in a smile edged with…relief?

She swallowed. Had he been concerned she would change her mind? Silly man.

In keeping with what he apparently considered a new tradition, he wore another kilt. She ran her gaze over his handsome face and form and was struck by the familiar pin holding the tartan in place at his shoulder. Having been worn by her father for as long as Piper could remember, the badge held a special place in her heart. She'd given it to Angus upon Da's death.

Her cousin spoke softly at her side. "Ye were yer da's pride, but second was that badge. I'm thinkin' he would want yer new husband to have it."

She swallowed past the lump in her throat.

"Let me take your cape."

Piper was slow to drag her gaze from her groom. When she did, she found Moira standing at her side wearing a wide grin. Behind her, Tilly's smile wobbled. *I love you*, she mouthed.

The prickling at the back of Piper's nose intensified as she mouthed the sentiment back.

Moira laughed softly and unsnapped the clasp at Piper's throat, sliding the cloak from her shoulders. "I know Wyatt Hunter is devilishly handsome, but you've got to pull yourself together, luv. You don't want him thinking you're too easy, do you?"

"There's no chance of that happening." Tilly snorted. "Look at him. He's sweating, wondering if you've changed your mind."

Piper jerked her gaze back to Wyatt's. The day was unusually mild for late February but, from what she could tell, he wasn't sweating. However, his brow was furrowed, and he looked as if he was about to stalk forward and take her hand instead of waiting for her to come to him. His obvious nerves somehow eased hers.

Tilly took the cloak from Moira's hand. "Go on with you now. Moira, start walking so Piper can put the poor man's mind to rest."

Moira laughed over her shoulder, then strolled down the runner to the archway. Clinging to Angus's arm, Piper followed, and the rush of excitement flowing through her veins increased with each step.

Less than three weeks ago, she'd despaired of ever smiling again. Yet, here she was, about to marry Wyatt. About to exchange vows with the man she loved here in this place where she'd woven her childhood dreams. She couldn't contain the helpless smile stretching her lips as she passed by CC and the girls and their husbands. Megan scrambled to her feet, but wasn't quick enough to stop Mandy from bolting into the aisle to throw her arms around Piper's hips to greet her *Auntie Pipah*.

Amid the laughter, Piper disengaged her arm from Angus's to stoop and give her new niece a hug and kiss her cheek. Once Megan had convinced the excited child to return to her seat, Piper took Angus's arm again, and they joined Wyatt, Tuck, and Moira where they waited with the vicar.

Taking her duties as chief bridesmaid to heart, Moira stepped forward to take the small bouquet Piper carried and adjust her train, then slid back into place as Angus kissed Piper's brow. Turning, he placed her fingers into Wyatt's waiting hand. Her cousin didn't release her other hand, however, and pinned Wyatt with a narrow-eyed stare.

"I'm trustin' ye with the daughter of me heart. Do right by her, lad."

Mutually touched and amused, Piper grinned, but Wyatt took the warning seriously. He dipped his head in a solemn nod.

"You have my word, sir."

Angus backed away, and Wyatt met her gaze. His nerves seemed to fade as the appreciative glow in his eyes grew. He lowered his voice to a rumbling purr. "You're beautiful."

She smiled and cocked her head, then couldn't help a teasing once-over of his very sexy wedding attire. She met his gaze once more. "So are you."

"It's the kilt. They do things to a woman." He matched her grin, but then sobered. "I love you."

The simple declaration sent a shiver through her system. "I love you, too."

Tuck cleared his throat. "Uh, folks. You ain't married yet. You're supposed to say I do first, then you can get to the mushy stuff."

"Oh, Tuck," CC moaned from behind to the sound of laughter.

"What?" Tuck glanced his wife's way with an innocent look. "The parson's waiting. Ain't that right, Parson?"

The elderly vicar, who had been making monthly trips to the village to say mass for the locals since before Piper was born, looked as if he weren't sure how to answer. Piper took mercy on him.

"We'll get to the I do's in just a moment, Vicar." She turned back to Wyatt. "But first, I want to thank you for my wedding present and ask how you managed to convince Broderick to sell you the cliffs?"

Wyatt glanced over his shoulder at the real estate mogul before answering. "Broderick didn't technically sell me the cliffs. We made a deal." Wyatt shot a quick glance at Tuck, who smirked.

She squinted between them. "What kind of deal?"

"A good one, I think." Wyatt took her arm and turned her to face the vicar. "I agreed to give Broderick access to the spot for certain occasions, with the proper notification, of course."

She blinked and found Broderick in the crowd. "You gave up the cliffs on the promise that you can borrow them occasionally?"

He grinned. "The view blew me away. I'd planned to use the space for outdoor parties for VIPs and the occasional wedding, which I can still do thanks to our deal." He tossed Wyatt a sharp grin before turning to Megan. "Your future husband and his sister are a very persuasive pair."

Piper arched a brow at the blush coloring Megan's cheeks and, shaking her head, looked at her groom. His smile was keen, but something wasn't adding up. "That's it? Broderick gets to throw a party here and you get the land?"

Wyatt squeezed her fingers. "*You* get the land. The acreage will be turned back over to you with the stipulation you grant the golf resort access a couple times a year." He turned to the vicar. "Parson?"

The vicar cleared his throat. "Dearly belov..."

"And?" she demanded. "What else aren't you saying?"

Tuck grinned, and Wyatt rolled his eyes. "And I'll be hosting a tournament to raise funds for Broderick's favorite charity."

Confused, she glanced over her shoulder, then back. "A tournament?"

"Okay, five tournaments." Wyatt's forehead creased with his self-deprecating grimace. "Plus, I had to convince a few of my friends to commit their time as well."

She slid her gaze to Tuck. He grinned and shrugged. Turning, she met Broderick's easy smile. In the row behind him, CC nodded her confirmation, then tossed her head toward the four remaining Gridiron Girls and their husbands.

Piper's jaw wanted to drop. "You all committed to this?"

V held up a hand. "Wyatt told us how important this spot was to you and we wanted to help him get your cliffs back. Besides, the funds go to the families of fallen soldiers. It's a good cause."

Piper shifted her gaze to each of Wyatt's friends and their wives. They all wore a warm smile that said V spoke for the group, but it was Gracie who had the last word, as usual.

She cocked her head, rested her hands on her pronounced baby bump, and met Piper's shocked gaze. "As soon as you say *I do*, you'll officially be one of us. The Gridiron Girls and their men stick together."

Wyatt squeezed Piper's fingers and she met his smile.

"What do you say, duchess? Are you gonna marry me?"

With her heart threatening to burst from her chest, she couldn't look away from the love in his eyes. "Go ahead, Vicar, and speak quickly, will you? I can't wait to say *I do*."

THE END

Meet the Author

Wife, mother and really young grandmother, Mackenzie Crowne shares her home with her high school sweetheart husband, a rambunctious Lab pound-puppy, and a blind cat. She calls Arizona home because the southwest feeds her soul. Her love of the romance genre has been a lifelong affair, both as a reader and a writer. A bout with breast cancer sharpened her resolve to see her stories shared with others. Today, she's a nine-year survivor, living the dream. Her friends call her Mac. She hopes you will too. Visit her website at mackenziecrowne.com, find her on Facebook, or follow her on Twitter at twitter.com/MacCrowne.